MICE of the Round TABLE

Merlin's Last Quest

JULIE LEUNG

HARPER

An Imprint of HarperCollinsPublishers

Library of Congress Control Number: 2018945993
ISBN 978-0-06-240405-3

Typography by Katie Klimowicz
18 19 20 21 22   CG/LSCH   10 9 8 7 6 5 4 3 2 1
❖
First Edition

For Brian Jacques
Eulalia!

Looking back on it, when they were old,

they did not remember that in this year it had ever rained or frozen.

The four seasons were coloured like the edge of a rose petal

for them.

—*T.H. White,* The Once and Future King

Merlin's Last Quest

PROLOGUE

Horatio Eavesdrip, twelfth of his name, was an excellent listener. With ears twice the size of his head, and as delicate as fairy wings, very little escaped the long-eared bat's keen hearing. Sometimes, if he hung at a certain angle and swiveled his ears just so, the mountains had much to tell him. Voices could travel long distances through the vast echoing caves—carrying their secrets.

This was especially true when those voices were raised in anger.

The mountains had become crowded as of late, with strangely dressed creatures roaming the upper chambers at all hours. Already, Horatio had gleaned that a witch of great power had moved in, making her lair in the abandoned Two-Legger mines. When the bat perched in his usual position, hanging by his toes in a crevice, it did not take long for her words to trickle down from high above.

"My spies tell me your plots have unraveled fast, contrary to what you've reported in your larks home," she chastised. "Camelot is weakened, but not enough. We need more magic. It's time for you to come back."

Another voice answered, this one more muddled, as if someone was trying to speak through water. "I think . . . found something . . . may help. Merlin's . . ."

Horatio tried to twist his ear closer to the walls as the words faded in and out.

"Forget Excalibur for now. The boy must come to us on his own terms. I have something bigger and more powerful in my sights. Bring me Merlin's scrolls."

The other voice became indistinct. As he strained to catch the next words, a sharp, high-pitched ringing started, and Horatio clamped his ears down in pain. Somewhere high above, a trumpet had sounded in the witch's room.

"We will discuss when you return, Red. Someone is listening in."

Horatio had been discovered! If the witch was using black magic to protect her conversation, it must be worth something.

The king should know.

Horatio unfurled to fly away deeper into the cave, back to his colony. But as he took off, something caught his wing tip, yanking him back. Black, smoky tendrils had clamped down on his thumb like pincers. He flapped helplessly in place.

"I know you're there." The witch's singsongy voice came from right next to Horatio's ear, wily and cruel. "Tell me, little spy, where are you?"

Horatio could feel the witch's magic worm its way into his mind, eating away at his thoughts. If she found out what he knew, all that he knew, it would endanger his entire colony—perhaps even all of Britain. He couldn't let that happen.

He wrenched out of the spell's grasp at the last moment. The bat flew away as fast as he could, through dark passages only a small creature could navigate.

Horatio was out of breath by the time he made it back to his colony's cave. He flew straight for the king's fine hanging stone. King Mir was settling in for his sleep, already upside down with his wings wrapped around him. Dawn was just around the corner.

"Flee! We must flee!" Horatio's words came out in alarmed hiccups. He flitted back and forth, waking much of the rest of the colony.

"Slow down, Horatio, quit flapping around. It's nearly bedtime." King Mir yawned and waved a dismissive wing at his chief listener.

"My liege, the situation is more dire than we'd thought." Horatio panted as his feet scraped against a crag. Flipping himself upside down, he was now eye to eye with his king. "We must wake the dragon from its slumber!"

CHAPTER
1

Raindrops lashed mouse-squire Calib Christopher's face, stinging like sharp nettles against his fur. Bolts of lightning ripped across the sky, illuminating the trees in stark black-and-white silhouettes.

"It's no use!" Valentina Stormbeak yelled over the accompanying thunder. "We can't fly on in this storm."

Calib clutched Valentina's wings tighter as a gust of wind threatened to throw him off the crow's back. He squinted into the dark, seeking any sign of Cecily von Mandrake and her kidnapper, Sir Percival Vole. What muddy tracks Calib had detected earlier were now washed away.

"We'll never find them if we stop now!" Calib shouted back. "They've had at least an hour's head start!"

His chest squeezed together like a tightening noose. None of this would have happened if it weren't for his own outstanding stupidity. His mistakes buzzed inside his head, stinging like hornets.

He, Calib Christopher, last of a line of brave knights and leaders, had unwittingly allowed Camelot's most dangerous traitor back into the castle when it was most vulnerable.

Not only had Calib let the enemy infiltrate the castle, he had also accidentally divulged Camelot's greatest secret to him: what the mice knew as the Goldenwood Throne was actually a legendary treasure called the Grail.

It had been entrusted to his family by Merlin all these years, its secret hidden in the designs of the Christopher crest. And now the Grail had fallen into the clutches of a Saxon betrayer, along with Calib's best friend, Cecily. Calib's stomach soured at the very thought.

He had to make things right again.

He had to defeat Sir Percival Vole, take back the Grail, and rescue Cecily.

If only this storm would let them catch up to the villain.

Valentina, the brave Darkling crow who had volunteered

to fly Calib in his pursuit, was losing her battle against the gusting wind.

"It's getting dangerous," she warned again. "We need to fly back to Camelot and wait out the storm!"

"Let's keep going!" he insisted. As long as he drew breath, he would hunt Sir Percival down. "I don't want to lose any more time than—"

Calib's world turned a blinding white.

Excruciating pain from the hottest heat he'd ever felt surged through his body. An acrid smell filled his sensitive nose— His fur was burning! But there was nothing to be done. Mouse and crow tumbled from the sky, plummeting out of control.

The wind screamed in Calib's ears, or perhaps it was *him* who was screaming.

Then suddenly, it didn't matter, for there was no sound at all.

Calib's eyes blinked open. A chandelier twinkled above him, the tiny candle nubs melted by flame into strange shapes.

Flame. Burning. Falling!

Calib sat straight up, jolted by the rush of painful memories. How had he managed to make it back to Camelot?

"Whoa, there, Calib!" Two sets of firm paws held him back down. "Steady there!"

His breath came in short jabs, and fellow mouse-squires

Devrin Savortooth and Warren Clipping pushed him back toward his pillow—but not before Calib caught a glimpse of empty beds lined up in rows against the wall.

He was in the castle infirmary. Most animals had recovered from the white fever that had ravaged the castle weeks ago. The air felt stuffy with the promise of an early summer day. It made his head throb, as though one of Sister Ysabel's fluttery wimples had been wrapped around his head.

"What happened? How long have I been out?" Calib croaked. The concerned faces of Warren and Devrin swam into his vision. Devrin was dressed in a green tunic that denoted her new rank of squire. Warren wore a white tunic from the infirmary and had a bandage wrapped around his forehead from when Sir Percival had knocked him out.

"When you set off with Valentina, Commander Kensington sent scouts after you," Devrin said. The brown mouse spoke in the gentle tone of an older sister. And in many ways, she was the closest thing Calib had to family since his grandfather had died. "She was worried you were acting reckless, out of panic. And—"

"Then you were struck by lightning," Warren interrupted, waving his paws in a mimic of an explosion. "*Kablow!* You've been out cold for two whole nights. I thought you were dead for sure!"

Devrin elbowed the gray mouse in the ribs. "Can you

stop being a cheesehead for two whole seconds?"

"Is Valentina all right?" Calib asked. The messenger crow was nowhere to be seen.

Devrin's jaw tightened, and Warren became somber.

"Valentina was badly burned. It seems her wings shielded you from the lightning," Devrin said. "Her clan came to bring her home to their crow healer."

Calib buried his head in his paws, the throbbing at his temples turning into a pounding. *He* was the one who'd insisted they keep flying in the storm. He couldn't let Valentina's injuries have happened for nothing. Calib tried to get up, but his friends held him back again.

"I have to," Calib protested. "Cecily is still out there!"

"You're not going anywhere." Devrin pushed a walnut shell filled with a steaming broth into Calib's paws. "Macie is leading another search party in the woods."

"You're on strict orders from Madame von Mandrake to rest and recover," Warren said. "And she said you had to drink this."

"What is it?" Calib asked as he sniffed the soup. It was odorless, even though he saw chunks of garlic floating in the broth.

"Er, there's one more thing we should mention. . . ." Devrin trailed off, and Warren looked down at his footpaws.

An awful dread loomed in Calib's mind. Tentatively, he

reached a paw to his snout. Where he should have felt long whiskers, there were only bristly stubs. Calib's paws trembled, spilling a bit of the soup. *His whiskers!* They were gone!

"They were singed pretty badly from where the lightning struck you," Devrin explained, her brown eyes apologetic. "We had to snip them off."

He gulped a few deep breaths, trying to keep calm. But it was impossible. What was a mouse without his whiskers? They were key to his sense of smell, balance, and direction.

"Are they going to grow back?" Calib asked, his snout twitching despondently.

"That's what the soup is for," Devrin said, nudging the bowl in his paws. "Witchbark is supposed to help with whisker growth."

Calib looked at the walnut shell suspiciously and then took a sip. His sense of taste was also dulled without his whiskers, but even so, the bitterness of the soup made him wince.

Footpaws pounded down the hall, and a moment later, a first-year named Dandelion burst into the infirmary.

"Macie is back!" the little mouse squeaked breathlessly. "The entire search party is in Goldenwood Hall! The knights are— Oh, Calib!" She stopped short and looked down at him in dismay. "Your *whiskers!*"

"Aren't *so* bad," Devrin said forcefully as Calib pulled a sheet over his snout, mortified.

"Er, that's right," Dandelion quickly corrected. "What I mean to say is, the knights are meeting in Goldenwood Hall right now to hear the scouting report."

As Dandelion bounded away to tell the rest of the castle, Calib looked at Devrin and Warren expectantly.

"No," Devrin said, already knowing what Calib was going to ask. "You are not going. You only just woke up. Madame von Mandrake still needs to check you for internal injuries."

"Other than losing my most important body part, I'm the picture of health." Calib kicked his blanket off to demonstrate. He tried to stand, but without his whiskers, the floor felt like it was moving out from under him. Devrin and Warren caught him and lay him back down onto the bed.

"Don't feel too bad. Maybe you'll grow noncrooked whiskers this time," Warren said.

"Aren't you curious to know what they found?" Calib asked. "Don't you want to know what happened to Cecily?"

"Yes," Warren said, "but Commander Kensington said we had to keep a watch on you from now on."

"You can watch me go to Goldenwood Hall, *and* we'll all learn what the scouts found."

Warren and Devrin looked at each other.

"He has a point. . . ." Devrin said.

With his friends' help, Calib gingerly dressed and clambered into a mouse-sized wheelchair made of empty spindles. Devrin and Warren then rolled Calib through the underground mole tunnels that led from the Two-Legger chapel to the throne room, carefully avoiding pebbles and potholes. The spindle-wheels squeaked loudly as they rolled, drawing other creatures' attention.

Calib felt his ears turn pink. He knew he must look ridiculous without his whiskers, but he pushed his embarrassment aside. All that mattered was that Macie was back from her search. She was the best tracker in all of Camelot, both inside the castle and out. Maybe she had already found Cecily and the Grail, and both were back.

But as soon as Calib entered the grand hall, he knew his hope had been foolish. The empty space where the throne had stood for generations yawned like a missing tooth.

A dozen mouse-knights had gathered on the stage at the far side of the arena, looking solemn in their gray armor—armor that had not been needed since the Battle of the Bear last fall. They were joined by Camelot's many ambassadors and advisers—General Fletcher from the bell-tower larks and Ergo Throgg from the moat otters.

And in the center of the creatures stood Macie Cornwall,

still wearing the green leaf cloak that allowed her to blend into the forest. All of Camelot's leaders seemed to be focused on something she held in her paws, but from where the squires stood, Calib couldn't make out what it was or hear what they were saying.

"This was a mistake," Devrin hissed. "You should have stayed in the infirmary."

"No," Calib whispered back hotly. "We need to get closer so we can hear!"

Before they could finish their argument, there was the loud scrabbling of claws on floor as Madame von Mandrake burst into the room, her apron flying behind her.

"What news? Did you find her?" Cecily's mother asked. Her fur was disheveled, and her eyes rimmed red. The sash of herbs she normally wore was missing.

None of the knights would look Madame von Mandrake in the eyes. Slowly, they shuffled back to clear a path to Macie. And for the first time, Calib could see what the squirrel held in her paws: Cecily's sword.

Calib was glad he was already in a wheelchair; otherwise, he was sure his knees would have buckled under him. Cecily would *never* willingly give up her beloved sword! She had saved up for months to have Quills, the porcupine weapons master, make it for her. The nimble rapier was perfect for Cecily's preferred style of fencing—fast and unrelenting. She had dubbed it Whirler.

"I'm so sorry, Viviana," Macie said quietly. "We found this in the woods."

There was a pause while Cecily's mother took in the abandoned sword. Then high-pitched wails filled the hall, the sound clawing its way into Calib's heart like a wild beast and tearing it in two.

CHAPTER
2

"There, there, Viviana," Commander Kensington said, placing a comforting paw on Madame von Mandrake's heaving shoulders. It was a show of affection Calib had never seen the commander display before. "We don't know for sure what happened. There is no need to assume the worst."

A few of the cooking assistants hurried to Madame von Mandrake and carefully led her to a corner chair. Slowly, her wails turned to stifled sobs, and finally, to silent, weeping tears. Sir Alric poured her a thimble of tea, which she accepted gratefully. Only then did the meeting continue.

"We have more news," Macie said. Her ear tufts twitched. "During our search, we found signs of doused campfires and berry bushes stripped from foraging. We think these are signs of a Saxon retreat and movement back toward the Iron Mountains in the west."

"Sounds like more Saxon trickery," a stout hare named Thropper observed. He was an ambassador from the Darkling Woods, sent on behalf of their leader, a fearsome lynx named Leftie Wildfang. The hare shook his head, and the many hoops on his ears jangled. "They only want us to *think* they are leaving."

General Fletcher ruffled his feathers. "And what does Leftie say?" he squawked. "We haven't heard a word from your leader these past few months—since the white fever hit. Could it be that he's turned tail on us?"

The hare surged to his hind legs and put his paws up in a boxer's stance. "Come a little closer and say that to me again!"

"Enough of your bickering!" Madame von Mandrake yelled at the top of her lungs. The entire hall hushed as Camelot's head cook surged to her feet. "Need I remind you that my daughter is kidnapped? None of your grudges matter now. We need to bring her back!"

Thropper lowered his front paws to the floor. "I apologize, General," he said stiffly.

The lark tucked his beak into his chest, preening angrily a moment before snapping out, "I beg your pardon, Ambassador."

The Darklings had fought Camelot for generations. They only recently became allies against the Saxons thanks to Calib and his friends' efforts. Still, peace among the two factions was often a fragile thing.

"Leftie has not been answering my letters, either," Thropper said, sounding worried. He looked toward Commander Kensington. "I'm sure there's a good reason."

Kensington nodded, her scarred snout wrinkling in worry. "That may be so, but I admit his absence in court is trouble— What in seven whiskers are you three doing here?!" she suddenly roared, striding through the scattering creatures to stop in front of the squires.

"You're supposed to be in the infirmary!" she thundered.

Calib cringed.

"It's my fault, Commander," Devrin said, quickly saluting.

"I wanted to know how we could help," Warren added.

"You've already given testimony, Warren," Commander Kensington said. "We know Percy took you by surprise, and you couldn't do anything to help. Now please go back to bed!"

"Hang on a moment," General Fletcher chirped. He narrowed his eyes at Warren. "Didn't this gray mousling once lie to everyone to cover up Percival's deeds?"

It was true. Warren had once lied for Sir Percival about what he saw the night of Commander Yvers's murder. Suspicion spread through the crowd like a contagious yawn.

Warren's eyes widened, and his lower lip trembled. "No, I didn't! I mean, I did. But that was different. *I'm different now,*" he babbled. His whiskers twitched nervously.

"Warren wasn't involved," Calib said loudly. Even though the gray mouse could be a total snot sometimes, Warren had saved his life at the Battle of the Bear. And he had more than redeemed himself in the months that followed by helping rid the castle of white fever.

Calib's paws shook as he hoisted himself out of the wheelchair. "It was my fault." The truth caught in his throat. Everyone would now know he was responsible for Cecily's kidnapping, including Madame von Mandrake.

"I know why Percival took the throne," Calib continued, willing his voice steady. "It's because the throne is Merlin's Promise, the last great Two-Legger treasure."

A confused silence greeted this revelation. Years ago, the great wizard Merlin had entrusted three magical treasures to the woodland realms before disappearing shortly after. The first was Merlin's Mirror, which had the power to see into the future. The wizard had given it to the

Darklings, but it was broken many years ago during a raid by the Saxons.

The second was Merlin's Crystal, given to the owls for safekeeping. Calib and his friends had discovered last autumn that it could unlock Excalibur from its stone.

Finally, the third treasure was called Merlin's Promise. This treasure was supposedly entrusted to the Camelot mice, but no one knew exactly what it was, and it had been commonly believed that the castle itself was the treasure.

Calib explained to the crowd how the Lady of the Lake had revealed to him and Cecily that Merlin had left the third treasure somewhere inside the castle. Calib had eventually figured out that Merlin's third treasure was actually a wooden Two-Legger goblet—the Grail—that the mice had used as a throne for many, many years. He also recounted how he had accidentally given the final clue to Sir Percival Vole, who pieced it together and stole away the Goldenwood Throne before Calib could warn anyone.

"And so, it's my fault that Cecily got captured," the mouse finished, a sob welling in his voice. The relief of admitting everything felt like releasing a dam. "I'm so sorry, Madame von Mandrake. I've failed you—I've failed you all."

He looked down at his footpaws, not wanting to see everyone's stunned expressions. Now that the truth was out, he was terrified of what would happen next. No one said anything. The room remained silent. A warm tear wet the fur around Calib's eye. Would they all despise him now?

Suddenly, a pawkerchief was dabbed at his cheeks. Surprised, he looked up to see Madame von Mandrake.

"There, there, *mon cher*," she said. "Don't carry it all on yourself. The only person to blame is that poisonous little vole." She whipped back her paw and brandished her pawkerchief in the air. "If he harms one strand of my Cecily's fur, I'll cut off his tail with my cleaver!"

Commander Kensington smiled slightly, but already she was strategizing, the look in her eyes distant. "If this is so, Calib—and I believe you—what does the throne do? What kind of power are we dealing with here?"

"I don't know." Calib looked at his paws. He was not being nearly as helpful as he wanted to be. "But I know that we need to get it out of the Manderlean's paws before it's used against us!"

There were murmurs as the knights and other leaders nodded their heads.

After the sorceress Morgan le Fay, the Manderlean was the most dangerous enemy known to Camelot—and certainly the most dangerous on four paws. No one knew where he had come from or even what kind of creature he was, as he always hid his face behind a golden mask, but he was the driving force behind the Saxon animal attacks.

The masked villain had eluded justice at the Battle of the Bear. For months, they'd had no word of him, until Calib had discovered a letter in Red's room with the Manderlean's signature paw print on it. It was only then that he'd realized the Saxons were working with Morgan le Fay and that the white fever had been another of their plots against Camelot.

"I need volunteers to go farther afield and search again," Commander Kensington said once Calib had concluded his tale. "Time is of the essence. We *must* recover Cecily and the Grail before Percival reaches the Manderlean."

Nearly everyone in the room raised their paws, including the squires, but Commander Kensington selected a handful of Macie's elite squirrel scouts, as well as Sir Alric and Ambassador Thropper.

"The search party will resupply with Macie and then head out tonight, under the cover of darkness. Everyone is dismissed."

The knights and emissaries saluted and began to leave the hall.

"Wait, what about us?" Calib asked, gesturing to himself, Warren, and Devrin. "We're the ones with the most information."

"You and Warren need to stay in the infirmary and heal," Commander Kensington said. "And I can't spare Devrin just yet."

"But—"

"What part of my order invited any discussion on the matter?" Commander Kensington said in a tone that invited no answer to that question at all. "The mark of a good leader is understanding how your actions affect others. Your grandfather understood that. I need you to rest and regain your health. Viviana?" she called across the room to Cecily's mother. "Would you please escort these two creatures back to the sick bay?"

Madame von Mandrake approached and took over wheeling Calib back to the infirmary while Warren trudged behind her. Devrin shot them a sympathetic look before she scurried away after the commander.

Calib stewed silently. Part of him was angry at Commander Kensington. How dare she lecture him, the last Christopher, about his own grandfather? But on the other paw, Calib could not deny the truth of her words. Because of his actions, many creatures had already been put in harm's way.

He sighed loudly.

"I know that you care about Cecily very much," Madame von Mandrake said as they entered the infirmary, startling Calib. A flush of color came to Calib's ears as Warren snickered quietly behind them. "But Kensington is right. There is no point in acting rashly. I do appreciate your dedication, and I know Cecily would too."

After she settled Warren, Madame von Mandrake

helped Calib back into his bed, gave him a quick hug, and left him to his own thoughts.

Calib had never felt so powerless. The Grail and his best friend were in enemy paws. He wished he still had some of Merlin's magic to fix this mess.

He paused.

He needed Excalibur.

CHAPTER
3

Galahad du Lac could feel beads of sweat forming on his forehead as he stood by the door of the throne room. Today, it was packed with the usual courtiers and knights, and more unusual guests, like the farmers and local townsmen. The air was stuffier than the kitchens. Only the slightest of breezes blew in from the broken window behind the throne. The ragged glass was a constant reminder of Mordred's escape from justice. With the sleeve of his tunic, Galahad quickly wiped his forehead and hoped his father, Sir Lancelot, had not noticed.

All afternoon long, King Arthur and Queen Guinevere had been holding court, listening to petitions and making decisions big and small that would keep the castle running smoothly. Ever since the white fever had passed two weeks ago, Arthur and his knights had been doing everything they could to put the castle back into working order. And while the king seemed content to work until sundown, everyone else seemed to have long since lost patience.

Galahad glanced around at the ladies-in-waiting who sighed and cooled themselves with paper fans. Knights stifled yawns and battled drooping eyelids. Even Queen Guinevere's gaze seemed to wander toward the windows.

Father Walter could not have been assigned a worse time to bring up their cause, Galahad thought. This late in the day, everyone would be too tired to listen. Plus, the knights were in a foul mood. They had just denied the last petition from the merchants' guild to improve the southern roads with cobblestone.

"Every rock is needed to reinforce the outer walls, especially at the rivers," Sir Kay said. King Arthur eventually agreed.

The head of the merchants' guild, a man with a woolly beard that would have looked at home on a sheep, protested, "Please, Your Majesty, just consider—"

"We are at war now," King Arthur cut in. "The Saxons could attack again at any time. We must think strategically about the resources we have left. Next petitioner, please."

Galahad clenched his jaw as he swung the door open for Father Walter, who had been waiting outside in the antechamber. This was *definitely* not a good time, but they desperately needed to resupply the infirmary.

The old healer slowly shambled up to the Round Table, leaning onto Galahad for support and guidance. The white fever had left the old man blind, and his joints had not recovered. Some days, he could barely get out of bed.

"Greetings, Father Walter. How are you feeling?" King Arthur said, his expression softening at the sight of the castle's oldest inhabitant and wisest healer.

"Not the spry chicken I once was, Artie," Walter said, using an old nickname from when he knew the king as a young squire.

A number of courtiers looked scandalized, but King Arthur laughed. "It's been a long time since I've been called that. Times were simpler then."

Father Walter let go of Galahad's elbow and eased into one of the wooden chairs that lined the Round Table. Galahad admired the Celtic knot designs that decorated the surface. The Round Table was the most important symbol of King Arthur's reign, representing his belief that a true king makes himself an equal among his people.

"The past only ever seems simple when the future is uncertain," Father Walter said as he drew out a scroll from his pockets. Galahad unrolled it and passed it around to the knights.

"We've finally had a chance to take stock of our apothecary. It seems that your nephew made a mess of things, destroying our rarest herbs and potions."

Mutters of anger rose in the room, and a trace of guilt passed like a shadow across Arthur's face. Red had been the king's guest in the castle, as an olive branch from his estranged sister, Morgan le Fay, who was Red's mother. Unfortunately, Red had proven to be less of an olive branch and more of a thorn.

While the king was expected to make a full recovery from Red's assassination attempt, Galahad was still taken aback to see how much it had affected him. Arthur now walked with a slight limp and often needed a cane. His hair, which had been the color of an autumn leaf, was now more gray than red.

"Thanks to Galahad and Excalibur, we've overcome the worst of the sickness," Father Walter continued. "But now our stores are sorely depleted, and we need to resupply as soon as possible."

Queen Guinevere, seated at King Arthur's right, nodded. "What would you require to accomplish this?"

The old healer inclined his head in the queen's direction. "A company of riders, strong mounts, and soldiers to stand guard as we gather the necessary herbs and—"

"Unfortunately, Father Walter," Sir Kay, Arthur's foster brother, interrupted, "all our riders are currently occupied in the countryside, rallying defenders to Camelot."

Father Walter frowned. "They could pick some of the items on my list while they travel. We need only send them a lark."

"I will not have my men picking flowers while we rally for war," another knight cut in. "We are more vulnerable than ever!"

Galahad opened his mouth to respond, but the queen spoke first.

"If our troops are injured, isn't it just as important that we can heal them?" Guinevere asked. "After all, last time our enemies attacked us with a fever, not swords."

"But the boy fixed everything with his magical sword, didn't he?" Sir Kay exclaimed. "Why couldn't he do it again?"

Galahad shifted uncomfortably on his feet as all eyes in the throne room fell on him. Since he had lifted the curse on the castle, rumors of Galahad's command over magic had quickly spread into outright exaggerations. He'd noticed that other pages and squires treated him with almost a servant's respect now. Knights had taken to tousling his hair for good luck before a tournament. And just last week, Malcolm, a page, had snipped a lock of his blond hair, saying it was for an experimental soup to heal boils.

"My sword is unpredictable," Galahad said, hoping his voice would stay steady. "I barely understand what it can do."

"Then maybe you should give it to someone smarter," Sir Kay groused.

"Watch your tongue," Sir Lancelot said, his gray eyes flashing. "Half of you are alive and standing because of my son. I agree with the queen. We need to make sure the healers have what they need."

Galahad bit back a relieved smile. His father—the greatest knight in all of Camelot—was still coming to terms with the fact that Galahad didn't want to follow in his steps. His defense was heartening to hear.

Sir Kay rattled the parchment list in front of Father Walter's nose. "Will anything on this list heal a soldier fast enough to turn the tide of a battle?"

"Nothing would," the healer replied calmly, "short of Excalibur's magic. But people will be injured, and they will need to be tended to."

"Not if we do the injuring first!" Sir Kay declared.

"That is enough." Arthur's voice rang out, silencing the chatter in the hall. He closed his eyes, as if he didn't want to say his next words. "Father Walter, I am afraid Sir Kay has a point. We have hard decisions to make in the coming weeks. All our resources must go toward battle preparations."

Galahad's jaw dropped open. Never in a million years did he think Arthur would come to the defense of someone as blockheaded as Sir Kay. Even Father Walter looked taken aback.

"What happens if there is a siege?" the old man asked. "Arrows will not stop a disease from spreading."

"No, they will not," Arthur agreed. "But I would rather ensure that a siege does not begin in the first place. Is there any other way you can get what you need?"

"There is one," Father Walter said slowly. "If we possessed the Grail again . . ."

Some of the knights in the room looked at one another and coughed. King Arthur's face became pale with anger. He raised his hand for silence.

"Do not say another word to me about the Grail," King Arthur said, his voice low and steady. "It is a fool's quest."

Galahad blinked in surprise. He didn't know the healer believed in the existence of the Grail. He knew of it from the stories his mother, Lady Elaine, had told him in front of the fireplace during the long winter nights when they'd waited for Sir Lancelot to return from a far-off war. But it had been lost years ago, and no one had seen it since.

Father Walter, who had become hard of hearing, barreled on, "I believe that Excalibur could be used to discover the Grail's whereabouts."

"No." This time it was Sir Lancelot who spoke. "I will not have my son wandering enemy territory alone, seeking something that was destroyed years ago—or may not even exist at all!"

"I appreciate your viewpoint, Walter, but I must continue on to the next petitioner," King Arthur said with an air of finality. "We need to make do with what we have now. Perhaps Guinevere can spare a few ladies-in-waiting to help you gather more herbs in the countryside."

"Gladly," the queen responded. "And may I offer my flower garden to your cause? Roses may be beautiful, but I would rather tend to something that is both beautiful and helpful."

"Thank you, Your Majesty," Father Walter said as Galahad hurried to help him up. As they exited back into the antechamber, the old man quietly muttered, "It won't be enough. If Morgan attacks with magic again, we will not be prepared." His eyes looked more tired than usual.

"Father . . ." Galahad paused, unsure of how to say it. "The Grail . . . Do you believe it exists?" When Father Walter nodded, Galahad rushed on, "Is it true, then, what they say of its healing powers?"

Father Walter let out a long sigh. "All I know is that whoever bears it will be invincible—that their wounds immediately close. Merlin wrote about it, you know. But no one paid any attention to his scrolls."

CLANG!

Galahad jumped in his skin. He turned just in time to see a suit of armor collapse into pieces on the floor.

CHAPTER
4

Calib's teeth chattered as the clang of the decorative breastplate echoed around him. He'd waited by the mice hole located behind a piece of loose tile in the throne room. The petition had ended sooner than he thought, and Galahad and Walter were already leaving.

Dodging between the long robes and dresses of the Two-Leggers in King Arthur's court, Calib just managed to slip under the door after Galahad and Father Walter. But they were walking too quickly for Calib to catch up to them, especially in the afternoon, when there were massive Two-Legger feet that needed to be avoided.

That's when Calib noticed the decorative suits of armor that stood at attention in the hallway. He'd only *meant* to climb onto one of the plumed helmets, but without his whiskers, he'd misjudged his speed—and the entire hollow suit had tumbled down.

Well, at least he'd gotten Galahad's attention. He began to wave a paw out of one of the visor's slits.

"Goodness, what was that?"

"A suit of armor, Father Walter, fallen over from a breeze," Galahad said. To Calib, he mouthed silently, "What are you doing here?"

"Must have been some breeze to make such a clunking noise on the metal. I could have sworn I heard the pitter-patter of mice just now."

"Ha-ha, Father," Galahad said weakly. "It's been a long afternoon. Why don't I take you to the garden for some fresh air, and I'll quickly clean up here?"

Calib heard the *rat-a-tat* of Father Walter's cane fading into the castle's hallways. After a minute or two of waiting, the helmet's visor suddenly flipped open.

"Calib!" Galahad scolded. "What on Earth are you— *Oh!*"

Calib had stepped out. He wobbled a bit, and the whole floor seemed to tilt sideways.

"What *happened* to you?" Galahad gasped. His right hand gripped Excalibur's hilt—allowing him to understand animals.

"I was struck by lightning," Calib said, trying to wave his paw loftily, but his dizziness put him off-balance, and he swayed. Galahad quickly placed his palm down for Calib to steady himself on.

"From the storm two nights ago?" Galahad asked incredulously. "Calib, you could have died!"

"I'm all right," Calib said. He focused on Galahad's nose to keep his vision from swimming. "But I need your help. We need to find R—"

But Calib stopped speaking as the doors of the throne room slammed open and the court spilled out, the king and queen seeming to have finished listening to petitions for the day. Without saying anything, Galahad gave a small nod of his head, and Calib scurried up his arm and into his tunic pocket.

They waited until the last noble, a woman with a conical hat and sleepy eyes, bustled out before Galahad reentered and bolted the door.

"We need to find Red," Calib finished as Galahad placed Calib on top of the Round Table.

"I know we do," Galahad sighed. "Sir Kay's sent out some scouts, but I don't really think they're trying. Why are you shaking your head?"

"You misunderstand me," Calib said, his words tumbling over themselves in their haste to get out. "*We* need to find Red. You and me. They've kidnapped Cecily and stolen the Grail!"

"Cecily!" The Two-Legger's mouth dropped open. "And . . . the *Grail*?"

Calib's whiskerless nose twitched. "You know of it?"

"Of course." Galahad began to pace now, long strides that took him from one end of the room to the other. In the past year, the boy had grown. Calib thought that someday not too far in the distant future, he might be as tall as his giant of a father.

"And Cecily!" Galahad exclaimed, swinging back to face the mouse. "I'm so sorry, Calib. What happened?"

Calib recounted everything, explaining how all three of Camelot's greatest foes seemed to have joined together to defeat them: the Saxons; the Manderlean; and Morgan le Fay, Red's mother. When he came to the revelation that the Grail had been in the castle under all their tails all along, Galahad fell back into a seat at the Round Table.

"The Grail," Galahad breathed. "I can't believe that it's real. That it actually *exists!*"

"I think if we find Red, we'll find the whole rotten lot of them—and Cecily," Calib concluded, slightly winded from all the talking. He was suddenly bone-tired. Maybe

Commander Kensington was right, and he was exerting himself too much.

Galahad placed his tiniest finger between Calib's ears. "Are you feeling all right, Calib?"

"It's my whiskers," Calib muttered miserably. He wished he weren't such a mousling about them—after all, it was Cecily who was now in enemy paws.

"I have an idea," Galahad whispered. Standing up, he unsheathed Excalibur and pointed the sword at the mouse's snout.

Calib's heart began to knock against his chest. "What are you doing?" he squeaked.

"I want to try healing with Excalibur, if that's all right with you."

Eyeing the sharp edge of the blade, Calib nodded. Galahad was his best friend, after Cecily. He had trusted the Two-Legger with his life before, and he trusted him still.

Closing his eyes, Galahad seemed to sink into himself, reaching for the soft hum of power that always emanated from Excalibur. Calib could feel the energy change in the air as the boy began to focus.

Galahad adjusted his grip on the hilt slightly. Calib was now aware of a second heartbeat that was not his own, though it pounded in his ears as if it were. The ripple of a draft blew through his fur. An ache throbbed somewhere behind his nose.

The pain began to cool, turning into a sensation as soothing as a babbling brook, as refreshing as a spring's day. Then suddenly—

Searing heat flashed through Calib's nose, as if he were being struck by lightning a second time.

"Ow!" Calib cried, placing a paw right on his snout. Galahad's eyes flew open. He jerked Excalibur's point up and away.

"Are you a-all right?" he stammered.

"It hurt for a moment, but . . ." Calib trailed off as his pawpads brushed against something long and thin. "Oh! My whiskers are back!"

Galahad stooped to examine his work and winced. "I think I got the color wrong." He held his sword like a mirror up to Calib.

"Oh . . ." Calib wasn't sure what to say. Where there had once been bright-white whiskers, there were now a bunch of black, unruly ones that curled outward like weeds. He wrinkled his snout back and forth, soaking in the scents that finally flooded his nose. He could detect Galahad's sweat, the musty woodwork from the table, and a strong spicy odor that seemed to come from the sword itself. The smell from the sword was actually a little over-whelming.

"Good . . . good as new," Calib managed to say. He put on a brave smile. Despite the surprising color, at least these new whiskers weren't crooked like his previous ones. Plus, they worked phenomenally well.

"I'm so sorry," Galahad said, and Calib noticed his skin looked ashen. "Red said I needed a proper teacher, but without Merlin . . . who's to teach me?"

Calib patted Galahad's thumb. "I love my new whiskers," he said, and meant it. "And now, we can search for Red."

Galahad sighed. "But no one knows where he went."

Sitting on the table, Calib twiddled his tail in his paws and tried to think where he would flee if he were Red. But it was hard. Camelot, with its turrets and secret crevices, was *home*. He supposed he would go live in the woods with Valentina and the rest of the Darklings. That is, if Valentina ever wanted to see him again, after the danger he'd put them in. Shoving the thought back with a hard push, Calib asked, "Where would you go if you had to leave Camelot?"

To Calib's surprise, Galahad answered without hesitation. "Easy—I'd go to St. Anne's."

Calib's ears twitched in confusion. "The *nunnery*?"

Smiling, Galahad reached into a pocket and pulled out a small locket. Inside was a portrait of a woman with long blond hair and a kind smile. Calib immediately recognized the smile, as it was identical to Galahad's.

"This is my mother, Lady Elaine," Galahad said

somewhat wistfully. "She lives at St. Anne's Nunnery. A few years after I was born, she left Camelot because she wanted to keep me safe. And I think she was often lonely while my father was away war campaigning for Arthur."

Excitement grew in Calib's chest. "What if Red would go back to his mother too?" Almost as soon as he said it, his hopes fell. "But, of course, no one knows where Morgan is."

"*Red* knew," Galahad said. "And he sent letters."

Now Calib truly smiled. "The *larks*."

Galahad grinned back and held out his open palm for Calib to clamber onto. "You know what?" he said. "Sometimes it feels like you know me better than most people."

"You say that as if you are surprised," Calib said as he braced himself against Galahad's thumb. "Mice are known to be *excellent* listeners."

Together, they traveled to the southernmost tower in the castle, up the exhausting spiral staircases leading to the aviary. Wide windows faced all four cardinal directions, and Galahad could see the Iron Mountains in the west as a thin range of gray. The air was breezy but smelled distinctly of bird poop. Dozens of cages hung on chains from the rafters, each housing a lark family. Feathers covered the ground like a layer of snow.

The loud chattering of larks quieted as Galahad entered

the room. The largest bird, General Felix, took off from his perch and settled in front of Galahad and Calib in a swirl of feathers.

"Squire Calib, you're not supposed to be out of bed," he chided, his head bobbing with each word. "Commander Kensington will not be pleased."

"It's my fault, sir," Galahad said. "I needed help."

The lark flapped his wings in surprise. Though all the animals had heard about Galahad's ability, not all of them had experienced it firsthand the way Calib had.

"Oh?" General Felix clacked his beak. "And why is that?"

"We want to speak with the larks who had delivered messages to Morgan le Fay on behalf of the traitor Red," Calib said quickly. "I have a lot of questions."

Felix's eyes darkened. "As do I," the general said. "Those messengers never came back."

The fur behind Calib's neck inched up. "They never came back? What do you mean?"

General Felix took a few agitated hops. "At first, we thought they stayed away because of the white fever, but the cursed sickness has passed, and no one's returned."

"Have you sent anyone to look for them?" Galahad asked. Felix cocked his head at the Two-Legger, looking slightly suspicious.

"The search party has yet to return," Felix finally said.

"I'll need to send another search party for them next."

"And where were they sent?" Calib asked.

"The Iron Mountains, in the path of the Dragon's Eye," Felix said. He fluffed his feathers and pointed a wing to the sky.

"All I see are clouds," Calib said.

General Felix rustled his feathers. "It's a star, squire. Of course you can't see it now, in broad daylight! But at night, it gleams with a reddish glow. And that's where the king's nephew sent all his messages. In the path of the Dragon's Eye."

Galahad bowed and said, "Thank you, Master Felix, for your help."

"Mmph," General Felix said with an odd head bob. "If I learn anything more, I'll be sure to let you know." Then with a farewell chirp, he flew high up into the rafters to give his report to the other birds.

Galahad looked at Calib. "I need some time to prepare," he said.

"We don't have time," Calib said, fear pulsing in his chest with every breath. "The treasure will be cared for—Morgan wants it. But Cecily . . . I don't know why they took her." He closed his eyes, trying to push out the worry. The fear. The *guilt*.

"I only need a little time," Galahad promised. "Besides, we can't follow the Dragon's Eye in the day."

Each second that passed was another weight on Calib's heart. But Cecily was brave and strong, and if anyone could take care of herself, it was her.

Calib nodded. "We'll meet on the bridge at midnight."

CHAPTER
5

The bells in the tower tolled half past eleven. Galahad had everything ready—a satchel of food, sturdy
boots, and a thick cloak that might be useful in the
cooler air of the mountains. But still . . . he wasn't ready
to meet Calib at the bridge, not yet.

He'd lost control earlier that day. When he had regrown
Calib's whiskers, the sword had felt odd in his hands, as if
it were a horse he couldn't command. That heat! He could
have really hurt Calib.

Or worse. Was it even safe for him to use the sword?

Perhaps Sir Kay was right. Perhaps he should give it to someone smarter. . . .

A soft knocking on his bedroom door startled him. "Who is it?" Galahad called out. He quickly shoved his travel bags underneath his bed.

"Father Walter."

Surprised, as it was many hours past Father Walter's usual bedtime, Galahad opened the door. In walked the old man, along with . . .

"Bors! Malcolm!" Galahad exclaimed. "What are you all doing here?" But Malcolm, a strapping lad of fourteen, ignored Galahad and promptly reached under the bed.

"Sneaking out of the castle again, Exacli-Boy?" Malcolm asked as he tugged out Galahad's packs.

"No! I mean, maybe, but . . . how did you know?" Galahad asked. Malcolm was usually too focused on coming up with new dishes for the kitchens to notice anything other than the frying pan in front of him. The one-time castle bully had since found a calling as a talented chef.

"Spied you in the cellars after dinner shoving your pockets full of cheese rounds and dried fruit." Malcolm removed a block of cheese from Galahad's bag. "I actually need this brie for a fish bake later."

"When Malcolm told me, we figured you were probably up to something, so we let Father Walter know." Bors folded his arms into his long sleeves. The former page was now the castle historian, tasked with documenting all its minutiae.

Galahad looked at the old healer, who had shuffled to Galahad's bed and was now resting his feet. "Are you going to say anything to the others?"

Father Walter bowed his head. "That depends. Are you leaving to gather supplies for the infirmary?"

"In a matter of speaking . . ." Galahad shifted uncomfortably. "I am going to quest for the Grail."

"Told you!" Malcolm said with a light punch to Bors's shoulder while Father Walter frowned. For a long moment, Father Walter didn't speak, and Galahad wondered if he had made a mistake.

But then the old man slowly nodded.

"The king has forbidden it, yes, but I believe that Merlin's secrets run deeper than most secrets," Father Walter said. "And you have already wielded one of his treasures with grace and courage." Galahad felt a blush rise in his cheeks.

"But while swords were made for war, the Grail was meant to maintain peace," Walter continued. "I'm not sure why Merlin hid the Grail, but perhaps he knew that Arthur would always fall back on war instead of looking for other solutions. Bors?"

The castle recorder hurried forward, and for the first time, Galahad noticed a scroll tucked under his arm.

"This is the only one of Merlin's Scrolls that Red didn't steal," Bors said. "And that's only because I had it in my chambers. I haven't been able to translate it at all, but maybe something in there will help."

"Thank you," Galahad said. "We—I mean, *I*—need all the help I can get."

"Merlin acted odd during his last days," Father Walter said, turning to face Galahad. Even though he could no longer see, the healer's eyes were full of kindness. "In the months leading up to his disappearance, Merlin would visit me often for elixirs of strength. Some thought he was dying or at least deathly ill."

"Was he?" Galahad asked, astonished that Walter had personally known the famed wizard.

"Not quite," Father Walter replied. "He seemed to be fading, more like. I saw him once wander into the woods as if sleepwalking. And another time, I thought I saw a white wolf walk in his footsteps, as if it were stalking him."

Galahad nodded, noting the information for later.

"Where are you going to start?" Malcolm asked.

"The Iron Mountains. Red said he was from there," Galahad said, keeping Calib and the rest of the creatures out of the story. It was for the best. Either Father Walter would believe him or he wouldn't, and Galahad didn't have time to try to convince the healer he was of sound mind.

"Then Bors, Malcolm," Father Walter said, reaching for his cane as he stood up, "I'm afraid I need you both to help me in the infirmary, where there are no windows facing the drawbridge, and we can easily say we never *saw* anyone leave."

Bors and Malcolm nodded and hurried to the door. "Best of luck, Galahad," Bors said.

"Remember," Malcolm added, "keep your wrist loose when you parry, and you'll be all right."

Galahad counted to one hundred before he picked up his bags and left his room. In order to preserve the castle supply of torches, only a few hallways were well lit, and he stuck to the shadowy corridors. Suddenly, he heard footsteps and soft voices coming down the hallway.

"Guinevere is right." Galahad's heart sank as he heard his father's voice. "We can't afford to look weak now. Word may reach the Saxons." Light from a torch flickered at the end of the hall. Panicked, Galahad dodged behind a hanging tapestry depicting the coronation of King Arthur, and a moment later, the real Arthur along with Guinevere turned into the hall, accompanied by Sir Lancelot.

"You know exactly how we should show our strength, Lancelot." King Arthur's voice soured with anger. "And yet you drag your feet when it comes to your son! Your boy and his sword are perhaps the best chance we have against the Saxons!"

Galahad's breath caught in his throat. He prayed that

the king was too distracted to notice his boots sticking out from under the tapestry. King Arthur would be furious if he found out Galahad planned on taking Excalibur away from the castle.

"He told me he wants to be a healer, not a fighter," Lancelot said. The trio was now right next to the tapestry, and Galahad caught a glimpse of maps and ink-stained hems. They had clearly been strategizing late into the night.

"I'm afraid he's still too soft-hearted," Lancelot continued. "Galahad's still a child with childish hopes. He's not ready to lead."

So that was how his father *really* felt about him. The fact that his father had hid his disappointment from Galahad somehow stung harder than any insult or embarrassment.

"Give your son more credit than that, Lancelot," Guinevere admonished, her voice fading as they drifted down the corridor. "There are different types of strength. . . ."

The torchlight grew dimmer and dimmer, until Galahad's only companions were the darkness and the sound of the chapel bell striking midnight, its dolorous chimes echoing in Galahad's heart like a warning.

CHAPTER
6

Calib held on to Galahad's ear as the boy slid into the cold water of the moat. Even though he'd spent a lot of the past spring sailing the ocean, Calib had never taken to swimming.

Meanwhile, Galahad treaded the water as silently as he could on his back, keeping to the shadow of the draw-bridge. He held his traveling pack on his chest.

"You'd think, after all the sneaking out we do, we'd be better at this," Galahad joked, teeth chattering. He coughed as a wave of river water splashed into his mouth and dripped onto Calib's tail. After climbing to the top of Galahad's head and then onto the travel pack, Calib wrung out his tail. In addition to bringing back his whiskers—albeit a different color than intended—Galahad had managed to heal Calib of his aches. Calib had pretended to be sick in the infirmary for the rest of the evening. Madame von Mandrake had marveled at what she thought was an extraordinary batch of witchbark broth.

"I should bottle it up and sell it to the balding moles!" she had exclaimed upon seeing Calib's fully regrown whiskers. "How potent!"

Flicking his tail free of the last of the river water, Calib glanced up at the night sky, scattered with starlight.

"We're coming, Cecily," he whispered, wistfully hoping that somewhere far away, under the same stars, his friend could hear him.

Once they swam to the other side, Galahad and Calib dried off as best they could, changing into the extra clothes they brought.

They journeyed in the dark through the fields, not daring to make for the road until they were far beyond Camelot's borders. As Calib passed the old cobbler's hut, which marked the last building in town, he turned to look back at the castle one last time.

From where he stood, the torches along the battlements

danced like fairies in the night, encircling the castle with a protective embrace. Calib's whiskers twitched, and he was filled with bittersweet melancholy. There truly was no place anywhere else quite like Camelot. And for as long as he drew breath as a Christopher, he would vow to protect it.

"Don't worry," Galahad said. "We'll be back soon."

Calib turned to face the opposite direction, singling out the brightest star, the Dragon's Eye. Its reddish light stood out in stark contrast to the summer night's velvety blackness. That's where Cecily was. That's where Camelot's hope lay.

Calib did not look back again.

Though it was late, the side roads weren't completely empty. Twice, a Two-Legger wagon trundled by, filled with siege supplies for the castle. The only creatures they encountered were a smattering of Darklings, skittish and huddled in small family-groups. Their slight silhouettes cast long shadows on the ground against the pale moonlight . . . including one that seemed familiar to Calib.

"Ruby?" he whisper-called.

The silhouette froze. "Calib Christopher?" the fox asked after sniffing the air.

"Go on," Galahad murmured. "I'll walk slowly so you can catch up."

Calib nodded, relieved that he didn't have to explain

to Galahad that a fox might not necessarily enjoy a Two-Legger's company.

"What are you doing here?" Calib asked, peering around the fox chieftain's legs to see a quartet of brand-new kits sleepily following their mother.

"I could ask the same of you," Ruby said, and bared her teeth in a smile that, had it been any other fox, might have sent Calib running. But Ruby was a friend of his and Cecily's—one to whom he owed his life.

"Something terrible has happened," Calib said, before sorrowfully rehashing Cecily's kidnapping. When he had finished, he heard a rumbling sound from above. At first, Calib thought it might be thunder, but then he realized the vixen was growling deep in her throat.

"Those villains," she said with a snarl. Her golden eyes flashed. "That's the fifth kidnapping this week!"

Calib swiveled his ears in her direction, unsure he had heard her right. "Fifth kidnapping?"

"Aye." The fox nodded, then quickly brought her nose to the top of each of her kits' heads. "Animals keep vanishing from the forest, not returning from the hunts."

Calib's fur prickled. "Are the Saxons attacking the Darklings?"

"Aye," Ruby said wearily. "They've been causing all kinds of trouble since the white fever started. Some other creatures have said that they're coming down from the Iron

Mountains at night, grabbing woodland folks unawares, and disappearin' 'em."

His breath caught at the mention of the Iron Mountains again, and Calib tightened his grip on Lightbringer, the sword given to him by Commander Kensington. More and more, the white fever epidemic unleashed by Morgan le Fay and the Manderlean felt like it had been a distraction. But if the fever—which had killed hundreds of creatures—was only a distraction . . . what worse kind of devastation could Camelot's enemies be setting into motion?

"That's why I'm bringing my kits to the castle," Ruby continued. "It's too dangerous, especially with some of my band missing. I'm hoping Ambassador Thropper can put in a good word for us."

"But Leftie hasn't sent any wo—"

"Leftie has already withdrawn his own camp from the foothills," the vixen interrupted loudly, accidentally startling her kits. They broke out into soft whimpers, and Ruby hastily began to lick their ears. When they had settled, she said with a sigh, "Merlin knows where Leftie is off to now."

Setting a paw on Ruby's much larger, clawed one, Calib thanked her. "Camelot will be happy to have you and your family," he said.

"We'll see about that," Ruby said, and then began to nudge her kits to their feet again. "But as Camelot produced such fine young creatures like you and Cecily, I am hopeful. I wish I could assist you in the rescue, but the kits . . ."

"It's all right," Calib said. "I have some help already."

"Good." Ruby nodded. "Then may Merlin guide you on your quest."

Calib bowed cordially and ran to catch up with Galahad, who was waiting at a crossroads many steps ahead.

"We better hurry," Galahad said, stooping to offer a hand for Calib to climb on. "There's still—"

"Shh!" Calib said. The earth beneath his paws had begun to tremble, and a moment later, his sensitive ears caught the sound of hoofbeats. And not just any plodding draft horse's steps, but the dainty fanfare of a royal horse.

"A guard!" Calib said. "They must have realized you've snuck out with Excalibur!" The boy snatched Calib up and dashed into the trees.

"Careful!" Calib squeaked as thin branches slapped against them. The hoofbeats were closer now—the rider had followed them off the path.

"Hide," Calib ordered, and Galahad threw them into a nearby yew bush. The smell of the crushed berries they'd flattened filled Calib's nostrils, and he tried not to sneeze as the rider thundered into the thicket and came to a halt.

There was a soft squelch of leaves as the rider hopped down from their mount.

"Galahad," the rider called out, "are you out here?"

The unmistakable voice, clear and regal, belonged to Queen Guinevere.

CHAPTER
7

Galahad heard Calib's squeak of surprise as he rose to his feet and stepped out of the yew bush. There was no point in hiding. He'd been caught. As best he could with berry stains on his tunic, he bowed to his queen.

"Your M-majesty," he stammered, and bowed. "It's a pleasure to see you this evening—er, morning?"

Holding her dappled mare's reins with one hand, Queen Guinevere gestured him forward with the other. In a finely crafted muslin dress—dyed a dark shade of green—and with a sparkling silver crown adorning her dark braids, she looked like a fairy queen beckoning to Galahad from another world.

Taking a tentative step forward, Galahad bowed again. This time, he felt Calib's tiny paws hop across his neck and into the hood of his riding cloak.

"Forgive me if I'm foiling any grand escapes," Queen Guinevere said with a slight smile. She walked around to the other side of her mount, her silk slippers barely making a whisper on the forest floor. She untied a saddlebag and began to rummage through it. "But I wanted to catch you before you were too far from Camelot."

"How did you find us? I mean, me?" Galahad corrected himself, remembering that the queen was not supposed to know about his ability to communicate with Calib.

Guinevere gave him another small smile. "The same way I find out about anything of importance."

From her bag, she gently pulled out her magical mirror—the same one Galahad had looked in last autumn. He shuddered at the memory of the flames that had emerged in the reflection. "I believe this mirror may be better off in your hands now. Along with this."

Guinevere handed him a diary bound in a soft red leather.

"I've written down everything I've ever seen in this mirror," Queen Guinevere said. "Though most of the time, I can barely make sense of the images at all. Go on, take a look."

Galahad did as he was told, wondering when the queen would order him and Excalibur back to the castle. But as he skimmed the pages, he forgot about being in trouble completely.

The visions varied in complexity—a garden overgrown with wild roses, a ray of light shining from a wooden cup. Underneath each one, Guinevere had written down possible meanings. A few of them were circled, where Guinevere had interpreted something correctly. Under an entry written just last summer, Guinevere had been able to foresee that a war with the Saxons was coming.

But as the pages progressed, Galahad saw grimmer and more foreboding visions appear.

A large shadow crawling over the parapets.

The moon turning bloodred.

The castle in flames.

"How long have you had the mirror?" Galahad asked. The diary was almost full, save for the last page, and as thick as the width of his palm.

"Years," the queen said, stroking her mare's nose. "When I first moved to the castle as a new bride, I found the mirror in my bedchamber. Later, I learned that the room once belonged to Morgan le Fay."

Peering at Galahad around her horse, she smiled sadly.

"I know I should have said something about the mirror to Merlin, but . . . I was young. And it used to show me pictures of my brothers and sisters in Cameliard. I missed them terribly, and I didn't want to give it up."

"The pictures, then," Galahad said, "do they show the past, too?"

Queen Guinevere shook her head. "I think not." Taking the diary, she flipped to a recent page, one that showed a sword in a stone. "That vision came a week before you arrived at the castle gates. But still, the visions have remained the same: Camelot still burns and falls to ruin."

Galahad's stomach twisted. "Why are you showing this to me, Your Majesty?"

"Because it showed me something new tonight."

Galahad took the mirror gingerly from the queen's proffered hand. He looked in but saw nothing but a swirling fog. Whatever visions it wanted to show Galahad, they were obscured by his own lack of Sight.

"I'm sorry," Galahad said, disappointed but also relieved. "I'm not sure what I'm supposed to see. I think last time was just a stroke of luck."

"I don't think *you'll* need to use it. I think you're meant to bring it back to its original owners. Those who possessed it even before Morgan le Fay."

A sharp pain pinched his neck as Calib dug his tiny claws in. Galahad shook his head. The mouse was getting very pushy lately.

"Who does it belong to?" he asked, holding the artifact delicately. He worried about breaking the fine glass and metal during the journey ahead.

"I'm not sure I truly know," Guinevere said. "Though," she said with a sidelong glance at Galahad's hood, "I do have some guesses. The only thing I am certain of, however, is that you are the one meant to deliver it. The Fates have their eye on you."

"Then you're not bringing me back to the castle?" Galahad asked.

"No, my friend," Guinevere said. "I would never ask anything of you that you do not believe to be *right*."

"But what about the king?" Galahad asked.

Guinevere sighed, and in that sigh, Galahad thought he detected a mix of sadness and frustration and deepest love. "The king is a good man," she said. "But he is scared—not for himself, but for his people. And fear can lead good men to folly. He believes there is no choice but war."

Weaving her fingers through her mare's mane, the queen leaped onto the horse's back. Picking up her reins, she looked down at Galahad. "For all our sakes, I hope peace is not out of the question yet."

CHAPTER
8

Calib waited until the sound of hooves faded into the
distance before he burst out of Galahad's hood. He
ran down Galahad's arm to examine the mirror.

His heart thumped wildly against his rib cage as he
took it in. Its glassy surface reflected the moon above in
perfect symmetry. "By Merlin's beard," Calib whispered
in awe. "It's here!"

"What's here?" Galahad asked. But Calib couldn't
bring himself to speak until he was sure. Reverently, he
reached out a paw to touch the cool handle. Upon contact,

his whiskers felt electrified, like they might vibrate off his snout. He jerked back. The magic inside the mirror was powerful—as strong as Excalibur, even.

Merlin's Mirror.

The wizard's first treasure, which had been given to the Darkling creatures.

Yes, it even had the metal thorns and roses that his grandfather had said distinguished the Darklings' gift.

Calib thought back to the stories Commander Yvers had told him about the mirror. How it had once brought much prosperity to the Darklings, allowing them to predict the weather patterns and maximize their harvests. How, after it was destroyed, the Darklings had resorted to raiding the creatures of Camelot to survive. Leftie said he had lost the mirror during a raid by the Saxons. And yet . . .

Calib put a tentative paw out again and felt the same strange tingle. There could be no doubt about it.

"This belongs to the creatures of the Darkling Woods," Calib said, looking up wonderingly at Galahad. "Everyone thought it had been smashed to pieces and lost, but it's been in the castle the entire time. For the last few months, all three of Merlin's treasures have been in Camelot, and we never knew!"

Even in the dim light of the moon, Calib could see that Galahad had turned pale. "Maybe that's how we were able to survive the Battle of the Bear and the white fever," Galahad said. "But now, none of the treasures are there. . . ."

From Galahad's expression, Calib knew they shared the same rising urgency.

"We need to hurry," Calib said. "Do you think we can use this to find Cecily and the Grail?"

Galahad held out the mirror for both of them to look into. "I'm not sure I know how it works," he murmured. "It only shows what it wants us to see."

A lump grew in Calib's throat. Galahad gently picked him up and set him back upon his shoulder.

"You can't get mad at a mirror for being what it is," Galahad said softly. "Don't give up hope. I have a feeling that it's trying to help us. We just need time to learn how to understand." He placed the mirror into his knapsack, carefully wedging it between the folds of his blanket.

And though it wasn't what Calib wanted to hear, he still felt the faint beat of hope inside him. Two of Merlin's legendary treasures were accounted for: the sword and the mirror—and Galahad had them both.

Surely that was a sign that the Grail wouldn't be far from their grasp, after all.

For four days, Galahad and Calib traveled almost without rest. At night, they felt comfortable enough using the main road to follow the light of the Dragon's Eye. But as soon as dawn arrived and the Eye faded into the sunlight, they'd go into the woods, trailing the path from afar and avoiding villages and towns. Sometimes, they found thin deer paths for Galahad to follow, but most of the time, the Two-Legger had to hack away at the underbrush with Excalibur to clear the path.

Calib thought not for the first time that it was a shame Galahad had not been born a mouse. He would have found it much easier to travel. But then again, it would have been much harder to carry Excalibur.

On the afternoon of the fourth day, during a short lunch break by a stream, Calib felt a funny tickle in the pit of his stomach. When a flock of camouflaged grouse hens took off in sudden flight, Calib felt relieved. He was sure it had been the watchful eyes of the hens that had given him that crawling sensation.

But after a few hours, far away from the river, the odd sensation had grown into a heavy unease. He couldn't quite place a paw on it. The Darkling Woods felt different since he was here last—eerie and off-kilter. The mouse surveyed their surroundings. The trees looked normal enough, greening with a summer lushness. He took a deep breath. It smelled normal enough, too—mulch, moss, and mud. And yet . . . Calib's new whiskers continued to twitch.

"Have you noticed?" Galahad whispered. They were moving slower now, the late afternoon sun's heat dragging down their pace. "The woods—they've been completely silent."

Galahad was right. The normal sounds of the woods were missing. No birds chirped. No crickets creaked. There was nothing beyond the crunch of Galahad's boots.

A tingle of fear shot through Calib's whiskers. He smoothed them down nervously.

Slowly, the soft give of fresh soil turned to rockier, harder terrain. The path was getting more difficult to see, and Galahad looked exhausted. His steps were slower, and his shoulders slumped. Calib had taken to riding in the knapsack to prevent from slipping off.

The sun began to set behind them, washing the woods in a deep lavender color. They had finally reached the foothills, where the trees grew increasingly sparse.

"There it is," Galahad said hoarsely. "Look."

Through the trees, Calib could see the Iron Mountains rise like sharp teeth towering over the horizon. The mountain range marked the end of the known realm for Camelot's mice. No mouse who had dared to cross over its jagged peaks ever returned to tell the tale. Even Calib, when he'd ridden on an owl, had only made it as far as Leftie's lair in the foothills of the Slate Rocks.

For besides its unforgiving heights, there was another

reason why most woodland creatures avoided the mountains.

"Do Two-Leggers also know about dragons?" Calib asked as he wrapped his tail around Galahad's ear to anchor himself.

"Only that they're great beasts of scales and fire." Adjusting his pack, Galahad resumed walking. "Why?"

Calib paused a moment, trying to remember how Madame von Mandrake had always started off the tale at bedtime.

"Long ago, when the world was wild and its magic young," Calib began, "a dragon roamed these lands. This area was once flat fields, but when another dragon landed, the two fought so mightily, the very earth underneath shattered and crashed together.

"Houses and castles shook, and creatures ran for their lives as the two dragons fought tooth, claw, and flame. A mouse named Lionel, whose home had been destroyed by the feuding lizards, went in search of a wizard to help. He made it all the way to Avalon and met Merlin as a young boy. When Lionel explained his plight, Merlin followed him back and put both dragons into an enchanted sleep.

"Merlin warned the animals, however, that if anyone ventured too deep into the mountains, they risked disturbing the dragons' slumber. And if the dragons woke up, they would rain such a destruction upon the land, all of

Britain would be destroyed in their rampage."

Galahad nodded thoughtfully. "I like that tale. And it makes sense why you have that story. Do you see over there?" The boy pointed. Calib followed the direction to see rising tendrils of smoke and steam from the mountaintops. "Some of the Iron Mountains have a liquid fire still inside them," Galahad continued. "Though none have erupted in our lifetimes—or our parents' parents' parents' lifetimes."

"Perhaps there was a kernel of truth in the myths," Calib said, trying to sound wise, even though his stomach churned slightly. He wasn't sure he wanted a truth with dragons in it.

The last of the sunlight left, and the Dragon's Eye again rose into the night sky. They adjusted their path slightly, and Galahad lit a torch to help them see the way ahead. The trees cast long, dark shadows that melted into the deeper darkness where the firelight could not reach.

Calib ducked back into the knapsack to check on the mirror for the sixteenth time that day. The mere act of touching it filled Calib with confidence . . . and his whiskers again with that strange, buzzing feeling.

Something was definitely odd about his new whiskers.

Suddenly, Calib felt Galahad stop abruptly. "What's happening?" Calib called. "Anything wrong?"

"I have to leave," Galahad announced, his voice slightly

muffled through the fabric of the knapsack.

"What?" Calib scurried up the rough cloth and poked his head out. "Why?"

"I have to leave," Galahad repeated, voice trembling. And without another word, Galahad turned around and fled.

CHAPTER
9

Calib gripped the strap of Galahad's knapsack to keep from falling out. Each jolt from the Two-Legger's frantic sprint threatened to throw him into the woods. Merlin's Mirror jostled in the bag, its thorns coming perilously close to slicing Calib's tail.

"Wait! Galahad!" the mouse cried. "Stop running!"

His shouts had no impact.

Desperate, Calib looked for a physical way to stop his friend. He spied his chance as a large branch loomed in their path. Timing the chaotic swings of the knapsack just right, Calib hooked the strap on a passing branch.

Boy, bag, mirror, and mouse came to a violent halt.

Galahad fell into the dirt, yanked backward by the force. The torch flew from his hands and sputtered out on the ground.

Calib lost his grip on the satchel and hit the ground on his haunches. He rubbed his tail, surprised it wasn't broken, then looked around for the knapsack. It had caught on the branch and now dangled precariously over them both. Gingerly, he got up and limped over to the dazed Galahad.

"Wh-what just happened?" the boy asked.

"I'm not sure," Calib said. "One second, everything was normal, and then the next, you were sprinting away, saying you had to leave."

"Really?" Galahad said, brow furrowed. "I don't . . . I don't remember anything."

"We should try again," Calib said. "But this time, maybe keep your hand on Excalibur's hilt."

Nodding, Galahad collected both mouse and knapsack and headed toward the mountains again. This time, they got a little farther before Galahad again turned heel and ran.

Again, Calib stopped him with the tree branch.

Galahad sat up, groaning. "I will be feeling that for a few days." He grimaced as he stretched his shoulders.

"Sorry," Calib said. "I didn't have any other way of stopping you."

"No, thank you," Galahad said, putting the knapsack across his other shoulder. "If it weren't for your quick thinking, I'd probably still be running back to Camelot, or straight off a cliff for all we know. What's happening here?"

This time, Calib had a theory—a strange, wild one that still, somehow, managed to feel true. "I think," he said slowly, "that there's some kind of protection around the mountains. A *magical* one. Every time we get close, my whiskers start to tingle."

Galahad tilted his head. "They tingle now?"

Twirling the ends of his black whiskers, Calib eyed Excalibur. "I think when you healed my whiskers, they grew back magical. I think they can sense when magic is afoot."

The boy looked puzzled. "You think I did that?"

Calib climbed back up Galahad's arm and settled onto his usual perch under Galahad's ear. "Or perhaps Excalibur intended it."

"If you say so." Galahad sounded doubtful, but he offered Calib his palm and put him back into Galahad's hood. "Why doesn't the spell work on you? Is that because of your whiskers, too?"

Calib shook his head. He couldn't help being amused

by his friend. "Two-Leggers are usually the first to be bamboozled, because of their size. I, on the other paw, am a mouse—easy to miss."

"Fair enough," Galahad said with a slight smile. "Now how am I going to get past the spell?"

"Swords cut, don't they? Why couldn't a magical sword cut through a magical barrier?"

Despite Galahad's misgivings ("It's just luck that your whiskers turned out magical and not poisonous!" he protested), Calib knew they were on the right track. And so together, they started back down the path with a relit torch and Excalibur unsheathed.

When they passed where Galahad had turned the last two times, Calib held his breath. But with Excalibur held out, Galahad merely hesitated and then pressed forward. A few more steps, and a burned oak suddenly appeared.

Calib eyed the black branches that spread out across the sky like a clawing hand. All around the tree, the ground was covered in ash. Nothing grew around it for about six feet.

Suddenly, he could feel the temperature around him drop sharply. Cold dread welled up in his lungs. A denseness clung in the air, making it hard to breathe. Part of him wanted to run far from this place. Another part sensed that some otherworldly force was almost certainly at work, trying to repel them. His whiskers felt weighted down with the dark magic. Calib focused on moving beyond his fear and forced himself to look past the dead tree.

Sure enough, the moonlight and the red light of the Dragon's Eye illuminated a shadowy barrier that shimmered in the air like a veil just beyond the tree line.

Calib tugged on Galahad's ear. "Do you see that black fog past the trees, but right before the mountains?"

Galahad squinted, then shook his head. "I don't see anything." He sounded slightly out of breath and came to a stop.

Was he about to run again? Calib had to get them out of there quickly. The spell must be incredibly strong if it could work against one of Merlin's treasures. But they didn't have just one of the wizard's treasures. . . .

"Use the mirror!" Calib said. "Not to see the future, but to see through the magic."

Galahad seemed unable to speak, but he reached into his bag and withdrew the mirror. Turning his back to the oak, he held it up to look at the reflection of the mountains.

Triumph surged in Calib's heart like a firecracker. For there, in the mirror, he could clearly see a thin dome of translucent blue light covering the nearest mountain peak.

"I see it," Galahad breathed. "That must be Morgan's home. That's where we'll find the Grail."

"And Cecily," Calib said grimly. He flashed back to

Cecily's whisker-kiss on his cheek after the victory feast of the Battle of the Bear, and the triumphant feeling fizzled. Until she was back with them, there could be no victory.

Using the mirror as a guide, Galahad sidled up to the ward. He raised Excalibur a little higher and pointed the blade at the barrier. The sword trembled in Galahad's hands, and Calib's whiskers shivered in response, as a wavering string of golden light emerged from the sword's tip.

"Do it," Calib said, his teeth clattering together as his whiskers danced, as if they had a mind of their own. "Cut the barrier!"

"What am I doing here?" Galahad asked.

Calib's heart fell. This close to the barrier, even Excalibur wasn't enough. "You're here for Cecily! The Grail! The Saxons!" Calib shouted any number of words he hoped might jog Galahad from the spell's clutches. "FOR CAMELOT!"

But the Two-Legger still didn't respond. Scampering up the boy's raised arm, Calib turned and saw Galahad's eyes had glazed over. The boy's body began to shake.

They were *so* close. As Galahad started to turn, Calib ran down the rest of the length of Galahad's arm and then chomped hard on Galahad's hand.

"Ow!" Galahad jerked his arm away in pain, slicing

downward with Excalibur in the process.

A gust of cold, damp air rushed out all at once, bringing with it the scent of rosemary and iron: the scent of dark magic.

Galahad's eyes cleared.

"*Go!*" Calib urged, dangling from Galahad's bleeding finger. Kicking his hind legs up, Calib somersaulted onto Galahad's arm and ran back to his shoulder. With the mirror in one hand and the sword in the other, Galahad hacked away at the rip in the blue light, creating a larger tear. With a last push of his shoulder, the Two-Legger tumbled through, bringing them to the other side—

And into a cave.

The trees, the forest—it had all been an illusion, hiding what was truly here: the entrance to an underground cavern in the Iron Mountains.

Calib's heart beat rapidly against his chest. This was the kind of magic the world hadn't seen for years. *Centuries*, even.

"I'm not sure where to begin," Galahad whispered, his voice echoing slightly as he looked up at the arched ceiling of rough rock and roots overhead. "Do you?"

"I do," a new voice said.

Calib gripped onto Galahad's ear tightly as the Two-Legger turned around.

A stocky boy of about fifteen with auburn hair stepped

out of the shadow of the cave. His brown eyes studied Galahad the same way a cat studied its prey.

"Had we known you were coming," Red drawled, "I would have put on a pot of tea."

CHAPTER
10

C alib felt Galahad tense as he quickly burrowed into Galahad's hood.

Mordred le Fay stalked forward, brandishing a sword that was the exact replica of Excalibur. Behind him, four heavily armed Saxon soldiers followed.

Calib couldn't help remembering how fast Red was with a weapon. Last time, Galahad had only managed to survive the fight because Calib tied Red's shoelaces together at the last minute.

That wouldn't be possible now—not with four Saxon

guards staring directly at Galahad. Calib's only hope was to remain very, very still. Galahad would have to talk, not fight, his way out of this one.

"Red," Galahad said. Calib hoped that Saxon ears, like other Two-Legger ears, couldn't pick up on the rapid beat of Galahad's heart. "I'm here to speak with Morgan le Fay."

"Are you now?" Red said, amusement lacing his voice. "Somehow, little Du Lac, I don't really believe you." He snapped his fingers, and the guards with their hooked blades began to close in.

Now, Calib's nose filled with the stink of Galahad's fear. *Come on,* Calib thought at the boy. *He's just a big bully! Stand your ground!*

"I know we left on, shall we say, complicated terms last time," Galahad said. "But . . . you were right."

Red's eyebrows shot up at that. "I was right?" he repeated slowly.

Galahad nodded vigorously, forcing Calib to cling on to the hood with both paws. "What you said back at Camelot," he continued. "Arthur and his knights know nothing. They only want to use me for Excalibur."

True bitterness clung to Galahad's words. Is that how the Two-Legger really felt?

Calib hoped he hadn't made Galahad feel like he only wanted him around because of the magic sword. Calib also had wanted Galahad on the quest because he was kind. Because he listened. Because he never overlooked anyone, no matter how small.

"I . . . " Galahad stopped for a moment, seeming to wrestle with himself. "I need to train with people who *know* magic. I want to learn from the best."

As Red narrowed his eyes, Calib sent out a wish to Merlin that the other boy would believe Galahad. The hero of Camelot had said those words so fervently that Calib would have believed Galahad himself if he didn't know his friend so well. And he *did* know his friend. He was sure of it.

Red's scowl slowly turned into a smile, and Calib wasn't sure which one was more terrifying. Red nodded at two of the nearest guards. "Search his belongings."

Before Galahad could say anything, one guard had yanked Excalibur from his hands while the other brusquely took his knapsack and began to rifle through it.

Calib's stomach lurched. The mirror! Taking a deep breath, he squeaked as loud as he could.

"What the—" the guard growled, looking up from the backpack and peering at Galahad.

There was a hard pinch behind Calib's neck as he was lifted by the scruff. A moment later, the world streaked by as he flew through the air. He landed with a soft puff of dust on the cave floor. Slightly stunned, Calib wobbled to hide behind a rock as Galahad let out a soft cry of alarm.

"What are you doing, Edgar?" Red asked.

"The boy had a mouse in his hood," the guard said, sounding disgusted.

"Fool," Red fumed. Calib heard the sound of approaching footsteps as Red walked in the direction Calib had gone flying. Red stopped and let out a hiss of breath. "It's too late now. He will have already scurried away. Next time, Edgar, catch the mouse—don't let it escape!"

"A mouse?" Galahad exclaimed, somewhat too loudly. "Disgusting! If he knew what was good for him, he would *stay away.*"

"That's enough," Red snapped, but Calib had understood the message. Sticking to the shadows, he climbed, paw over paw, to a narrow rock ledge where he could see what was happening.

Nodding at the Saxons, Red said, "I will escort our guest from here. You are dismissed." The guards retreated into the shadows, the sound of their stomping boots echoing down various tunnels.

Red shoved Galahad's satchel back into his arms. Then he pointed at the sconce on the cave wall, and it immediately extinguished, plunging them into darkness. Before Calib's eyes could even attempt to adjust, an orb of blue light popped into existence. It illuminated Red's face as he held it up. "Now follow me."

Red turned to go farther into the cave. Galahad glanced back once before following Red. Keeping to the edges and the shadows, Calib trailed the Two-Leggers and the small patch of bobbing blue light.

Calib soon heard the sound of running water. Slowly, it grew louder until finally, Calib felt a gentle mist upon his face.

The light in Red's hands surged forward and grew brighter, illuminating more of their surroundings. They stood on the edge of a vast underground lake whose black depths were impossible to see through. Calib's stomach twisted. For someone who despised swimming, he somehow always seemed to find himself near water.

"*Verum aqua,*" Red whispered, and as he did, his hands moved in complicated gestures, as if he were playing an invisible lute.

The lake's water became translucent, turning a bright-turquoise blue.

"Do not stray from the path," Red said. "And remember: the pikes are always hungry." And then he pushed Galahad. The Two-Legger hit the magicked waters, disappearing beneath the ripples.

A second later, there was another splash as Red dove after.

"Galahad!" Calib shouted. "GALAHAD!" His words

echoed around the cave's walls, but there was no one to hear him. The top of the lake remained even and unbroken.

Neither Red nor Galahad resurfaced.

CHAPTER
11

Galahad instinctively gasped for air as the ice-cold water of the subterranean lake poured into his mouth. To his surprise, he did not choke.

There was a sharp prod in his side, and he looked over to see Red treading water, his hair fanned out around his head. Catching Galahad's eye, he pointed down.

Below, Galahad could see a glowing spiral staircase emerge, step by step, reaching all the way down the depths of the lake. There seemed to be some kind of mirror at the bottom, making the steps look inverted, as if they kept going beyond the ground. Near the bottommost stair, a door marked with the carvings of mermaids and sea monsters stood upside down.

Red kicked toward the steps. With one last look back at the surface, Galahad followed. He had lost track of Calib after the Saxon had thrown him. He hoped his friend was all right. The water was shockingly cold, a stabbing sensation prickling up Galahad's body. He resisted the urge to splash back out. If Red could do this, so could he.

As he swam toward the steps, Galahad noticed something strange. He could have sworn he had started by diving down . . . now, it looked as though the whole world had been inverted.

Ahead, he saw that Red had placed his feet onto the stairs and was walking toward the door, as if he were climbing a normal set of steps. Galahad moved to do the same. As soon as his feet touched the stairs, the water warmed, and he discovered he could breathe the water. Instead of floating, his body weight readjusted. It felt like he was no longer underwater.

Morgan le Fay must be very strong indeed to maintain such an enchantment in her lair. When he'd seen Red in front of him, he hadn't had time to plan, and so he'd blurted out the first thing he could think of: *I need to see Morgan le Fay.* But what would he say to her? *Please stop attacking Camelot, stealing our friends, and taking our treasures, thank you very much*? Or was Red not even taking him to her?

A school of fish swam by close to the staircase—close enough that Galahad could see the razor-sharp teeth lining one fish's mouth. *Pikes*. But though Galahad braced himself for an attack, one never came. The pikes swarmed by with teeth chomping, but they stopped about five feet short of the staircase itself.

Distracted by their swirling patterns, Galahad suddenly slipped on the steps.

Instead of falling down, he felt himself falling up, toward the surface. Galahad tried to place his foot down on the next step, but he was already floating away. Galahad saw the school of pikes take notice and turn around as one cloud of ravenous fish. They were coming for him now, moving with the speed of a war horde.

"Red, *help!*" he shouted.

Or tried to. All that came out were bubbles.

Far below him—or was it above him?—Red had already reached the door and opened it. On the other side of the door was what looked like a long hallway lined with torches. The ruddy glow was a stark contrast to the glowing blue of the water.

Red turned around and looked at Galahad with a small smirk.

Galahad swam desperately toward the door, diving

straight down, clawing the water with his hands and feet. He could feel the teeth nipping at his heels. He kicked a few of the fish in the face.

The opening was finally within reach!

Galahad launched himself through with a final burst of effort. He flew through the door and fell face-forward onto the dry, stone ground of a fortress.

Red slammed the door shut.

"Thanks for nothing," Galahad gasped. To his surprise, he was completely dry. He hoped Calib would find an easier way than that into Morgan's lair.

"You're in my house now," Red said. "Nothing is going to come easy for you from this point on."

The unassuming castle-like conditions of Morgan's underground fortress took Galahad by surprise. For an evil sorceress's lair, it lacked any skulls or spiderwebs like in the stories his mother used to tell. Rather, the stone floors and tapestried walls reminded Galahad of Camelot. He hoped Calib was all right and that he had understood his message.

Thinking of his little friend made his chest feel tight. Galahad took some deep, soothing breaths. On the first inhale, the smell of dusty relics and moldy paper reminded him distinctly of the castle library.

But as Galahad exhaled, the scent changed in his lungs. He caught a hint of rosemary and something burned and metallic, almost like fresh blood. He wondered how much magic must have been used to create a staircase like that in the underground lake.

Galahad kept his mouth shut, pulling back a biting retort. He tried to memorize their path from room to room, but Red seemed to intentionally pick a confusing path around the drafty, cavernous halls. After so many twists and turns, staircases and sharply sloping tunnels, Galahad lost track of where they were and how they had gotten there.

Morgan's lair was a maze, each hall branching off one another in a network of caves tunneling into the mountains. They seemed to walk past countless armories and strange-looking libraries. Rows of Saxon guards marched in tight formations down the corridors. A few of them gave Galahad a curious glance in passing. The mountain fortress reminded Galahad of a busy anthill, with a queen ant at the very center, commanding her workers.

Finally, the hall grew as wide as two horse carts, and they arrived at a pair of doors made from a wood stained so red, it gave the unsettling impression that it was covered in blood. Galahad held back a shiver. Red placed both his hands on the door handles, which were each carved into the shape of a sea creature not unlike the pikes. He glanced back at Galahad.

"Good luck," Red said, then threw open the doors to

reveal a long room lined with stone columns. At the other end, high on a dais, was a throne made of black onyx. It dominated the chamber, seeming to suck in all light, as if it were some great beast's eye. Vines of thorny roses clung to the back of the throne. And at its center sat an elegant woman.

She was dressed in fine white silks, the color starkly contrasted against her seat, and her sheet of auburn hair fell past her shoulders. On her head, she wore a crown fashioned out of jewels that were as black as the throne. But despite her otherworldly beauty, there was something familiar about her . . . in the intensity of her gray eyes, in the color of her hair, in the lines of her features.

She was truly the king's sister.

"Welcome, Galahad du Lac." The enchantress's voice was oddly sweet, like careful notes plucked on a lyre. "Step forward."

Tentatively, Galahad began to walk down the aisle. The torches in the columns flickered as he passed. There was no one else in the chamber except for them. He stopped at the base of the dais, mere feet from Camelot's greatest enemy.

Unnerved by the resemblance to the king he so admired, Galahad wasn't sure whether or not to bow. Considering she was the enemy, he settled on a nod instead.

"I've heard much about you," Morgan continued.

Red was easy to deceive, but judging from Morgan's demeanor, she did not seem to take kindly to empty compliments. So Galahad responded with the simple truth: "I've heard many things about you, too."

Morgan's face steeled just a little bit, but she still let out a tinkling laugh. "Exaggerations from my brother no doubt."

Standing up, Morgan walked down the steps from her throne. She circled him slowly, as if she were appraising a work of art. "Tell me, Galahad, why are you here?"

"I want to learn how to wield Excalibur," Galahad said, and it was a version of the truth. He did want to learn how to use his sword properly to heal and protect, but he didn't want to learn from Morgan.

Morgan stepped closer to Galahad.

"You lie," she said, no longer smiling. "Or rather, you're *half* lying. Tell the truth!"

Suddenly, Galahad became dizzy from the strong smell of magic rolling off Morgan in thick waves. To his horror, his mouth opened against his will. His throat tightened, but he couldn't stop the truth from flying out.

"I'm here to stop you!"

His words echoed in the vast throne room, repeating again and again, with no way to silence them. The scent of magic dissipated, and he braced for Morgan's next attack, but instead, she simply smiled.

"There we are," she said approvingly. "But why would you want to stop me? Arthur has spent the majority of his reign questing for personal glory, seeking out war and its trophies."

She fluttered a hand. "My foolish brother is bored by peace—you recall how he left the kingdom when it grew calm, in order to seek more adventures. In order to *steal* more for himself."

"King Arthur doesn't steal!" Galahad shouted, knowing it was dangerous to confront the sorceress but not caring. If she could force him to speak the truth, what was the point of holding in what he really thought?

"No?" Morgan asked. "But he stole the throne of Britain."

Trying to take full steadying breaths, Galahad said, "Arthur is our rightful king. *He* pulled the sword from the stone."

"Funny how those in power get to assign themselves the role of the righteous," Morgan commented as she trailed back up the steps. "Have you not considered why it is that I, the eldest child, was not crowned queen? It is not simply because I am a woman, no," she continued. "Our father had more sense than that."

With a graceful sweep of her skirts, she sat on her throne. "As the oldest, *I* was meant to pull the sword from the stone on my sixteenth birthday. I trained *years* for it . . . but Merlin saw to it that twelve-year-old Arthur got there first." She tilted her head at Galahad. "And so, one man with magic on his side gets to flout the rules and pick whomever he wants? Does that seem *like justice* to you?"

Galahad had never heard this version of the story before. But if it were true, he could see how it might seem unfair to Morgan. But it was hard to trust the word of someone who'd sent her son to kill her brother or who had cursed the very castle she claimed belonged to her.

"I see you are thinking," Morgan said with a nod. "Good. You are no fool. So let me ask you . . . What do you know of the Grail?"

The room again filled with the smell of dark magic, but this time, Galahad didn't need Morgan's prodding to tell the truth. "I know nothing," he said.

Galahad knew the moment Morgan's patience had ended. A slight wind swept through the windowless chamber, and the torchlights danced wildly.

"Very well, then," Morgan said. "Perhaps you need more time to think."

She pointed to the doors, and they flung open to reveal Red with a cohort of Saxon soldiers behind him.

"Take our guest to his room," Morgan commanded. Once again, Galahad found himself surrounded by Saxons.

"And while you're there," she continued, her hard gaze falling on Galahad, "think on this: for Arthur, the world has always been black and white, good versus evil. It's harder to figure out which side to fight for when all the world is gray." Her eyes flashed. "I, on the other hand, don't see the point of petty warfare, and I hate to see talent like yours wasted in it."

As the Saxons led him out of the chamber, Galahad felt something uneasy bloom in his belly. What Morgan had said was not unreasonable. In fact . . . he had thought the exact same thing not too long ago.

What a strange feeling it was to agree with Morgan le Fay.

CHAPTER
12

In the hour since Galahad disappeared underwater, Calib felt as though he were the one holding his breath.

Neither Galahad nor Red had resurfaced. Perhaps an entrance lay below the lake. But anytime Calib so much as put a tail tip near the lake, a school of pikes swarmed to the surface, their terrible teeth gnashing every which way.

The mouse would have to find another way into the lair. Retreating deeper into the cave, Calib let his whiskers guide him.

To his dismay, Morgan had her lair well protected

with not only magic wards but more conventional traps as well. As he ventured farther in, Calib saw that there were paths that led to false floors, giving way to pits full of sharp spikes. He tiptoed around stone columns where an accidental nudge might bring a pile of boulders onto unsuspecting heads.

Calib scampered on. Had Galahad not granted him his magical whiskers, he would have already walked into a trap. As ugly as they were, he had to admit they were a huge improvement over his previous ones.

Perhaps when they got back to Camelot, Galahad could heal Valentina as well. Calib thought how his crow friend might enjoy magical wings that could help her fly as fast as a storm worthy of her name, Valentina Stormbeak. Guilt lingered in his heart. Magical wings were the least he could do for his crow friend.

The mouse closed his eyes and tried to discern where to go next. He wanted to go where the sensation of magic was strongest, for that would most likely lead to the Grail—and to Cecily. He picked up his pace, following the undertow of magic deeper and deeper into the cave.

Gradually, Calib noticed that the height of the tunnel was shrinking, becoming as large as the opening leading to the Goldenwood Hall. The darkness seemed to retreat, and glowing blue lights began to dot the empty sconces on the corridor's walls.

This was the same light Calib had seen in Merlin's Cave near Camelot, and it was the same blue of the crystal that had freed Excalibur from the stone.

For a moment, his fear was pushed aside by a sense of wonder. Magic was rare—the Lady of the Lake had even said that it was seeping away from this world. So how could there be so much magic contained in one place?

The odious scent of weasel musk now mingled with the scent of earth and stone. Calib set his teeth. He'd taken on the Saxon weasels before, and he would do so again.

Suddenly, he hit a dead end. A stone wall blocked the tunnel, and a sculpture of a hissing ferret had been carved into it.

Calib was stumped. He'd been so sure this tunnel was leading somewhere big.

He studied the statue more closely. The detailing was incredible, as if every last strand of fur had been carefully carved. The statue also sported a pair of sparkling eyes—pieces of black onyx set into stone. Calib had the uncomfortable feeling that the statue was watching him.

Cautiously, he reached out a paw . . . and bopped the ferret on its nose.

Nothing happened. Maybe if he twisted its ear?

The feeling of being watched intensified. It was hard to think with the statue's judgmental eyes glaring at him.

He placed a paw over them—and suddenly, the right eye gave way.

Calib jumped back as the entire wall swiveled open about two inches, revealing a set of stone stairs that led down into the darkness. The scent of weasel musk was even stronger now. Though his eyes watered, Calib nearly cackled with delight. He had discovered a secret stairwell!

The steps were shallow and long, sloping down like ramps. They were low enough for a mouse to go down on four paws at a run. In the darkness, he could make out different doors and passageways sprawling away from this center path.

Doubt filled Calib's chest like steam in a kettle. There was no way to know how big this place was, and any number of tunnels could lead to Cecily. How would he find her?

Not knowing what else to do, Calib kept to the main path. At least he'd be able to find his way out again if he needed to. That was less likely if he started to take turns. After some time, he heard the echoes of rushing water, accompanied by the sound of metal clinking and shouts. The smell of burning wood and sulfur filled the tunnel, and the air grew hot and humid.

Calib rounded the last step and suddenly found himself on a stone balcony. Slinking down in case anyone was watching, he scrambled toward the edge. For a moment, his head swam.

The balcony overlooked a cavern that was taller than the highest spires of Camelot. Heights had stopped bothering him after he'd ridden owls. What made him dizzy was the vast underground city that had been carved into all sides of the cavern.

Steep stairs receded into the cave walls, leading to rows on top of rows of roughly constructed huts, each one glowing red with fire inside. Calib noticed a rhythm to the constant clanging, like the banging of a thousand pots and pans. From his vantage point, it looked like a hedge maze in Camelot's gardens—only at least three times as big, and vertical. Far below lay an underground lake with steam rising from its surface.

Warships crowded on the pebbled shore—*hundreds* of them, each sleeker and deadlier than the one before.

With growing horror, Calib realized he was looking at the might of the Saxon weasel army.

The Saxons had not left Britain after all. They had retreated here . . . and by the looks of it, they were preparing for another attack.

He went to flee back up the stairs. Camelot had to be warned before it was too late! But at that moment, the sound of approaching pawsteps blocked his escape route.

Panicked, Calib jumped behind a basket half full of

firewood. As the pawsteps came closer, he quickly leaped into the container and covered himself with the branches. He peered through the loose netting, and a pair of burly weasels came into view on the balcony.

Each one wore the rank of a knight on their armor, as well as the Saxon emblem—a red dragon against white. By the looks of them, they'd seen many battles. The taller weasel had a wooden leg, while the shorter one wore an eye patch over his left eye.

"A Two-Legger from Camelot? Here?" the tall one asked, pausing to tie the laces on his boots by propping his footpaw on Calib's basket. Inside, Calib held his breath.

"True as I'm standing here," the other replied. "I just saw him through the water gate. He demanded to be trained in magic."

"I thought we were here to go to war with them, not teach them magic tricks," the tall one complained as he lifted his footpaw off Calib's basket.

The weasels continued to mutter to each other as they stomped off, and soon, Calib couldn't hear their voices anymore. Slowly, he poked his head out.

The coast was clear—so why were his whiskers tingling so hard that he thought they might fall off?

Something pinched Calib behind his neck, and suddenly, he was yanked out from inside his hiding place.

"I thought I smelled a dirty little mouse," someone snarled.

Twisting, Calib glanced back to see the wicked gleam of weasel teeth.

CHAPTER
13

The eye-patched Saxon guard cuffed Calib so hard in the head that stars exploded in his eyes. Then he threw him to the ground.

"The last prisoner I caught for slacking, I whipped him with his own tail—after I removed it!" the weasel growled. He cracked the whip that had been at his side.

Not daring to blow his cover, Calib tried to play along.

"My apologies; I got lost."

The guard yanked him up by the tunic collar, peering

at him in the eye intently. "Now where would you be headed, with a sword, no less?"

Calib looked at Lightbringer, his heart dropping to his stomach. He needed to think of an excuse quickly. "Th-this old toothpick?" he stammered. "I'm delivering it to the Manderlean. I was just polishing it up."

"I'll take it to our glorious leader; might even get a few boons for it," the weasel said. Calib watched helplessly as the Saxon guard pocketed his beloved sword. Would the Manderlean recognize the design when he saw it?

"Now where do *you* belong?" the other guard snarled.

"B-b-belong?"

Another slap across the snout sent Calib's whiskers stinging. "Where. Do. You. Work? The eastern or the western forges?"

"Er . . . the eastern one?" Calib replied.

"Then run back there!" barked the weasel. He prodded Calib with the butt end of his club. Stumbling a bit, Calib caught himself and began to walk away.

There was the crack of a whip, followed by a sharp sting in Calib's ear.

"Did you not hear me?" the weasel growled. "I said . . . *run.*"

Calib ran.

He had no idea where the eastern forges were located, but he sprinted down the stairs as if he did, praying that the guard would not follow. It was only after he'd fled down two landings and twisted out of sight that he slowed back down to a walk.

Passing some of the fiery huts he'd seen from afar, Calib realized they were actually forges. And the incessant clanging noises came from the animals working at them, heating metal over the fires and then pouring the molten metal into curved, wicked-looking molds.

They were creating scimitars, maces, and axes.

Weapons to maim and kill.

But that wasn't what made bile rise to the back of Calib's throat. Because for the first time, Calib could clearly see that each of the creatures who worked the forges wore chains.

They were shackled to each other, links of metal running from paw to paw.

Some wore unfamiliar garb and bore tattoos he'd never seen, but others looked familiar . . . including a massive badger. Though the badger was not wearing his signature tortoise shell armor, Calib recognized him as Lylas Whitestripe—second-in-command of the Darkling army and a hero of the Battle of the Bear.

Lylas wore a rough cloth sack and was wielding a massive hammer, and red sparks flew in all directions as he beat a sheet of steel. The badger turned slightly, and Calib's heart lurched. Fresh red scars scored the badger's back.

How did a great Darkling warrior like him end up in a place like this?

Without thinking, Calib began to run to his injured friend.

Crack!

Instinctively, Calib ducked. But the whip hadn't been directed at him, it'd been cracked above the heads of a line of creatures—hares, otters, squirrels—who were being ushered to another forge, and they were momentarily blocking Lylas from Calib's view.

Some of the creatures bore bandaged paws, others visible burns. All carried expressions of misery and exhaustion, made worse by the sheen of black dust and oil from the forge fires. The workers kept their eyes down, and they flinched whenever a guard walked by.

Ruby the vixen's warning came back to Calib: *Animals keep vanishing from the forest, not returning from the hunts.*

So this was where the missing animals had gone.

A big plume of black dust enveloped Calib from behind. His fur was instantly covered in clinging black soot.

Coughing, Calib looked up to see the badger standing over him. "Lylas!"

"I thought that was you," Lylas murmured from the side of his snout. "And if I did, others will too. Make sure you keep dirty."

"What's happened?" Calib asked. "Lylas, what's going on?"

But Lylas just shook his great head and rolled his eyes in the direction of a sentry who was stationed within earshot of their conversation. The weasel, however, was deeply engaged in gorging himself on a slice of blue cheese. Calib's stomach growled. It had been a long time since he'd had a proper meal.

"Hand me the bellows!" Lylas said loudly. He grabbed a set of chains on his worktable and hastily clipped them around Calib's footpaws. The metal was cold, but not tight, and if Calib wasn't careful, they would slip off.

Lowering his voice, Lylas said, "Keep going *down*. And whatever you do, don't—"

The crack of the whip snapped the air just above Lylas's ear, making both of them wince.

"No talking among the prisoners!" the weasel guard barked, crumbs tumbling down his tunic as he stood. "Or do you need another lesson in humility, skunk-beast!"

Lylas's eyes burned with defiance, but he turned back to his forge and again picked up his hammer. The weasel turned to Calib and squinted. "And what are you? A rather large mole?"

"I'm a mouse, actually—"

But the guard wasn't listening. Instead, he had grabbed Calib's paw and was marching him forward. "Moles belong in the mines," the weasel barked, and before Calib knew it, he was shoved onto a small platform, along with other moles—proper moles with dull black fur that didn't look too dissimilar to Calib's soot-covered body.

Suddenly, the floor beneath him began to move down. It was sinking!

"Rat whiskers!" Calib cried, clutching the cart, as if it were somehow more secure than he was.

"Get ahold of yourself," whispered one of the moles.

"Be nice, Charles," the mole on Calib's other side admonished. Then he turned his head to Calib. "They're lowering us down into the mines—there's a pulley system that will bring us back up later."

The mole smiled sympathetically at what Calib guessed was the stunned expression on his face. "You must be new. Just keep your ears down and your tail close."

Calib looked up at the elongated tunnel above him and wondered how far they would go underground. And even though he knew Cecily had to be somewhere in this cavernous place of lakes, hidden cities, and mines, he felt as though the stars must be closer. At least for them, he knew where to look. His ears popped as the creaky pulleys lowered them farther down, the platform inching deeper and deeper into darkness.

Finally, the lift came to a screeching halt. As the moles filed out, Calib gave his whiskers a quick pat. The presence of magic was strongest down here, and his whiskers felt like they were burning again.

Stepping off, he saw that they had arrived at another

subterranean alcove, smaller than its counterpart thousands of feet above. A row of five armored Saxon weasels with whips and swords greeted them.

"Move out!" they barked. "Faster!"

Not knowing what else to do, Calib followed the kindly mole, avoiding rogue kicks from the guards. As his eyes adjusted to the darker cave, he was taken aback by the number of ragged animals gathered here in loose lines—moles, foxes, and badgers . . . all the natural diggers.

Their eyes squinted against the torchlight being carried by Saxon guards. Like Lylas, the animals too wore sack-like clothing. They were covered in a fine layer of dust. Calib could count the ribs on some of these creatures. Many of them were coughing from the poor, uncirculated air.

From a distance, Calib could hear the steady strike of pickaxes chipping against rock.

"Here," the kindly mole said, handing him a pickax. "This way."

Not knowing what else to do, Calib followed the mole to a rocky wall. "Like this," the mole demonstrated, swinging his tool. Rubble and grit showered down on them. A group of younger moles, maybe only half Calib's age, scrambled forward to begin to pick through the rock.

"What are we mining for?" Calib asked as he swung his own pickax at the wall. Dust exploded, filling his eyes, nose, and lungs. He began to cough.

The mole shook his head. "No one knows," he whispered. "But whenever we find an interesting-looking rock, we're supposed to bring it to the guards."

"How many of you are down here? Have you met a mouse named Ce—"

"Shush!" another mole with a star-shaped nose digging near them cut Calib off. "Are you trying to get us killed? No talking allowed!"

Taking a swing, Calib joined the steady beat of the axes breaking into the mountains. Soon, his footpaws grew weary. It had been night when he and Galahad had broken the barrier, and Calib thought that it must be well into the next morning by now. Each strike against the rock shot pain into his shoulders.

Just as he thought he could bear no more, a Saxon struck a large gong with a hammer. Immediately, silence washed over them as the miners abandoned their work and ran toward the entrance.

"Food," Calib's mole neighbor murmured. "Come on!"

Dazed from exhaustion and hunger, Calib allowed himself to be swept into the rush. Mice wearing aprons had formed a line with their carts, and already the rest of the digging animals were holding out acorn caps for teaspoons of soup and mush.

When Calib approached a calico-furred kitchen mouse, the mouse paused a moment and whispered, "Not . . . *Calib Christopher?*"

Calib's paw flew to his ear, and when he drew his paw away, it was smeared with soggy soot. His disguise was slowly slipping off.

"I'm sorry," Calib said to the kitchen mouse. "Do I know you?"

"Oh my whiskers," the mouse whispered excitedly. He was even a little younger than Calib. "I've seen you before, but you wouldn't remember me. I was there, in Leftie's den, when you first arrived to ask the Darklings for help last autumn. But what are you doing here?"

"I'm on a mission for Camelot," Calib said, keeping his voice low and his eye on the guard. "I just don't know how I'm going to get out of the mines. . . ."

The mouse's whiskers twitched. "Switch places with me! I'm a server. We have more access than most of the prisoners."

"No," Calib said, shaking his head. The hollow desperation he'd seen in the miners' eyes told Calib this wasn't nearly enough food for the hard labor they were doing. It was certainly no place for a mouse even younger than him. "It's miserable down here."

"You're going to save us, though," the mouse said earnestly. He was already untying his apron. "The Saxon weasels can't be bothered to learn who we are. They only count that the same number of creatures who came down, go back up."

The rough burlap apron was thrust into Calib's paws.

"Please," the mouse said. "We can't last much longer. And I know you can help."

His heart sinking, Calib nodded and handed the mouse his pickax. "What's your name?" Calib whispered as he tied the apron around his waist.

"Fennel Fraytail."

"Do you know Dandelion Fraytail?"

"Yes." Fennel bobbed a nod. "She's my cousin."

"Hey!" All the creatures, including Calib, jumped as a Saxon guard strode over to them. "You," he said, prodding a paw at Calib. "Get behind your cart. And the rest of you, keep it moving. Don't make me say it again!"

"Yes, Commander," both the miners and kitchen staff said despondently, and with that, young Fennel was swept away into the bowels of the mines. His heart squeezing, Calib picked up a teaspoon ladle and began to scrape at the bottom of the pots.

The food was going rapidly. With a sinking stomach, Calib saw there wouldn't be enough soup to feed half the line of hungry miners before they ran out. When the food had been emptied from each tray and trough, the kitchen mice were ushered back into the pulley box.

"Are we bringing more down?" Calib whispered to his neighboring mouse.

The mouse looked at him disdainfully and didn't bother answering what he clearly thought was a foolish question.

Calib had to bite his tongue from lashing out at his fellow mice. How could they be silent? The injustice of the situation was unbearable. Britain was where all creatures could live as equals. That was the foundation upon which King Arthur built Camelot and his Round Table. How had Camelot let this happen, right under their snouts?

Calib stood with fierce determination as the lift moved upward. He had come here to rescue Cecily and the Goldenwood Throne, but what was another few thousand souls added to that tally?

He would save them.

He would save them all.

CHAPTER
14

Galahad drifted into an uneasy dream that felt more real than it should. He was standing on top of a mountain. A glowing white shadow in the shape of a wolf swam just out of focus. He could hear only the faintest of whispers in the wind—nothing he could actually understand.

"I can't hear you," he said. He tried to reach out and touch the wolf, but suddenly, a great pain exploded in his hands. He looked down and saw that he had grabbed Merlin's Mirror, the thorns cutting into his palms. Inside the mirror's reflection, Camelot was engulfed in flames.

Galahad bolted out of his dream, gasping for air.

"Finally, you're awake," Red drawled, standing over him. Groggy and confused, Galahad took a few moments to remember where he was. After Morgan had dismissed him last night, Red had lead Galahad to a small room with a rickety bed and a dresser. He had locked Galahad in, with not only a key, but also, Galahad suspected, with magic. With no way to escape and look for either Calib or the Grail, he had fallen asleep, exhausted from both his travels and his nerves.

Red yanked the covers off Galahad. "You're no pampered hero of Camelot here. In my fortress, you *work*. Get up and get dressed," he said as he strode to the door.

Galahad rose from his bed and got dressed for the morning. His body felt heavy and groggy, his mind fuzzy. His conversations with Morgan the evening before felt like muddled memories from long ago. Was it true that she had been wronged by Arthur?

When Galahad had put on a fresh tunic from his pack, he stepped out to see Red waiting impatiently for him.

"Let's go," the older boy grumbled. "You're making me late for training."

"Where are you taking me?" Galahad asked.

"You don't get to ask the questions here," Red said, and began to walk quickly down a passageway . . . and then another . . . and another . . . and another.

Red marched Galahad confidently past an underground quarry, which had been turned into a makeshift battle arena. Saxon soldiers sparred in pairs. Others practiced beating on straw men with iron clubs, spraying stuffing and sawdust everywhere. The clanging and shouting were constant and deafening. Galahad thought back to the gentlemanly jousts and chivalrous fighting King Arthur employed among his knights. He couldn't see how that code of honor could outlast the Saxons' brutal melee training.

Red prodded Galahad to move faster. Galahad blinked. They had just made a quick left down a corridor that he could have sworn wasn't there a second before.

"How do you find your way around in here?" he asked, the question tumbling from him before he could stop it.

"My mother's security at work," Red responded, waving casually at a carved door Galahad thought they'd already passed earlier. "The halls are enchanted. Once you know how to master the magic, the right room will come to you." Galahad deflated. He was used to having people working against him—it was quite another to have an entire fortress against you.

He wondered where Red was taking him. The dungeons? He didn't think so. But wherever it was, he was sure it couldn't be good.

Red eventually opened a door and ushered Galahad

inside. They were standing between two long bookshelves at least three times his height. They were filled with yellowed books and rolled-up scrolls. The shelves extended for many feet beyond him. Red walked them to the end of the aisle, where Galahad was astounded to see rows and rows of shelves in a room as big as Morgan's throne room. Rays of yellow beams poured from the cavernous ceiling, where crystals were embedded into the stone roof as skylights.

This book collection puts Camelot's to shame, Galahad thought jealously. He leaned in closer to look at some of the titles, admiring the gilded spines and fine leather bindings.

"Finally!" a voice called from beneath the stacks. "Lord Mordred, you're late. The scrolls aren't going to translate themselves!"

A girl about Galahad's age popped her head up from the opposite side of the shelf. She had spritely features—a heart-shaped face that framed inquisitive brown eyes. Her brown hair sprouted in a thick mass of curls that she kept in a high bun, making her a foot taller than Galahad.

"Actually," Red said, pushing Galahad forward, "I've brought you a new assistant."

The girl's eyebrows shot up. "The queen didn't mention that," she said. "In fact, she said that you, Red, were supposed to—"

"This," Red interrupted, "is Galahad. Galahad, meet Britta, Mother's head researcher."

"Hmm," the girl said as she stepped out from behind the shelves. Her arms were full of scrolls. She was dressed in a page boy's long black tunic with many pockets filled with quills and ink. "Do you know Gaelic?"

"Yes," Galahad said, puzzled.

"Thank goodness," Britta said, and shoved her bundle of scrolls into Galahad's arms. "You can start by copying that entire stack." And with that, she bustled off.

Galahad glanced down at the thick scrolls in his arms. Tiny letters in narrow lines marched up and down the parchment on both sides.

"Copying this will take days," Galahad said, dismayed. "A *year*, even."

"Who says you'll be leaving anytime soon?" Red smirked, and as he exited the library, Galahad heard the door lock shut.

CHAPTER
15

Calib kept his head down as he scurried back to the kitchens with an earthenware tray. For the past three days, he'd been working as a server in the Saxons' kitchens, joining the rows of mice and shrews carrying out trays of bread and cheese through the swinging doors and delivering them to the Saxon guards.

When he'd first returned from the mines, Calib had tried to find Lylas again. But the head cook, a hare by the name of Jasper, refused him leave to depart the kitchens until the next morning. By then, to Calib's dismay, Lylas was nowhere to be found.

He'd also been trying to locate the dungeons without being noticed by a Saxon guard. But there were as many tunnels as holes in a piece of Swiss cheese. He'd snuck into the passageways willy-nilly a few times and gotten hopelessly turned about. After that, he'd realized he needed to be more organized in his approach. Slowly, he would work his way from east to west, making sure that not a single possible place would be overlooked.

For three days, he'd found neither fur nor whisker of Cecily's. No one—not any of the miners, forge workers, or kitchen staff—seemed to have seen her.

Calib entered the smoky, brick hovel of the kitchens, passing the rows of cooking pits that had been dug into the ground like trenches. Cauldrons and griddles hovered above each pit, bubbling with soups and grilled cheeses. The heat was drier, possibly even hotter, here. But at least the smell of rotten eggs from the sulfur mixed with weasel musk had subsided.

Looking around, he finally spied Jasper, who looked like he was in danger of dipping his ears into the soup every time he reached in to stir it. The white hare ladled out a sample to taste and made a disgusted face.

"Bad batch! Pour this down the chute," he instructed a nearby pair of shrews. The two nodded solemnly and came over to maneuver the cauldron off the fire. Then the hare picked up a small sack and hopped over to the garbage chute.

Calib hurried over to him, careful to avoid slipping on his loose chains, and tapped his shoulder. "Jasper, could I—"

The hare jumped around, raisins flying from the sack. "I'm sorry! I'm cooking as fast as I can!"

"It's just me, Ca— I mean, Warren," Calib said, almost forgetting he'd given the other prisoners a false name.

Realizing it was only a mouse, the hare sighed, exasperated and visibly relieved. He gave Calib a hard shove. "Don't go sneaking up on creatures like that. Thought you were the guards!"

"Sorry," Calib said, stooping to pick up the raisins. "I only wanted to know my next assignment. I was hoping maybe you could assign me the dungeons today." He handed his pawful of raisins to Jasper, who quickly chucked it down the garbage chute.

"You've asked me that every morning since you've been tasked to the kitchens," Jasper said, his large foot thumping the ground in exasperation. "And as I've said every day, we don't serve the dungeons."

"But—"

"Warren, Warren." The hare shook his head and sighed. A sadness lingered in his eyes. "I know your mommy probably taught you to be compassionate and stand up for what's right, but that only gets you killed around here—or worse. If you want to survive, the only one you can look out for is yourself." The hare sniffed loudly, then changed the subject. "Did you know your name means 'home' where I'm from?"

Disappointed and hungry (*always* hungry), Calib shook his head, not feeling much like talking. He took a nibble from one of the fallen raisins. Sweetness bloomed in his mouth.

"These taste fine," he said to Jasper.

"Shows how much you know about cooking," Jasper snorted, snatching the last raisins out of Calib's paws. "But since you're so eager to seek dangerous knowledge, I have a new task for you, one that will definitely take courage."

Throwing the last of the raisins down the chute, Jasper gestured for Calib to follow him to a long table, where he had laid out a fresh-yolk omelet topped with tomato skins, chives, and goat cheese on a meal tray. Calib's mouth watered at the sight of all that food, though it was placed next to a bowl of raw, stinking mackerel bits. "Deliver the Manderlean his breakfast."

The Manderlean.

At the sound of his name, Calib felt something hard— either courage or fear—wedge itself into his chest. Calib took the tray, trying to keep his paws steady.

"The Manderlean will be in the war tents near the docks," Jasper said. "The omelet is for our dear warlord. The fish is for that terrible hawk. Don't mix it up—and don't let the hawk see you."

With a gulp, Calib nodded and quickly ducked out of the kitchens. He checked his reflection against the silver tray to make sure the white patch around his ear was still hidden. He'd taken to rolling inside any extinguished fire pit so that he might pass as a gray mouse rather than a mouse with the tawny gold-and-white fur of a Christopher. He wondered if the Manderlean might recognize him from the Battle of the Bear—even with all the soot covering his fur.

As he approached the docks, he tried to keep count of how many warships lined the shore of this underground lake. Commander Kensington, he knew, would want to know. There were at least fifty Two-Legger ships, and each one could contain perhaps one hundred Two-Leggers and who knew how many additional creatures inside.

While an attack on Camelot by sea was nearly impossible due to its position on the lip of a cliff, an attack from the river was a different story. If even just one of these ships made it to the moat, who knew how much damage it could do.

The underground lake let off a constant steam that stung Calib's eyes. The rotten-egg stench was so strong here, it made him gag if he breathed too deep. Saxon weasels marched in formation around the shore, running through training exercises and obstacle courses. Calib stayed alert, keeping careful balance of his tray while skirting past any drilling troops.

Canvas tents were pitched all along the side of the lake. He headed for the largest one with the most guards lining the entrance.

"Breakfast for the Manderlean!" Calib said to the nearest weasel, perhaps more brightly than he intended.

The burly guard sniffed the plate, wrinkling his snout at the fish. He stepped aside, giving him just enough space to squeeze past.

Calib entered alone into a waiting area that was separated from the rest of the tent by a curtain. From the other side, Calib could hear voices.

"My lord, I assure you, we are looking for him." The voice spoke quickly, but Calib would recognize it anywhere: Sir Percival Vole! Calib's paws began to shake—not because of the weight of the breakfast tray or even fear—but in anger. Percival had been responsible for Commander Yvers's death. He'd kidnapped Cecily and stolen the Grail. The Manderlean may be Camelot's greatest enemy, but Percival was its greatest traitor.

"We've questioned the weasel who brought you the sword. We have turned the eastern forges upside down looking for the mouse," Percival continued, "but you should keep your focus on the question of the Grail—"

"Silence!" The Manderlean's bark made Calib nearly jump and upset his plates. "The Grail is about as useful to me as a drinking cup right now!"

"I believe the old commander took the Grail's secrets to his grave." Sir Percival's voice trembled. "But the young Christopher may know more."

"*I* will take matters of the Grail into my own paws going forward," the Manderlean snapped. "Just find me that mouse."

"Yes, m'lord," Percival mumbled. He was quiet for a moment, seeming to have a debate with himself. Finally, he said, "And the mouse-maid?"

"What of her?" the Manderlean snapped again.

"Have you perhaps questioned her? She was very close with the young Christopher. Perhaps she knows something about unlocking the Grail."

Calib's heart jumped. Cecily! They were talking about Cecily! He tried to lean in to catch the next words.

The Manderlean snorted. "I doubt it. You may do with her as you will. Put her in the mines."

There was another hesitant pause from Percival. Then: "I don't think . . . She's not exactly a *tame* mouse."

"Then kill her," the Manderlean said as casually as if he were planning to take a stroll. "There are many mouths to feed, and she is of no use. She can be Theodora's dinner tonight."

CHAPTER
16

A gasp escaped Calib before he could stop it, and a
second later, the curtain whipped open.

Sir Percival Vole snarled down at him. His eyes
were still rimmed with leftover kohl from when he had
masqueraded as Mistress Pearl. He'd lost some weight,
which made his previously plump cheeks sag like slack
sails. His teeth were black as ever, but Calib could no
longer distinguish the smell of his rotten breath from the
smell of sulfur all around.

The vole stood with his arms crossed and his footpaw

tapping impatiently. For a second, Calib thought a flicker of recognition crossed Percival's face, but then it passed.

"You're late with the breakfast, prisoner," the traitor of Camelot said. He stepped back a little so that Calib could enter with the tray.

"My apologies," Calib mumbled out of the side of his mouth, disguising his voice a few octaves lower. He wished he had his friend Barnaby's gift for accents at that moment. "I didn't want to interrupt."

Sidestepping Percival, Calib made his way to the large rectangular table at the center of the tent. At its head sat the Manderlean, studying an open scroll.

Calib suppressed a shudder. The golden mask still covered the creature's face, making it impossible to tell what kind of animal he was. The lack of features made the Manderlean even more mysterious—and terrifying.

With eyes that seemed to be lit by coals, the Manderlean scrutinized Calib intensely. Calib dropped his eyes to the table and saw that it was covered with maps. Carefully, Calib set the tray of eggs and raw fish in front of the creature, and bowed.

The Manderlean stayed still, making no move to eat— or dismiss Calib.

"Aren't you forgetting something?" Sir Percival snapped.

Calib's breath caught. He'd messed up somehow. *They*

know—A screeching caw from outside the tent interrupted his swirling thoughts.

"Theodora becomes very cranky when she's not fed in a timely manner," the Manderlean said. "And when she's cranky, she's known to put *mice* on the menu."

"Yes, m'lord," Calib grunted, quickly grabbing the bowl of fish from the table. "I'll take care of it straight away." And before the warlord could examine his new prisoner further, Calib scurried out of the tent.

Theodora the hawk was roosting in a birdcage near the back of the tent. She was hooded, wearing a leather helmet that covered her eyes, blinding her to her surroundings. Still, the claws of her talons gleamed and looked as if they'd been freshly sharpened. Her beak hooked cruelly.

"I hear you, groundling." Calib jumped as Theodora clapped her beak together. "Come closer. Have you brought me my fish?"

Gritting his teeth, Calib hurried toward the cage and pushed the bowl through the bars.

"Y-yes, ma'am," he stuttered from the ground. Though he was terrified, he was slightly in awe of the hawk's sense of hearing. She couldn't see him because of her hood, and as far as he could tell, hawks weren't known for their keen sense of smell. By only listening to him walk, she'd been able to tell what he was.

Suddenly, Theodora flared her wings, and the gust of

wind from her feathers knocked Calib back onto his tail.

He scrambled to his feet as Theodora let out a piercing burst of laughter. *"Sieer! Sieer!* Careful, groundling, unless you want to end up in the Wolf's Mouth. That's where the misbehaving beasts go!"

There was an awful squelching sound as Theodora dug her beak into the fish and began to gulp down strips of scales. Feeling queasy, Calib turned and left the war tents.

Things weren't looking good.

Calib was a prisoner for Camelot's biggest threat. Sir Percival was still at-large, plotting Camelot's fall. And Cecily was almost certainly going to die at sunset.

But for the first time since he'd arrived, Calib had a confirmation that he was on the right track. He'd learned that Cecily was still alive, along with some idea of where she might be.

The Wolf's Mouth.

Cecily was somewhere in this fortress, and he *would* find her—before it was too late.

CHAPTER
17

Galahad's hand cramped with exhaustion. For three days, he'd been transcribing the most boring of scrolls from Gaelic into Latin, the only break being when Red would come to collect him, and with two or three Saxon guards, escort him back to his room.

Galahad wanted to scream with frustration. He was no closer to discovering where Morgan was hiding the Grail, and he hadn't even seen Excalibur since the first night it had been taken from him. Thankfully, he still had Merlin's Mirror, but it had remained simply a mirror, showing

Galahad only his own tired eyes.

And yet, no matter how many hours Galahad spent in the library, Britta always seemed to be there more. She was there when he arrived, and she remained when he was escorted off.

The girl was relentless, barely taking time to eat the food the guards would bring in. Occasionally, she would stop and ask Galahad for help with a word. If Galahad knew the answer, he'd tell her, and her quill would scritch-scratch across the parchment once more.

But today, for once, Galahad couldn't hear the *scritch-scratch*. Looking up from his scroll, he saw Britta's curly hair spilled out across the table as she lightly snored. Her quill was still in her hand, ink dripping from the tip onto her notes. Galahad scanned through what she had written, and realized Britta was creating a code to translate Merlin's ciphers.

Galahad frowned. He was running out of time. He needed to master Excalibur before Britta could unlock the wizard's secrets. As quietly as he could, he stood up and moved to the section of the library that had caught his eye the first day: Magical Properties.

He scanned the spines and the fluttering tags of the scrolls: "Henges," "Divination," "Prophecy," "Magicians" . . .

"What are you doing here?"

Galahad jumped at Britta's voice. Turning around, he saw her standing with her arms crossed. Her quill was tucked behind her ear, dripping droplets of ink onto her neck. "We have to keep translating!"

It would have sounded much more intimidating but for the loud yawn that escaped her.

"Why don't you take a break?" Galahad asked. "You'll be able to work faster if you're not so tired."

"No." Britta shook her head adamantly. "I'm not . . . sleepy." She yawned again. "Fine, maybe just a little." She plopped into a nearby armchair.

"Why do you work so hard?" Galahad asked, hurrying over to the table where a guard had left a bread-and-cheese plate.

"It's hard to justify taking a break when you're trying to save Saxony," Britta said wearily. She took a bite of bread.

"Saxony?" Galahad asked, surprised. "Why would anyone want to save Saxony?"

"Why? Because that's my home, silly!"

"You're a Saxon?" Galahad exclaimed. In his experience, the Saxons were a ruthless, warlike bunch. Nothing like the studious researcher before him.

"Yes, I studied at the best schools there," Britta said, pride glowing in her voice. "That's why Her Majesty brought me here. So I can help my country."

Curious, Galahad asked, "What's wrong with it?"

"The land is drying up," she said matter-of-factly. "Crops are dying. Animals are fleeing. So we had to flee too. But I believe in Morgan le Fay. She's the smartest sorceress I've ever met. The only orchards that are still blossoming are the ones she's enmagicked. She's our best hope for survival."

Galahad could barely wrap his mind around Britta's words. He couldn't imagine the queen he'd met helping farm the lands and calling trees to burst into bloom. That didn't match the stories he'd heard about her at all.

But then again, Britta didn't match his image of a Saxon. He'd only ever met Saxon guards and warriors on the battlefield. He'd never stopped to think that they too must have families. Children his age. Academies.

Speaking about her home seemed to have woken Britta up. She headed back to her desk. Looking down at where she'd left off, she read something, then asked, "How do you translate this?" She tapped her finger at a word, and Galahad walked over to look at it.

"'Potion,' I think," Galahad said, reading over her shoulder. "And you say your research is going to save Saxony?"

"Yes." Britta nodded as she jotted something down. "Queen Morgan believes that many answers can often be found in libraries— Oh!" she broke off, and stared at her parchment. "I think I've figured something out!" Standing up, she rang a little bell on the wall. A moment later, a Saxon guard strode in.

"Give this to Her Majesty," Britta said. "Quickly!"

She turned to Galahad, her face aglow. "Thank you!" she said. "I think with that last word, I might finally be on to something!"

But Galahad was barely paying attention. His heartbeat had jumped into his throat as he scanned the scroll Britta had asked him to look at. The handwriting was oddly familiar. He'd seen it before in Camelot's own library—the hasty scrawl of Merlin.

His mind flashed back to the library scrolls Red had stolen from the castle.

"Britta," Galahad forced out, feeling as if he were choking. "What have you been translating? How, *exactly*, is your research going to help save Saxony?"

Brushing a curl off her forehead, Britta smiled at him. "I've been working on translating Merlin's secrets. We're trying to figure out how to use the Grail, you see. And once we've figured that out, no one will dare fight anymore."

Oblivious to Galahad's growing horror, she tapped the scroll in front of her. "I've seen your land. It's more than big enough for both Saxons and Britons to live together peacefully. Your island is fertile. It can easily grow enough food for both nations, if we stop fighting long enough to care for it."

The door opened, and Red waltzed in, wearing full-plated fighting armor—a chestplate, helmet, and lance. His metal boots clanged and echoed in the large library.

"Very good, Britta!" he said with a smile. "Her Majesty is ready to try something based on your latest finding." He pointed at Galahad. "Mother will see you now."

CHAPTER
18

Calib mulled over the puzzle of the Wolf's Mouth as he returned to the kitchen, after delivering breakfast to the Manderlean and his hideous hawk.

The rest of the kitchen workers were awake and busy, cooking breakfast for their fellow prisoners. Jasper stirred a gigantic casserole made of corn kernels and bread crumbs, yelling over his shoulder the whole time.

"For the last time, Fennel, there is nothing to be afraid of. Just keep your eyes straight ahead and walk right on past."

"I don't want to!" whimpered the mouse Calib had encountered in the mines. The young Fraytail had since snuck back into the kitchens by hiding in an emptied soup cauldron. "That place makes my fur stand on end."

"Oh, for hoppin' out loud, just because something is carved like a wolf, doesn't make it an actual one!"

Calib's ears perked up. "What did you say about a wolf?"

"Fraidy Fennel here would rather let the miners in the east end of the mountains starve than walk past a tunnel that spooks him!"

Fennel crossed his arms. His eyes were brimming with tears.

"Would it help if I walked with you?" Calib said. "I'd like to see this tunnel for myself."

Before Fennel had a chance to respond, Jasper waved them both away with his spoon. "Fine, just get out of my fur and do something useful!"

Fennel pulled on Calib's tunic and motioned for him to follow him. He pushed a food cart laden with two vats of mushy pea gruel onto the lift that led to the mines. Once inside, Fennel began cranking a lever that lowered them deeper into the depths of the mountains than Calib had ever gone.

Fennel said, "Everyone's afraid of the deeper tunnels. They think they're haunted. So the miners at the very bottom always get fed last." Calib's ears began to pop. "Jasper's right, I am being a coward."

Calib patted Fennel reassuringly on the shoulder.

"A wise mouse once told me that being brave does not mean lacking fear," Calib said, remembering Commander Yvers's words. "If you were never scared, you wouldn't know what it means to be brave. I know you are not a coward because the day we met, you took a great risk to save me. That is not a coward's way."

At this, Fennel beamed. "I can see why Dandelion thought so highly of Camelot."

Suddenly, the lift came to a stop with a screech and then a thud, and Fennel's smile vanished.

"We're here. Now, the wolf tunnel is on the right. But we'll need to turn left to meet the miners."

"You should go on without me," Calib said. "There's something in the tunnel that I need to see."

"You can't be serious!" Fennel cried. "Creepy voices come up from there!"

"I will be fine," Calib said, puffing up his chest. "I need to see if my friend is down there."

Not looking convinced, the mouse nodded.

"Good luck, Calib. I hope you know what you're doing." Fennel wheeled his food cart away, leaving Calib facing the tunnel's mouth alone.

The entrance to the tunnel had been carved to look

like the open mouth of a snarling wolf, complete with fangs, bordering a staircase that sloped downward. He didn't know where it led, but he knew at once this was where Theodora the hawk had been referring to. A wailing sound reached Calib's ears, and he steeled his resolve as he peered in past the wolf's teeth. It could have been just the wind, but in truth, it sounded like crying animals.

Mustering all his courage, and chanting Camelot's motto under his breath, he walked into the tunnel. The path corkscrewed deeper than Calib would've thought possible. The air was stuffy and unbearably hot. Gradually, the incline of the stairs leveled out into a low-ceilinged hallway. The way was poorly lit, with torches only every few feet. But even so, Calib could clearly see the tightly packed cells lining either side, each filled with Darkling animals. Many were asleep and snoring, but others paced their cells, appearing to have gone rabid in captivity. Hungry eyes followed Calib's every movement.

"Cecily," Calib whispered, hoping she was within earshot. "Cecily!"

"Cecileeeee C-c-celi!" mimicked a nearby crow.

"I'm trying to sleep over here!" roared a fox with a bandage across his eye. He banged on his prison bars, which woke another fox, who gnashed his teeth.

Soon, all the prisoners were arguing about who woke

whom. Someone started calling for the guards. In the noisy chaos, Calib ran deeper into the prison, trying to peer into every cell—trying to find Cecily.

Eventually, he sprinted past empty cells—ten, twenty, thirty of them. On one paw, Calib was glad they weren't all filled, but with each empty cell, he felt his hope slip away. If Cecily wasn't here . . . then where was she? What if Sir Percival had already ordered for her to be brought before Theodora? What if—

There was a splash of color up ahead. A bit of plum and opal—Cecily's favorite colors!

"Cecily!" His footpaws pounded the rock floor, and a moment later, he was there. Cecily was sitting on the ground, her back to the cell doors. Why hadn't she turned around? Was she sleeping?

"Cecily!" he said again, "it's me!" He reached a paw through the bars and tried to shake her awake. "Cecily, wake—"

But Calib's words caught in his throat as Cecily's head rolled clean off her neck and struck the ground with a hollow wooden sound.

When it rolled over, Calib realized his mistake. What he had thought was Cecily was just a corn-husk doll made up to look like a mouse-maid, complete with a walnut nose and leaf ears.

"Calib Christopher, what a surprise," a voice whispered.

Sir Percival Vole stepped forward from the shadow. "For you, I mean. A little soot is not enough to fool a master of disguise like myself."

Calib had fallen into another trap.

CHAPTER
19

"I've brought Galahad, Mother."

Galahad's stomach churned as Red announced their presence in the throne room. By helping Britta translate a single word, he had given Morgan an idea of how she could possibly use the Grail. With the Grail's power on her side, it would be only a matter of time before she launched her attack on Camelot.

And it would be all Galahad's fault.

Morgan, who'd been pacing the dais upon which her throne sat, now stopped and smiled.

It chilled Galahad to the core.

"It's good to see you again, Galahad," Morgan said. "Especially after I hear you've been *most* helpful."

Galahad's mouth twisted into a scowl, and he was surprised to see Red wear a similar expression.

"It was my idea to assign Galahad to translating," Red reminded his mother.

Morgan waved a casual hand as her dress whispered past the rosebushes on the dais. The bright-red flowers looked to Galahad like droplets of blood.

"Yes, Red," Morgan said. "Though I suspect your wish for Galahad to take up your chore was the motivating factor and not a strategic plot."

Red's face flushed, and he mumbled something to the ground, but Morgan wasn't listening. Instead, she was striding toward Galahad, her white skirts trailing behind her like tendrils of smoke.

"With this new information," she said, "I have a theory. Please humor me."

Morgan held out her hand and then plucked the air, and her hand, which had been empty, was suddenly not.

In her palm stood a wooden cup that glowed a buttery yellow in the torchlight. It was perfect in its symmetry except for a small divot where a piece of it had broken off.

The Grail—mere inches from Galahad's face!

His heart pounding, Galahad resisted the urge to

snatch it out of her hands. He had gone too deep into enemy territory. He would not make it far if he tried to run for it now.

But then, with a flourish, Morgan held the Grail out to him. "Take a sip," she instructed. Peering down, Galahad saw an inky black liquid slosh about. The smell of black magic was so thick, he thought he might be sick.

"What is this?" he asked.

"No dawdling," the sorceress said, and holding the cup to Galahad's lips, tilted the chalice toward him. "Just trust me."

Begrudgingly, Galahad allowed one sip before sputtering. The liquid inside was burning hot, and it traveled down his throat like liquid fire.

Morgan nodded, and with a final flourish of her hands, the Grail disappeared back into the air.

"And now," she said, walking back up the dais and settling into her throne, "let's test my new theory—and your mettle."

"What?" Galahad managed to ask, still coughing, before Red ran at him from behind, sword drawn.

Galahad had only a second to throw himself out of the path of Red's swinging sword. He hit the black marble floor with a gasp. As he looked up, he saw Excalibur's hilt sparkling on the floor next to him.

Not questioning how his sword had suddenly appeared

there, Galahad lunged for it, his fingers wrapping around its hilt before he bounded to his feet. He ducked again, just managing to keep Red's blade from slicing his face.

The clangs of Excalibur and Red's sword echoed in the throne room as Galahad and Red dueled once again. But this time, there would be no army of creatures to help Galahad.

Galahad was utterly alone against Red's onslaught; the older boy's slashes fast and unrelenting, his sword moving in a blur of fury.

His breathing ragged and his arm numb from Red's attacks, Galahad found himself backing up farther and farther . . . until he felt the cool stone of the wall against his back. Red had him pinned.

Galahad spun away to avoid getting gutted. Red, anticipating this move, stuck out his foot. Galahad tripped and landed with a thud on the stone floor. The force knocked Excalibur from his hands, and the sword spun away from him on the polished floor.

"Don't—" Galahad gasped as Red's sword came swinging down with unforgiving speed and cut into Galahad's forearm.

Warmth flooded Galahad's arm as blood spilled out. A moment later, the pain followed, a blinding ache that made black dots swim in front of his vision. He couldn't move; he could barely *think*.

"Halt!" Morgan cried, a command imbued with magic.

Galahad blinked away the fuzziness and watched as an invisible force yanked Red's sword from his hand. It stayed suspended in the air, frozen and harmless.

Red whirled on his mother. "Tell me when you're ready to stop playing favorites!" he yelled, and stormed out of the room, armor clanging.

With ragged breaths, Galahad tried to push himself up from the ground, his vision swimming.

"Stay still," Morgan said, and she moved to sit next to him on the floor, her white dress unfurling around her like a blooming lily.

Through his fading vision, Galahad watched as Morgan clicked her wrist, and suddenly, a ball of blue flame danced and crackled.

Morgan clamped her flaming hand onto Galahad's forearm. Where she touched, Galahad sensed a dry heat and the smell of woodsmoke.

But then, the pain rolled back. His vision cleared.

Struggling to sit up, Galahad looked at his arm.

The wound had instantly healed.

If it weren't for Morgan le Fay, Red surely would have killed him.

"How did you do that?" Galahad asked with wonder.

"There is power in all living things," Morgan said, walking down the aisle. "A skilled magician can harness that power and do with it as she pleases."

Staring now at the smooth, unbroken skin on his arm, Galahad marveled at the sorceress's power. The power to heal *completely*, not just *patch*, as Father Walter did with herbs and elixirs.

He remembered what Britta had said, how Morgan had come to Saxony and saved their fields. Could Arthur have stopped the war, if he had been generous with Camelot's harvest? If he had sent his knights to Saxony to help till the land instead of sending them out on personal quests for glory?

"Ma'am?" Galahad said, thinking quickly, "Do you think . . . Is it possible . . . Could I do that?"

The sorceress smiled. "I can teach you, if you'd like."

There was something about Morgan's smile that Galahad still did not trust. Yet . . . if he learned how to heal from her, how could that harm Camelot? And besides, if she thought he was becoming interested in her version of events, perhaps she would allow him to work with Britta on Merlin's Scrolls. He could misdirect Britta's research while seeking the knowledge of the Grail for Camelot.

Mouth dry, Galahad nodded. "Yes, please."

Morgan smiled. "This time, I believe you. Pick up Excalibur. You have earned the privilege to keep your sword. Tomorrow, we will begin your training in earnest. For now, I'm afraid I've just received news that I am needed elsewhere."

No new messenger had entered the throne room as far

as Galahad could tell, but as Galahad exited the throne room, he had the sense that someone was watching him. Turning around, he looked once more at the dais. No one was there. All looked the same. Except for one thing.

The rosebushes around the throne still hung heavy with red blooms—except for one empty spot, where instead of a rosebush, there were only a few brown petals and a mound of ash.

CHAPTER
20

The blindfold was yanked away, and the sun glared into Calib's eyes. He squinted against the yellow-white light, trying to make sense of his surroundings. He was surprised to be standing outside on a thin stone ledge overlooking the rest of the Iron Mountains. A strong wind blew away the bits of soot that still clung to his fur. Sir Percival stood before him, smug with his new triumph.

If Calib weren't shackled, he would have kicked himself.

He couldn't believe he'd fallen again for an enemy's trap. He surely must be the worst Christopher ever to come out of Camelot. Jasper was right: his reckless heroics endangered everyone he held dear.

After catching Calib, Sir Percival and his guards had blindfolded him. "March," the guard had growled.

Calib had been led to a twisting stairwell and made to climb out to this precipice outside the mountains, where he now stood. The sun was low in the sky and approaching sunset. Calib could hear the sound of the rushing river far below; likely the same one that the hot spring fed.

"Well, well." Sir Percival had smiled widely. His teeth revealed themselves like two rows of rotten tree stumps. "I knew you would come calling sooner or later. Like grandfather, like father, like son. Christophers always let their foolish pride get the better of them."

"It's called honor," Calib spat. "Something you obviously know nothing about, traitor." His ears flushed hot from Percival's barbed words. The greedy old vole might have the upper paw and the Grail, but Calib's family name was unimpeachable.

"I know about honor—just not for the great lie that is Camelot." Percival shook his head in mock wonder.

"Tell me where Cecily is!" Calib said, fixing his eyes on Percival. "What have you done with her?"

"You want answers, and you'll have them. After we get

ours," Percival said. "What do you know about the Grail and its powers?"

"Nothing. You killed the only mouse who knew anything before he ever got the chance to tell me." Calib's mind flashed back to the terrible moment when he saw his grandfather's shadow twist in pain from the assassin's blade. Nothing would ever bring his grandfather back, but his death still left Calib with the bad taste of injustice. Even though the assassin had been vanquished at the Battle of the Bear, Percival was the true murderer.

"Now *you're* the one who is lying." Percival grew impatient, and paced around Calib like a bird ready to pluck a worm from the ground. "Yvers and Merlin would not have left you completely in the dark."

"I'm telling you, I don't know anything!"

"How did you discover where the Grail was, then?" Percival asked.

"Cecily helped with the final clue." Calib shrugged. "Maybe if you had smarter friends . . ."

"I've had enough of your insolence!"

The vole raised his paw, as if he might strike Calib across the face. Calib cringed and closed his eyes for the impact, but it never came.

When he opened his eyes, he saw why.

The Manderlean had appeared.

"What did I say about your temper, Percy?" the

Manderlean spoke in a rasp. The warlord had appeared soundlessly at Percival's side, catching the vole's arm and twisting it around his back. "You should have told me sooner that you had a Christopher caught in your little web. Why was it Lieutenant Johann who had to tell me?"

"My liege," Percival said, his face twisted with frustration and fury. "I wanted to make him tell us the secret to the Grail. I was going to tell you once—"

Percival stopped speaking as the Manderlean held up a paw. "Once you found out the Grail's powers?" the Manderlean said, eyes flashing. "If I didn't know better, I would think you were trying to keep secrets from me."

The gold mask was blinding in the sun, giving the Manderlean an otherworldly glow. "Step aside, Sir Percival. There is something I would like to try one-on-one with our guest."

With a wave of his paw, another set of weasel guards came forward, bearing the Grail on their shoulders. Calib expected his whiskers to detect whatever powerful magic was inside the Grail, but there was nothing coming from the cup. Calib was confused. Was this a trick of some sort?

The only thing that pulsated with any power was the Manderlean.

Once, Calib had thought of the Grail merely as a broken Two-Legger cup turned into a throne for the mice commanders of Camelot. It was only after Galahad made the cup whole again with Excalibur that Calib finally had seen the cup's resemblance to the one on the Christopher coat of arms.

The mouse was beginning to realize that his grandfather had probably given clues to the Grail's true identity through the years. Perhaps if Calib had paid closer attention, he would have discovered the Grail sooner.

Some sort of liquid sloshed inside the cup. Calib's guards pulled him up to his hind legs and brought him to the lip of the Grail. Calib sniffed at the liquid.

"You must be thirsty," the Manderlean said.

Calib was parched, but he was also suspicious. "Is this poisoned?" he asked.

"No." Without warning, the Manderlean shoved Calib's head into the cup.

Surprised, Calib sucked down a few sips. He fought to resurface, but the Manderlean's grip on the back of his head was ironclad. For one awful second, Calib thought he would drown.

Suddenly, the grip released.

Calib burst out of the water, sputtering and choking. He expected water from the Grail to taste different—possibly magical—but it didn't.

The Manderlean gestured, and the guards unchained Calib. When he was free of the weight, the Manderlean stepped back and threw Lightbringer at his footpaw. "Surely you didn't think I would forget a sword such as yours! Now time to test your mettle!"

Calib grabbed the hilt and pointed the blade at the Manderlean, but one of the Saxon guards stepped between them. The weasel was clad in leather armor and carried a heavy wooden cudgel. Calib made a feint to the left and then darted right, trying to reach the Manderlean, but the Saxon was not fooled

With a casual swing, he leveled the cudgel at Calib's head. Calib was barely able to scamper out of the way in time.

The weasel turned to follow him, dull eyes watching impassively as Calib repositioned his footpaws. Desperately trying to remember all his dueling lessons, he advanced slowly toward his opponent, holding Lightbringer before him. He very much wished that the Manderlean had given him a shield. It was no use trying to parry a cudgel with a sword. The weasel swung again, and Calib dove away. A stinging blow landed on his tail, leaving it bruised and numb.

Springing back to his feet, Calib tried a different tactic. He charged at the weasel, ducking below the cudgel to land quick slashes wherever he could. Most of them glanced harmlessly off the armor, but a few found the unprotected fur of the weasel's shoulders and hindquarters.

The weasel hissed but gave no other indication that he even felt the cuts. He stood unmoving as Calib darted in for another attack. But at the last minute, the weasel took a quick step backward, swinging the cudgel low instead of high. The heavy club caught Calib in the midsection, knocking him on his back and sending Lightbringer clattering away. Calib lay on the ground, gasping for air, waiting for the killing blow.

CHAPTER
21

"Stop!"

The weasel withdrew on the Manderlean's command and marched back to his place with the others. The Manderlean sniffed derisively, and Calib picked himself off the floor, ears flushed with embarrassment.

"Mediocre." The Manderlean sighed. "I had expected more from someone who has twice thwarted my plans."

"What is this about?" Calib asked, wincing with every inhale. His lungs felt bruised by the blow.

"Merlin did love to play favorites," the Manderlean

said. "I wanted to see if he might have twisted the Grail's magic to work only on Camelot's animals."

Calib knew the answer to that question was an obvious no. He had been soundly defeated. And if the Manderlean had not stepped in when he did, Calib would have been nothing but mouse jelly on the end of the weasel's cudgel.

"It is only a matter of time before we discover how to unlock the Grail's powers," the Manderlean continued. "I have all the cards in my paw, while Camelot has none. It's time you realized that you are fighting for a lost cause. Your friend Galahad at least has seen the error of his ways. He has agreed to train with Morgan le Fay."

At this, Calib's heart filled with some hope. So Galahad had infiltrated the Two-Legger fortress successfully. But Calib squashed down his happiness and faked a scowl. "Then what's stopping you from attacking?" Calib demanded. "Could it be you're still afraid of Merlin's protection over Camelot?"

Calib couldn't tell for sure, but the Manderlean seemed to be frowning behind the golden mask. "Guards, take him back to his cell. No," he said after a thought. "Take him to the Deep."

Calib was marched far past the hallway of cells in the Wolf's Mouth, until he thought they must be at the very belly of the mountains.

"Here," Sir Percival said as they finally came to a halt

in front of what must have been the Deep. "Your precious Christopher name won't do you much good here."

The guards stepped back and let the odious vole be the one to shove Calib into the cell and lock the door. The air was so hot now, Calib could breathe only through his mouth.

"Better to be a Christopher locked away than a traitor who walks free," Calib gasped.

Sir Percival bared his teeth. "And yet, Christophers can be traitors, too. Didn't you ever wonder how Sir Trenton perished at Rickonback River?"

Calib's heart squeezed at the mention of his father's name and the battle that had taken his life.

"It was an ambush from the Darklings," Calib said, reciting what he had been told since he was a small mousling in the nurseries. But the familiar words caught in his throat. Calib knew that the story was no longer true. Merlin had said as much when Calib met him in his crystal cave. Back then, the wizard was hiding under the guise of a white wolf named Howell. Calib wished more than anything he could have Merlin's guidance now, in whatever form.

The Darklings had become Camelot's allies, and in many cases, his friends. All the other nasty rumors he'd ever heard about them—the many things for which they'd been blamed—had turned out to be unfounded. Calib swallowed hard, unable to hide the doubt in his eyes.

"Perhaps you're finally catching on." Percival smiled knowingly. "The truth is, your grandfather *framed* the Darklings for your father's murder. It was a *Saxon* raid, not a Darkling one. But in order to avoid a new war he could not win, Yvers blamed it on the innocent Darklings instead."

"That's not what happened!" Calib shook his head. His heart refused to believe, but the tremor in his voice betrayed him. "That *can't* be what happened!"

"Your heroes are not the perfect mice you think they are," Percival said softly. "Sir Trenton was trying to sneak the Goldenwood Throne out of the castle. Steal it away from Yvers and sell it to the Saxons. Except your father underestimated the Saxon tradition of just taking what they want without paying for it."

"But they didn't take it!" Calib pointed out, desperate to poke a hole in Percival's tale. "The Grail has been in Camelot's possession all along, until you came along."

"You are right in that the deal never went through, thanks to Merlin's meddling and the owls' intervening. But the Manderlean got enough of it."

In between his words, Calib realized what Percival was suggesting: that his father was the original traitor to the throne.

"Not *all* of the Grail was recovered," Percival said.

"It fell during the skirmish between father and son and cracked. Mull on *that* while you rot here in the Deep."

"You lie!" Calib shouted at Percival's retreating tail. "You're a *LIAR!*"

But the Manderlean's creatures had already disappeared up the stairs, leaving Calib all alone in the stuffy, stinking dungeons.

Not even a single Saxon was left behind to guard him. He was too deep in the bowels of the earth for anyone to be able to reach him.

As Calib laid back on the hard bench that served as his bed, he tried to forget all the things Percival had said—but they would not be ignored. His gut told him that perhaps—maybe, just possibly—this was one thing Percival was not lying about.

Stewing in his sour thoughts, Calib lost track of time, and he drifted in and out of a fitful sleep. The noises from the forges never seemed to stop. How loud they must have been to echo down even to the Deep. He began to imagine that the sounds were coming closer, growing to a manic crescendo, suffocating him. . . .

He sat up with a jolt, his ears twitching. That wasn't the forges at all—that was the pitter-patter of paws. His ears twitched.

"Who's there?" Calib demanded as he surged to his feet. "Stop skulking and face me in the light!"

"I like what you've done with the whiskers," said a new voice in the shadows. A very familiar voice.

And then she stood in front of him: Cecily von Mandrake.

Safe. Unharmed.

Alive.

CHAPTER
22

"Cecily!" Calib cried, nearly melting with relief.

Cecily held up a torch, illuminating her wide grin. "Found him. Let's get him loose, boys."

Half a dozen squirrels and mice stirred out of the shadows, hollow-eyed but determined. Their chains dangled from their lank limbs in broken pieces.

"Stand back, unless you want to lose an eye," one of the squirrels said.

He brought forward what Calib thought was a small, thin candle. The squirrel winked at Calib and shoved the unlit end into the keyhole on his cell. It made a sizzling sound that Calib had never heard before. The squirrel ran back to the rest of his group.

"Do as he says!" Cecily shouted, clapping her paws to her ears. Calib pushed himself against the back of the cell, just as the lock suddenly exploded in a crackling flash of light. When Calib's eyes adjusted, he saw the lock had been broken and now hung uselessly warped. The door swung open.

"What was that?" Calib was dazzled by what he'd just seen. "Magic?"

"It's something found inland, far from here," Cecily said, sounding a little impressed herself. "They've been using it to make more tunnels in the mountains."

"Two-Leggers call it fire powder because it explodes in reaction to flame," the squirrel said. He looked at Cecily. "I hope this little mousling was worth the trouble we spent looking for him. It's very valuable."

"He's worth it, I promise." Cecily gestured for Calib to follow them. "Come, we don't have much time."

The group wound through more twisting tunnels full of unoccupied cells, until finally, they found themselves at a wall of rock, with no more turns to take.

"What now?" Calib asked.

"Help us push!" Cecily said, leaning her weight against the stone. The rest of the squirrels followed suit. Slowly, it began to pivot around on an axel. It was a hidden door!

"How do you know about this?" Calib asked.

"I've met some very interesting creatures since I've arrived," Cecily said, smiling mischievously. "I escaped the very first night they brought me here. Percival must have figured that you would come along after me, so he set up the trap."

"Why didn't you try to leave?" Calib asked.

"You'll see why," Cecily said. Her mouth was set in a grim line.

On the other side of the wall, there was no tunnel; only a large horizontal crack in the mountains, just tall enough for the squirrels to go through if they ducked their heads.

Ahead, Calib could see the ruddy flickering of a fire against a cavernous dome.

"Head toward the bonfire," Cecily said from behind.

The pathway was roughly hewn, with rubble scattered everywhere. Calib had to tread carefully for fear of getting his footpaw caught in a hidden crack in the rocks.

Eventually, they arrived in a large underground quarry where a whole new group of animals was gathered around the bonfire in question.

"I've brought him!" Cecily called out to the group. "I *told* you he would show up!"

Calib counted nearly fifty creatures gathered, including

a number of the messenger larks who had gone missing from Camelot. They were the first to surround Calib with questions.

"Did General Fletcher sound angry when we didn't arrive home?" asked one.

"It's such an embarrassment. I have never been late with a message, ever," lamented another.

A familiar voice cut in.

"Stop pestering Calib with useless questions," said Ginny, one of the Camelot kitchen mice who was supposed to be spending the season learning Darkling cuisine. "There are more important things to worry about than what General Fletcher thinks of your punctuality."

"Ginny!" Calib exclaimed. He ran to give her a hug, and she squeezed him tightly in return. "What are you doing here?"

"Obviously, I'm not here for my health," Ginny said, pointing at the split ends of her whiskers. The mouse's reddish fur had lost much of its luster and volume. "We were captured by the Saxons a few weeks ago, with Lylas and the others. I got put to work in the kitchens, naturally. And with some help, we were able to escape."

"I see you caught on to my clue," Lylas remarked as he roamed into the bonfire's light. "Welcome, Calib."

Calib smiled at the sight of the badger. He looked much more refreshed than when Calib had last seen him.

"I did," he said, "though it took me longer to get down here than it should have."

Lylas smiled. "What matters is that you're here, though." He turned to Ginny. "How are we on supplies?"

Ginny looked troubled. "We're running low. If we rescue any more, we might not be able to provide enough every day."

"Well, I don't plan on staying here for another day," growled a deep voice. "Not with Calib Christopher here to assist us."

The largest creature stepped forward. He was broad-chested and fearsome, with wild yellow fur, and Calib immediately recognized him.

"Leftie!" Calib exclaimed. He gave a swift bow to the leader of all the Darklings. "It's good to see you, sir."

"You too, mouse," Leftie said, strolling forward to clap a massive paw on Calib's back. To Calib's surprise, even the wildcat supported broken chains. "Though I wish it were under better circumstances."

Calib nodded solemnly. "How long has this been going on? No one has heard from you in months. Camelot, well, they were getting nervous."

"Feared I was turning traitor, eh?"

Calib cleared his throat. "Something like that."

Leftie sat down on his haunches and smoothed his whiskers. "Winter was only just starting to end, and I was weak," the lynx growled. "I hadn't even had time to get my wits about me before they captured and brought me here to work in their forges."

Leftie snarled at the memory, revealing both his fangs. "There are others who have been here even longer, held captive since the Battle of the Bear. We now realize that Morgan and the Saxons only provoked that fight with the hope of storming the castle and stealing the Grail. When that did not work, Morgan le Fay cursed Britain with the white fever, in order for the Manderlean's creatures to sneak into the castle and find it."

"But what's she waiting for?" Calib asked. "She has it now."

"Yes," Leftie said as he threw an extra piece of coal onto the fire, making it hiss. "But she doesn't know how to use it."

Cecily nodded solemnly. "My first night, they questioned me about it." Her right ear twitched, and for the first time, Calib noticed nicks in it that hadn't been there before. His blood boiled, but he tried to stay calm, the same way Commander Yvers would have.

At the thought of his grandfather, Sir Percival's words rose up to sting him again. He no longer had time to think about that now. He didn't want to linger on the past. Part of him was too afraid to.

"How did we not know this?" Calib asked, reeling

from the information. "How could they have done this right under our whiskers?"

"We were too distracted by the petty squabbles between Darklings and Camelot," Leftie said. His bobbed tail began to swish in agitation. "But now we know better. We've managed to free a good number from their chains."

"But it's not enough!" Cecily burst out. "They still manage to capture more to replace the ones we've freed! They work the miners until they die from exhaustion, and the smiths until they're so tired they nearly fall into their fires. We need to fight for their freedom!"

At her words, a hum went around the group of freed prisoners.

"Don't speak of what you don't know, mouse-maid," Lylas said. "You've seen battle, but you haven't seen *war*." At the badger's words, the animals around him murmured in agreement.

"You've only just arrived here, little groundling," a wizen old crow added. "You haven't seen what we've seen."

"But we can't keep tunneling forever," Cecily said with a stomp of her footpaw. "If we can convince *all* the prisoners to revolt . . . There's an army here that we could use *against* the Saxons! Don't you agree, Calib?"

Though he admired his friend's bravery, Calib hesitated. Remembering the many warships that edged the sulfuric lake, he asked, "How many Saxons are there?"

Leftie stroked his chin. "From my estimate, at least one thousand animals and five hundred Two-Leggers, with more coming every day. The Manderlean and his Saxons outnumber us free folk, ten to one, and with the stink of magic everywhere, I don't see how we can do anything yet."

The wildcat looked at Cecily. "I'm sorry." The flickering red flames threw shadows across Leftie's face, but even the shadows couldn't hide the sadness in his eyes.

This wasn't how it was supposed to go. Calib was supposed to find Cecily and bring both her and the Grail back to Camelot triumphantly. He wasn't supposed to be stuck in the Iron Mountains for the rest of his days.

"What can we do?" Calib asked, feeling helpless as he looked at the older and wiser creatures around him.

Lylas handed him a shovel. "We keep digging. We keep exploring. We keep holding faith that one day, we will see the sun and sky again."

CHAPTER
23

"Healing has two sides: life and death," Morgan had told Galahad as she'd ushered him into an underground garden nearly a week ago. This deep into the mountains, there was no sunlight, yet a large yellow crystal embedded in the rock ceiling gave off a warm glow that seemed to be enough for the potted saplings and rosebushes that grew in the stuffy garden. For the past week, Galahad had toiled under its dim light.

"The line between both is thin," Morgan had continued, "which is why you must work hard to be able to reach out and grasp the spirit of a living thing. Life is potential. *Potential* is magic."

She'd then set a potted oak sapling in front of Galahad. "When you can draw this sapling's potential into Excalibur, we can move on to the next lesson. Do you understand?"

At first Galahad hadn't. But now, as he pointed Excalibur at an oak sapling in a pot of sandy soil, he thought he heard a quiet whisper from the plant. Stunted and frail, the sapling had lived all its brief life in the caves. But it still dreamed of the forest. For a moment, Galahad could feel the essence of it through the sword: a wispy hint of moss and loam and sunlight. But then it was gone. Excalibur felt heavy in his hands.

"You are too passive," Morgan observed from her high-backed chair situated among the wild rosebushes. "The sword is only a tool. It cannot do the work for you. You must *bend* it to your will, or magic will always escape you. If it helps, imagine that the sapling has within it what you most want. Direct that want down your sword, and *take.*"

Though tired and exhausted, Galahad nodded. Taking a deep breath, he wiped sweat off his brow. What he most wanted was easy: the Grail.

Galahad had not seen the Grail since Morgan had first made him sip from it, but he knew Britta—who was crushed that her theory had proven incorrect—was still hard at work trying to unlock its secrets. Occasionally, in the evenings, if he was still awake after training sessions with Morgan, he'd join Britta and pretend to assist her. All the while, he tried to slow down the Saxon researcher's progress and glean new hints for himself on how to work the Grail.

As Galahad adjusted his grip on Excalibur and fixed his mind's eye on the Grail, another image replaced it. A memory from long ago, of a young Galahad situated between Sir Lancelot and Lady Elaine. Each held one of his chubby hands, and they swung him by the arms as they walked by the river, singing a silly ditty with him. It was one of the few memories Galahad had of his family together, a rare moment when Sir Lancelot wasn't out on Arthur's orders. It was a rare memory of peace.

Suddenly, Galahad was again aware of the sapling's yearning for the sun on its leaves, its dreams of rich dirt in its roots. And this time, instead of letting the sapling's thoughts slip away, Galahad gripped them. Excalibur's hilt grew warm in his hand.

"Good," Morgan said softly from behind him. "Now, tug, pulling the sapling's potential into Excalibur."

Barely breathing, Galahad tugged at the sapling's essence, as if it were a loose thread from his tunic. The sapling shrieked!

Startled, Galahad let go of Excalibur, and the sword

clattered to the ground, breaking his concentration and his connection to the little tree.

"I can't," Galahad said, looking toward Morgan. "The sapling said it hurt!"

"Sometimes, to heal, you have to hurt first. To grow something, you have to burn something." Morgan frowned, an expression halfway between impatience and disappointment. Galahad was becoming very familiar with that look. "Galahad, you lack conviction. This should be easier for you."

She gestured toward the sapling with a casual flick of her wrist. Through Excalibur, Galahad felt a surge of magic, and a moment later, he saw the sapling writhe like a snake as its leaves turned brown and withered. He caught a sense of dry heat and pain, a forest on fire. Then the skinny branches crumbled into a fine gray dust. In Morgan's hand, a ball of blue flame danced and crackled.

"Remember, all living things have power. A skilled magician can harness that power and do with it as she pleases."

Morgan closed her hand into a fist and walked over to a stout little tree. When she touched the blue flames to its trunk, the ball extinguished, leaving a curl of smoke and the scent of rosemary and iron that lingered in the air. A second later, the leaves of the tree rustled as large plums, dusky purple and fragrant, hung heavy on the formerly bare branches. Morgan plucked a fruit from a branch and gently tossed it to Galahad, who caught it.

"Anyone—even Red—can accomplish this task. But you, Galahad, are barely trying."

"Why bother with me, then?" Galahad asked. Resentment swept through him, and he was surprised at how hurt he was at her words. But then, Morgan smiled

"Because you are special. Anyone, with some studying, can channel power, just as any skilled forester can walk through the forest and identify the birds by their song, or the trees by their leaves. They may even learn to interpret the behavior of the birds or to determine which trees are healthy and which are sick. But they will never be able to understand the emotions of a rowan tree, nor translate the language of the larks.

"Excalibur chose you, and once you have mastered Excalibur's magic, you will find that you can move a forest as easily as you can listen to it."

Galahad shivered. She knew so much about Excalibur, and he remembered again what she had said on the first night he'd arrived: that the sword in the stone had been meant for her.

"Why did Merlin not let you pull the sword?" Galahad blurted out before he could stop himself. Immediately, he winced, preparing for the sorceress to punish him for his impudence. But instead, she sighed.

"I don't know why," she said sadly. "But I never quite fit in with the others of Camelot. My thirst for knowledge proved a nuisance to the court after they realized I was no longer going to be queen. They whispered about me in the castle, plotted to marry me off to some lesser noble."

Again, Galahad felt uncomfortable. Morgan's experience in the castle had some similarities to his own. Awkwardly, he tossed the plum from one palm to the other.

"Arthur," Morgan continued, "for all his weaknesses, tried to be understanding. And when he realized that Merlin had stolen my inheritance away from me, he personally requested that the Sisters on Avalon take me onto their island and teach me their ways. He hoped that if I could not have the throne, perhaps I would be placated by knowledge."

She shook her head, and her auburn hair shimmered down the length of her back.

"Avalon was home for me—for a little while, at least. The Sisters, despite their powers of foresight, did not understand their role in the world. Why cultivate all this magic and knowledge, only to hoard it away on an island? In this, Merlin and I agreed. Where we differed is how we proposed to use it. Merlin wanted to use his magic to prop up weak kings like Arthur. But I believe that only those with power belong in power. Only the people who can make difficult decisions should lead. In order to survive, Camelot needs a strong ruler."

Galahad's mind flashed back to all the bickering at the Round Table during those hours at court. What if King Arthur had simply gone with his gut?

"Enough of this," Morgan said, and then she plucked the plum from his hand. She took a bite from it and swallowed, the plum's sweet juice so fragrant that Galahad could smell it from feet away.

"Pick up Excalibur. Try again."

CHAPTER
24

For days, Calib had been looking down his snout at only rock and darkness and more rock. The rebellion had found several passageways that had been dug out long ago by some other creatures, but many had caved in or led to nowhere. None led to the surface.

That evening, around the campfire, there was somber news. One of the more promising tunnels had collapsed, nearly killing two moles.

"We have to start over!" Lylas said, his jaw set with frustration. "This is the fifth time this has happened!"

"What is causing these cave-ins?" Calib asked.

"No idea," Lylas said. "Everything seems to be going well when we leave to sleep, but then our supports come loose in the night. If I had to guess, I feel as if someone or something is purposefully sabotaging our efforts."

"Badger," Leftie growled warningly, "heed your words. Who among us wants to stay here forever? We must continue to trust one another, or else all is truly lost."

Lylas looked into the embers. "I'm sorry, Leftie. Of course I don't think any creature within our ranks is hindering our efforts."

"I think those tunnels are cursed," Ginny said softly, wringing her apron with her paws. "I hear spooky noises coming from them at night."

"There's no such thing," Cecily said. "It's just bad luck."

Leftie the wildcat fixed his single yellow eye on Cecily. "You haven't seen any other creatures when you go exploring, have you, Von Mandrake?"

"Whatever do you mean?" Cecily asked in the same tone Calib recognized from when Commander Kensington used to ask who had used the Hurler without adult supervision.

"I know when you go to collect food, it takes twenty times longer than when Ginny here does," Leftie said, his voice gruff, though there was amusement in his eyes.

"So I ask you: Have you seen anything in your explorations?"

"No," Cecily said. "Not anything."

Leftie nodded, but something in Calib's stomach wiggled. He wasn't so sure he believed her.

When Cecily next went to forage for food, Calib asked if he could come along.

"I haven't been yet, and I think I'll go mad if I just keep digging the entire day," he said truthfully.

"As long as you can keep up—you never could in Camelot!" she said with a smile, and Calib smiled back at the memory of them and the other pages scurrying to the Two-Legger kitchens to help scrounge food for the castle feasts.

They raced through the different tunnels, until Cecily gestured to what looked like another dead end. But she leaned against one side of the stone and began to push.

"Come on, help me," she grunted.

Bracing his shoulder against the stone, he pushed. Slowly, the wall revolved, and the sour smell of rancid food filled Calib's nostrils and lungs. The stench made him cough and his eyes water. In the darkness, Calib could see bits of eggshells, peels, and rotten bones strewn across the ledge on the other side.

"Blech, what are we doing here?" said Calib, breathing through his mouth to dampen the smell.

"Waiting on our food delivery from Jasper," Cecily said, also holding her nose.

"Food delivery . . . from Jasper . . ." Calib was beginning to put the pieces together.

"He's the one who has been secretly sending us food this whole time," Cecily continued. "He pretends it's gone bad and—"

"Sends it down the garbage chute," Calib finished as the last puzzle piece clicked into place. Jasper didn't hate his cooking—he'd been feeding the rebellion! They were standing on a small ledge overlooking a large mining shaft of untold depths. If the drop was positioned properly, it would land right here where they were waiting, making it easy pickings for an intrepid mouse.

Calib's admiration for the brave hare grew tenfold.

"This is how Leftie has kept his rebellion fed the entire time," Cecily said. "But, well, there have been hiccups. Hopefully, Jasper won't be late this time. He's missed his previous two deliveries, and as you heard Ginny say, we're running low."

"Incoming," a hushed voice from somewhere high above echoed down.

Cecily pushed Calib close to the wall. Four parcels, bound multiple times in cheesecloth, crash-landed on the ledge with loud splotching sounds.

Calib and Cecily ran forward to grab the satchels and

pull them back to the other side of the door, where things were not so smelly.

Unwrapping one of the packages, Cecily revealed a perfectly serviceable pile of vegetable pastries. They were still steaming, despite being a bit crumbly and smashed from the fall. The smell of one sent Calib's stomach into a growling frenzy.

Cecily took a bite. "Mmmm, absolute perfection," she murmured, her ears flat against her head and her grin unmistakable.

Calib sampled one for himself. The flaky piecrust gave way to a comforting mush of broccoli, onion, and carrot. He closed his eyes to appreciate the flavor of the gravy-like broth mingling with the buttery potatoes.

"This is as good as Madame von Mandrake's," Calib said. But as soon as the words left Calib's mouth, he regretted them.

Cecily looked like someone had smacked her on the snout. Her eyes filled with sudden tears. She swallowed her bite slowly and turned to Calib.

"Is Maman beside herself?" Cecily's whiskers trembled. "Does she think I'm dead?"

Calib patted Cecily's shaking shoulders, at a loss for what else to do in the moment. "Of course not. She's worried, but she knows you're smart and quick on your paws."

"I hope you're right," she said, wiping at her eyes. "It's

just been so long since we've had a good, peaceful day. I've almost forgotten what it's like *not* to be scared of what the next day will bring."

Inwardly, Calib cringed. It was true; Camelot always seemed to be in danger these days. He wondered if the Saxons would ever give up their onslaught, or if this would be their new reality for decades to come.

He handed Cecily his pastry. "Go on, eat some more," he said. "You'll feel . . . Maybe not better, but stronger if you're not hungry."

Cecily nodded and bit into the soft vegetable pastry.

"Ow!" she exclaimed.

"What's wrong?" Calib looked around, wondering if he'd missed a hidden attacker. But Cecily was staring at her pastry. In the dim light, Calib could see something gleam inside the pie. A glass vial.

Quickly, Cecily extracted it and held it up to the torchlight. Inside was a note.

"What is this?" Calib asked.

"A message from Jasper," Cecily said, wedging her tail into the narrow opening and wrapping it around the parchment. "This is how he communicates with us sometimes. Last time, Lylas nearly choked on it."

There was a soft pop as the message came free. Huddling next to Cecily, Calib began to read the hare's skittish handwriting:

A Two-Legger has joined Morgan's ranks.
Judging by his sword, he's even more powerful than her.

"That's just Galahad," Calib said, a wave of worry for his friend crashing down on him. "He's pretending to be on Morgan's side so that he can find the Grail."

"If you say so," Cecily said. At Calib's glare, she hastily added, "We better get going. Ginny's going to cry with delight over these pastries."

Calib nodded, and they scurried back up the passageways that led to the friendly campfires. But as he handed out the fresh food from the kitchens, he noticed that a few of the pastries seemed to have gone missing . . . and that Cecily was no longer near the glowing red embers.

CHAPTER
25

In the moments when Galahad didn't have to deal with Morgan's odd tests or confrontations with Red, he found refuge in the library. There, he worked with Britta, helping her translate and, in some cases, preventing her from getting too close to the truth.

Even though the Saxon girl was working against them, he couldn't help being impressed at how far she'd already gotten by herself. She was a dangerous ally for Morgan to have. Part of him hoped he could convince her to join Camelot's side instead.

Today, Galahad was looking at a scroll that detailed an eyewitness account of the Grail at work. It recounted the final battle between King Arthur's forces and the last Saxon army to be driven from Britain:

Great drops of golden light fell upon the battlefield. Where they touched, the dead and injured arose anew, unscathed by arrows or swords. Afterward a great wolf stood where the wizard had been. And he bore the treasure away.

Galahad paused. He had nearly forgotten about his dream of the white wolf.

"I'm starving. Do you want any food from the kitchens?" Britta asked. "I can bring some back."

"Some bread and cheese does sound nice," Galahad said.

"That's it?" Britta asked. "I'll do us one better. I saw there were some dried figs in the larder this morning."

"Figs?" Galahad asked. He'd never heard of figs.

"You've never had figs?" Britta's brown eyes grew wide. "Not a fresh one?"

Galahad shook his head.

"Are you in for a treat! Back before Papa's land dried up, we had entire orchards full of fig trees, and oranges and grapes." Britta closed her eyes, as if savoring an imaginary delicacy. "Maybe when this is all over, we can try growing some in Britain."

"When did this drought begin?" Galahad needed to understand exactly what had happened in Saxony. Perhaps that would explain why they were always attacking Camelot.

"It wasn't a drought, though," Britta replied, shoving her hands into her pockets. She looked down. "It rained just as much as it had any other year, but the ground would not take it. Everything green was dying, withering away into dust and ash."

Britta sighed, a sound full of wishes and melancholy. "We had to abandon our land and move to the coast. Papa became a fisherman. He's terrible at it—could only net fistfuls of minnows. There was never enough food for my younger sisters. So when Morgan came to town, promising a new green land for us, I signed up for the cause without hesitation. I can't handle a sword very well, but I can solve any type of word puzzle."

"Did anything strange happen before the drought started?" Galahad asked. He wanted to see if any connection could be made to Morgan. "Were any animals acting weird?"

"For a while, we thought it *was* the weasels who were causing it," Britta said. "Papa and the other men would set traps and go on hunting parties. But one day, they all disappeared, and the land didn't get better."

Galahad's face paled as he realized the Saxon weasels may have just been escaping persecution themselves.

"What's the matter?" Britta asked. "You look as if someone sneezed on your soufflé."

"Oh, nothing," Galahad said. "It must have been hard to deal with, leaving your family behind."

"Morgan has promised she'll send for them as soon as we figure out the Grail," Britta said. "That's why I work so hard."

Silence hung in the air between them.

Finally, Britta said, "If you'll excuse me, I'll be right back."

Britta left the library, and Galahad sank into his chair.

He'd been actively working against her this entire time, but maybe, once he figured out the Grail, he could negotiate with King Arthur on Britta's behalf as well.

CHAPTER
26

There was another cave-in a few days later. The rebellion was lucky—only one tail was broken and some whiskers crumpled—but Calib worried that the next time they might not be so fortunate. He wished he had paid more attention in Sir Alric's innovation lessons. As it was, Calib had been too interested in trying to prove himself as a swordsmouse to listen during the less glamorous parts of his training. As Camelot's head engineer, Alric would have known how to dig tunnels that didn't collapse. Maybe Cecily would remember something useful.

But when he checked the tunnel she'd been assigned to, she wasn't there. The tips of his fur rose on end.

"Hi, Ginny," Calib said, scurrying to where the chef-in-training was busy cutting up a pitiful parsnip. "Have you seen Cecily?"

"She just came by," Ginny said. "She went that way." She indicated with her nose a tunnel Calib had only gone down once before. After saying a quick thank-you, Calib headed that way.

Calib was sure she hadn't been caught up in the cave-in, but he still wasn't sure what Cecily had been up to with the food filching. She clearly knew something the others didn't. He flew down the dark path, and even his sensitive eyes had a hard time adjusting to the light.

"Oof!" Calib ran into something solid, warm, and very furry.

"Calib!" Cecily exclaimed. "What are you doing here?"

"I could ask you the same thing!" Calib retorted. "You're stealing food from the kitchens! Cecily, how could you? If you're hungry, you can have some of my—"

"Excuse me," Cecily huffed, her pink nose becoming even more pink with anger. "Do you think I'm taking this food to feed myself?"

"I—" Calib stopped, his ears twitching. "No, I don't really think that," he admitted. "But I know you're up to something. Please tell me."

Cecily hesitated a moment, her ears twitching, before she finally nodded. "All right . . . but you have to promise to be quiet and listen to me. Got that?"

Calib nodded, and Cecily led them down the tunnel. It became shorter and narrower the farther they went. Here, in the heart of the mountains, the rock was dark and dense.

"Who could have done all this?" Calib asked, marveling at the smooth stone under his footpaws. The path had been worn down by many paws before him, and like so many hallways he'd encountered within the mountains, it branched off, with paths leading in seemingly random directions. Cecily had brought pieces of chalk to mark the walls so that they could keep track of where they had gone and which tunnels had already been explored. Judging by the tight walls and low ceilings, Calib could tell this rock must have been difficult to carve.

They came to another abandoned quarry, like the ones they had passed earlier. However, this one was much larger than the others. Cecily led him to a round room that looked like it once served as a mine shaft. It smelled of coal and . . .

Calib's hackles rose. "Stop," he whispered to Cecily. "I smell weasels!"

"Actually—" But before Cecily could finish whatever she was about to say, three weasels—all armed—appeared.

"Get back, scoundrels!" Calib's fighting instincts kicked in. He dropped his food and picked up a pebble. He chucked the stone at the closest weasel—a brown, furry fellow with a white tuft on his chest. It whizzed by his ears and ricocheted off the wall, striking one of the two weasels behind him.

"Ow!" a voice yelped.

"Stop!"

Calib felt something tight around his paw and looked to see Cecily gripping him. "They're not the enemy," Cecily said firmly, then released him.

Calib looked at the three weasels more closely and saw that they looked no older than he. In fact, they were children. Calib felt a wash of guilt and embarrassment as he realized he'd struck a young weasel-maid.

"I fink he knockt out my toof," the weasel-maid said, running a tongue over the top of her teeth.

"I'm so sorry," Calib said, mortified.

"Thath all right." She smiled, a gap where one of her teeth used to be. "I was thoo afraith thoo pull it outh."

The foremost weasel sauntered forward.

"Some welcome from the hero of Camelot," he said sarcastically. "Or should I say the dentist of Camelot?"

"You surprised me," Calib protested. "And what sort of welcome do you expect as invaders to our land?"

"Ahem!" Cecily stepped between them. "Calib, this is

Thomas Steepaw, and his siblings Rosy and Silas. I think you'll want to hear what he has to say."

"I doubt that," Calib grumbled, giving Thomas a sideways glance.

"Thomas, tell Calib your story," Cecily said.

"Are you sure he wants to hear it?" the weasel asked, glaring at Calib.

Cecily waved her paw dismissively. "Calib's just being cheeseheaded right now. But he *knows* how to listen to creatures he thought were his enemies. He's the one who united Camelot and the Darklings . . . isn't that right, Calib?"

Calib felt as if his heart had been pinched. Shame flooded him. While the Saxons may not be Britons, they deserved to be heard. He nodded. "My apologies, Thomas. Please, tell me."

"Very well," Thomas said, and sat back on his haunches. "My siblings and I grew up in Saxony. I was studying to be a scholar, but then the famine struck. Something terrible happened to our crops back home. They all dried out and turned to dust in the field. There was not enough food to eat. I had to do something for my brothers and sisters, or they would starve."

As if in response, a stomach growled loudly.

"I brought Jasper's latest delivery," Cecily said, rummaging in her satchel for some of the scraps Ginny had given her. The two younger kids nearly bowled Calib over to get to the food.

"Thank you," Thomas said. "My poor parents didn't survive the winter, and since I'm the oldest, I stopped my studies to take care of my brother and sister. One day, these weasels showed up in town, talking a big talk and recruiting others to join them in a journey to settle new lands. They promised food for the journey and money to start a new life. All we had to do was promise to work for them for a year. I immediately signed up, thinking I had solved our problems forever. Except . . ."

Thomas gestured to the place around them. "I didn't realize what we were in for until we arrived. They were looking for labor in their war against Britain."

Calib was horrified. He saw the shabby state of their clothes and how Rosy still clutched a doll made from bits of rope and a bead. How Silas ravenously munched on the parsnip, like he hadn't eaten in a year.

"How long have you lived like this in the Iron Mountains?" he asked, voice hushed.

"I don't know how long exactly; it's hard to keep track without the sun, but we arrived shortly after what the Saxons have been calling the Battle of the Bear."

"About seven months," Calib whispered.

"Seven months," Thomas repeated, his eyes widening. "It feels like longer."

"Why hide away here?" Calib asked. "Why didn't you join the rebellion?"

"The others don't trust the Saxons," Cecily explained. "Something about Merlin's Mirror being broken."

With a twist of guilt, Calib suddenly remembered that he had not told Leftie about Merlin's Mirror yet. They had to get to Galahad as soon as possible to make sure another of Merlin's treasures didn't fall into the wrong hands.

"But don't you see," Cecily continued, "they deserve our help, just as much as the others. This problem with their food . . . This is Morgan's doing. Her magic drained the crops in Saxony; it's killing their land!"

Thomas bobbed his head. "It'll start happening here too. The witch turns everything she touches to ashes, draining it of all life."

Calib thought back to the burned-out trees that had been dotting the Darkling Woods since spring and nod-ded. Thomas's words seemed to be the truth, but still . . .

"And you're not causing cave-ins, right?" he asked.

Cecily glared at Calib, who quickly held up his paws. "Only needed to check."

"No," Thomas said with a dignified sniff. "Certainly not."

"Actually," Cecily said with one last scowl at Calib, "Thomas, Rosy, and Silas have been exploring tunnels back in this area. No exit yet," Cecily said hurriedly, "but they did find some tunnels marked with old runes. I think they may have been made by the druids."

"Druids," Calib whispered, remembering the term from Sir Owen's history lessons. "The mystic mice who helped build the giant stone circles throughout Britain?"

"Yes, and I think some of that stone came from here. See?" Cecily pointed to something marked on the ceiling above a tunnel that branched away from them. "If you go down that way, you'll run into an old quarry."

"Those rocks are boring," Rosy piped up. "Silas and me like the sparkly ones, don't we, Silas?"

"Yeah!" Silas said. "We have a rock collection. Do you wanna see?"

Cecily tousled the weasel's fluff. "Maybe next time, but Calib and I best be getting back. We'll be missed."

"You should tell your story to Leftie," he told Thomas. Even as he spoke the words out loud, determination straightened his spine. "I'll vouch for you."

Thomas wrinkled his snout. "I'm not sure. . . ."

Taking a few small steps toward the weasel, Calib tentatively reached out and patted the Saxon's shoulder. The weasel's fur was thick and soft, and even though Calib knew that Thomas, too, must emit the usual weasel musk, he realized that he hardly noticed the smell anymore. He had gotten used to it.

"You are incredibly brave," Calib said. "And facing creatures you think are the enemy will prove that you're braver than all the knights of the Round Table combined. You've already faced so much, but this isn't the life you want for your brother and sister—or for yourself. Think about it?"

Thomas didn't say anything, but he looked at Rosy and Silas, whose eyes were starting to drift shut now that hunger pains wouldn't keep them awake. He turned to Calib. "Yes," he said softly. "I promise. We'll think about it."

CHAPTER
27

Red's relentless assaults showed no sign of stopping. "Yield," the larger boy panted through his face-plate. "You know I've got you beat."

Galahad retreated across the flagstones of Morgan le Fay's throne room. Red was trying to force him into a corner, and no matter which way Galahad turned, it seemed like Red was always one step ahead of him.

Red was a flurry of attacks: high left, high right, high right again, low right. Galahad barely got Excalibur in place to block the last one. Excalibur had always felt surprisingly light in his hands, but since he'd been in Morgan's fortress, it seemed like the sword had become ten pounds heavier.

"Watch your back," Red warned. Galahad had half turned his head before he realized it was a trick, but by then, it was too late. Red charged, slamming his shoulder into Galahad's chest and knocking him backward. Galahad stumbled, trying to keep his balance, but it was a hopeless effort. He went crashing to the floor.

"You cheated!" Galahad shouted, furious.

"No such thing in a fight," Red sneered. He looked very pleased with himself.

Galahad was sick of this. Every part of his body hurt, and he was no closer to besting Red. With a frustrated cry, he lashed out with Excalibur, catching Red in the shin. His smirk turned into a grimace of pain as he fell to his knees in a clash of metal.

"Enough." Morgan was standing over them both. She held out the Grail, full to the brim with the same inky black liquid from before. "Drink from the Grail again and heal Red with Excalibur."

Galahad sighed. He almost wished that Morgan would go back to letting Red pummel him. He was black-and-blue, and every muscle in his body ached, but at least he seemed to be making progress at sword fighting. With healing, however, he could not figure out what Morgan wanted him to accomplish with the Grail.

He pointed his sword back at Red and reached out with his mind toward one of the rosebushes surrounding the throne. Now, after many days of practice, he could easily sense the bush's yearning for the sun.

Galahad tugged half-heartedly on the bush's life, urging it to cooperate, but it resisted. It wanted to live. It *pleaded* with Galahad to let it live.

Feeling sickened, Galahad released. "I can't do it."

"What's the point of keeping him around, Mother, if he can't do anything you ask?" Red said. With his own flick of the wrist, one of the red blooms disintegrated into ash, and the cut on his shin healed. Only a few flecks of blood on the floor indicated that Galahad had ever injured Red.

Morgan pursed her lips, then gave a sharp nod. "Follow me. Both of you."

Without waiting for a reply, Morgan stalked out of the throne room. Red sprang to his feet and hurried after his mother, throwing Galahad another sneer. Galahad sighed and followed.

A spiral staircase led down into the depths of the fortress. Galahad could hear Red's heavy footsteps several turns below, but he could not see him. A quiet word from Morgan occasionally echoed up from even farther down the stairwell. Galahad tried to hurry, but he never seemed to get any closer.

The stones of the curved walls grew larger and more misshapen as they descended, as though the higher levels had been built one atop the other over many centuries. The steps grew wider and deeper, great slabs of stone piled into uneven ledges. After a while, the stone seemed more like a cave than a castle. The air felt thick, and the candles in their sconces struggled to push back the shadows.

Quite abruptly, the staircase ended. Galahad found himself in a vast cavern, though how vast he could not say since the ceiling and all but the nearest walls were lost in darkness. Morgan le Fay was holding a torch above her head; the only source of light. She was kneeling on a narrow wooden bridge that spanned an underground river, its current swift and white. Red stood to Galahad's left, watching his mother.

Morgan was leaning out over the edge of bridge, perfectly still as she stared into the churning foam below. With no warning, she plunged her free arm into the black water. As she stood up, Galahad saw a pale-white carp wriggling in her hand.

"To make something, you must first take something. To build a house, you must break the stone," she said, gazing intently at the fish. It gasped and gaped, white eyes blind and bulging, its scales glistening in the torchlight. "That is power. If you tried to listen and accommodate every life and every thing, *nothing* would get done. Do you understand?"

Galahad's mind flashed back to Father Walter's first teaching: if someone hurts, you help, no matter peasant or king. Somehow, he didn't think Morgan shared the same view.

"Do you feel this fish's thoughts, Galahad?" Morgan asked.

Galahad nodded. With Excalibur at his side, he could sense the creature's desperation.

"Tell me," Morgan commanded.

"It's afraid," Galahad said slowly. "You're hurting its fins, and the air burns its gills."

Morgan bowed her head, looking almost contrite, and let go of the fish. Instead of splashing back into the river, it floated in the air, still gasping. Morgan turned her hand in a scooping gesture and siphoned some water off the surface of the river, forming a ball around the carp as it hovered. The fish stopped gasping and started swimming back and forth in the sphere. Galahad could feel its clammy sense of relief and confusion.

Red stepped to the river's edge, watching the fish.

"I don't know what it's feeling," Red said thoughtfully, "but it doesn't matter. It was hatched down here in the dark; it will die in the dark. It could live an entire life that will have no meaning. But we can change that. We can use it to do something that actually makes a difference for us."

"No!" Galahad cried, but he could feel Red already conjuring some spell.

The carp twisted, and Galahad felt its pain. He knew enough of Morgan's magic to sense the carp's life draining away as Red wrung it of its essence. Without even thinking about what he was doing, Galahad reached out with all of his crude magical skill. He did not know what to do; he just knew that if he did nothing, the fish would die to satisfy Red's cruel whims. He couldn't let that happen, so he reached out and *stopped* it.

Red turned to Galahad, a shocked look on his face. The carp was still writhing in pain, but the flow of energy had stopped, its life force suspended somewhere between it and Red.

"That's it," Morgan le Fay cried in excitement. "You can save it!"

But Red was not giving up without a fight. He redoubled the spell, and the flow of energy resumed. Galahad could almost see it now, a slender thread hanging in the air above the water. He tried to picture himself grabbing hold of it, pulling it away from Red. But Red was much stronger, and Galahad still did not know how this magic worked. The carp's struggles were growing weaker.

"Use Excalibur!" Morgan called from the bridge.

Galahad tried to reach through the sword, the way he did when he talked with Calib. He focused all of his concentration on that thread, and as he did, he felt Excalibur come alive with energy.

The strength of it was amazing. Galahad had never felt so much power before. He was giddy with the thrill of it. It reminded him of the first time he realized he could speak with Calib, except ten times better.

With a wave of his hand, he broke the spell Red was casting. Red stumbled backward, shrieking, tripping over the uneven rocks as he fell. His face grew as white as parchment, and he let out a whimper of pain as his hands flew to his throat.

It was an odd reaction, but Galahad couldn't think on it now. He had expected the thread of energy to vanish, but instead, he was shocked to find it flowing toward himself. He got a sense of something cold, wet, and powerful as the carp's life force touched him. He shrank from it in revulsion, pulling his concentration away from Excalibur, and as suddenly as it had appeared, the power was gone.

Morgan's sphere of water dissolved, and the carp returned to the river with an indignant splash. With a flick of its tail, it turned into the current, swimming away as fast as it could. Galahad breathed a sigh of relief, then braced himself to face the sorceress.

"Impressive," Morgan said, her face impassive. "I believe I just learned a lot about you, Galahad."

CHAPTER
28

With the discovery of Thomas and his siblings, Calib's days of toiling in darkness grew a little more bearable. Thomas had a funny way of looking at the world, and could make any story—no matter how humdrum—interesting, almost bringing a smile to Calib's face. No easy feat in the labyrinth of the Iron Mountains. In the hopes of avoiding suspicion, Calib and Cecily took turns sneaking food to the Saxons, but occasionally, like today, they both managed to sneak away together.

"Jasper's messages are getting fewer and further between," Cecily said, pacing Thomas's cave. "If we wait too much longer, we will lose any opportunity we had to fight. We'll be too hungry to even lift a paw."

"Shh," Calib said as he took a rock from Rosy's collection and placed it on top of a tall tower of pebbles he and the young Saxons were building.

"Careful," Silas warned. "You don't want to—Whoops!"

The young weasel's tail had begun to whip back and forth with his excitement and accidentally knocked down the whole tower.

"Again!" Rosy cried, delighted with the game, and Calib smiled at them. They were really no different than the mouslings at Camelot.

"You'll have a hard time convincing Leftie to take action," Calib said to Cecily, picking up a pebble and beginning again. "Nothing has changed in our favor. . . ."

"Could you send a message to that Two-Legger?" Thomas asked as he carefully sorted the remaining food. Calib noticed that two portions were much larger than the third.

"I don't see how," Calib said. "I haven't seen him since we got separated when we first arrived. I wish we could, though. It would be a different story if we had Excalibur or the mirror, much less the Grail."

Cecily scowled at her paws. "I hate feeling helpless," she said. "What's the use of training to be a knight when you can't do anything to help?"

Thomas stood and handed Cecily a long, thin root. "Show me again some of your fencing tricks?" With a tight nod, Cecily stood, and the two began to fence.

Calib carefully placed another pebble on the tower. In the dim light of Thomas's flickering torch, it seemed to sparkle a light blue, as if it were a bit of crystal in the sea. Calib blinked, then quickly plucked the pebble from the tower.

"Hey!" Rosy protested.

"One second," Calib said as he burnished the pebble against his fur to remove its thin layer of dust. His whiskers twitched. Holding the pebble up to the torchlight, he gasped. Now he was certain. It was a bit of blue rock that looked just like Merlin's Crystal. It was the same color of magic.

"Rosy, where did you get this rock?" he asked, trying to stay calm and not alarm the little Saxon kit.

"Thomas found it," she said, and sucked her paw.

"Thomas?" Calib said. "Where did you get this?"

Thomas and Cecily lowered their roots and came over. Cecily's eyes widened. "Is that—?"

"I think so," Calib said, heart pounding. "I think we might finally know why the Manderlean has creatures mining the mountains. They're looking for magic crystals!"

"Magic crystals?" Thomas scrunched his snout skeptically and shrugged. "It's pretty, though, and I remember I found it at an entrance to one of the lower tunnels."

"Do you remember which one?" Calib asked.

"Yes," Thomas said promptly. "Do you want me to show you?"

After making sure Silas and Rosy understood that they were to stay put in the cave, Calib, Cecily, and Thomas inched down a tunnel, ducking to avoid scraping their ears on the ceiling. Calib led the way. Thomas, who was taller than the mice by about four inches, had to crawl on all fours. Cecily brought up the rear. Their torches gave off enough heat to make Calib sweat, but he barely noticed.

His whiskers were jumpy again.

The whiskers on the right side of his snout tingled, pulling him forward. It was a very familiar sensation, and it continued to grow stronger, even when Thomas stopped them outside the mouth of a new tunnel. Far below, Calib thought he could detect the faintest blue glow, as if it were distant starlight.

"What does that rune mean?" Calib pointed up, where someone had carved a peculiar creature above the tunnel's entrance. From where he stood, the rune looked almost like two webbed wings sprouting forth from a rounded body.

"It says 'beware,'" Thomas said in a hushed voice.

Cecily's fur rose. "You mean out of all the hundreds of tunnels down here, we have to go into the one with a warning?"

"There's definitely something down there," Calib said, gripping his whiskers with both paws now to keep them from shaking.

"What is it?" Cecily asked.

"Magic," Calib said.

"Do you have the Sight?" Thomas asked. "Do you know what's going to happen in the future?" From his tone, Calib could tell Thomas had been mulling over this ever since Calib had told them about his magically attuned whiskers.

"No, I don't." Calib touched his snout self-consciously. "I can only sense if there's magic around, but I can't do anything with the magic—I don't think. Let's go."

They passed another engraving of a winged creature, this one more sinister and detailed than the last, with scales and a forked tongue. It reminded Calib slightly of the gargoyles on Camelot's roof. But it reminded him even more of . . . Calib shook his head. He didn't want to think it.

But someone else already had.

"Wait a moment," Thomas called from behind. "This engraving . . . It looks like a dragon."

"Dragons don't exist," Cecily said coolly. Calib heard a scraping sound as Cecily marked the wall with chalk. "There's no historical proof."

"That's not true," Thomas said. "In Saxony, we found the skeleton of a great beast. It was taller than five Two-Leggers standing one on top of the other! It is said that the land was once infested with great wyrms that ate magic stones and breathed fire."

Calib's fur prickled, but he couldn't tell if that was from Thomas's words or just the drifting magic in the air. "What happened to them?" he asked.

"A great wizard chased them into the mountains, where they were forced to hide from the rest of humanity," Thomas said. "Or so legend has it."

"We share a similar story in Camelot," Calib said, surprised. "When Merlin was young, he stopped two dragons who were fighting and banished them to the Iron Mountains."

"Who's Merlin?" Thomas asked.

Calib opened his mouth to explain, but caught a mouthful of spiderwebs instead. Even though he had the torch, Calib kept walking into the sticky nets and tripping over rocks. Only the blue glow ahead of him gave Calib any sign that they were going in the right direction. And it was growing brighter.

"A great wizard," Cecily murmured. "And an even

better wolf. But be that as it may, most real scholars agree that it's just made-up."

"Do the Saxons still believe in dragons?" Calib asked.

"Of course," Thomas said, sounding surprised. "Isn't that why the mountains here have so many holes inside? No Two-Legger or creature could have made so many tunnels and disappeared without a trace. It would have taken forever!"

"Pish," Cecily sniffed. "I'll believe in dragons when I see one with my own two eyes. Let's keep going."

The magic was now so thick in the air that Calib's whiskers began to ache and sting, as if something was yanking at each individual hair. Invisible tendrils of magic eddied around his paws and clung to his fur. He could feel it permeate the air, filling his lungs, making it hard to breathe.

A sense of foreboding wrapped around him—heavy and gut-wrenching. This place was protected by magic far stronger than anything Morgan could conjure. This was *old magic*, the kind that ruled the world before man or beast ever roamed it.

But as they walked into a larger cavern, the feeling of dread lifted as suddenly as it had come. In its place was wonder.

Because in this cavern, the rock wasn't dense and thick. It was lined with crystals, dangling from above like chandeliers. They were as wide as tree trunks and glowed blue, the same as Merlin's Cave and Avalon's lake. It was a color Calib now recognized as the presence of raw magic. Each was an identical copy of Merlin's Crystal—the same one that had unlocked Excalibur from the stone.

"This is incredible!" Thomas cried, his jaw open. He spun around with a torch.

"I think this is where Merlin's Crystal must have come from!" Calib exclaimed.

The light seemed to pulse in agreement.

"This is definitely what the Manderlean is digging for," Cecily said, letting out a low whistle. "If that one little crystal was able to unlock Excalibur and give Galahad such powers, imagine what this could do."

Cecily gestured at the largest crystal, which was as big as a Two-Legger carriage. Calib could see right through it.

"But somebody must have carved out this tunnel," Thomas said, puzzled. "Why did they leave it all here?"

"I don't know," Calib said, looking up. "But I'm beginning to think that Thomas may be right about dragons." He pointed to the ceiling, where deep slash marks in the stone looked like the work of some very lethal claws. "What do you think, Cecily?"

Cecily's eyes widened as she looked past Calib's shoulder.

"C-Calib, now, I need you to remain calm. . . ."

"What?" Calib asked, turning around.

There, behind him, were the glowing eyes of a dragon.

CHAPTER
29

"Who dares disturb the Dragon of the Iron Mountains from its slumber!" the dragon thundered. A shower of dust and grit clattered down around them. "Who intrudes upon my sacred lair!"

Calib clapped his paws to his ears and squeezed his eyes shut as the dragon's large wings swept up and extended in a frightful display. His heart lodged in his throat as he ducked to avoid being hit by a wing.

"We meant no harm by it, Your Dragon-ness, sir!" Thomas pleaded, trembling from nose to tail. He bowed so low that his snout touched the ground. "We're just trying to find our way out of the mountains!"

"None shall live who enter our—I mean, MY domain!" The dragon's eyes burned bright blue. "Run before I kill you!"

Calib was prepared to turn tail and sprint when he felt Cecily brush against him.

"Buy me time," she murmured into his ear, and then she slunk away, tail whipping out of sight. Calib almost laughed from sheer nervousness. Sure, he would distract a dragon. What could go wrong? Drawing from the thin reserve of courage that once allowed him to speak to the owls, Calib stepped forward.

"Wait but a moment, oh great dragon!" Calib proclaimed. "You don't want to kill us yet!" He kept his eyes averted. He was too afraid to look at the blue pupils directly, lest he lose his courage entirely.

The dragon tilted its massive head. "And why not?"

"Because . . . because I have a lot of questions!" Calib wanted to kick himself.

"We don't have time to give you answers!"

Thomas let out a whimper.

"Well, we might have useful answers for you!" Calib said, not thinking beforehand of what he'd say, just letting the words come as they did. "Don't you want to know why your mountains has been invaded by Saxon weasels?"

"We know that answer," the dragon roared. "It's because of that witch!"

"Yes," Calib said hastily. "But we can help you get rid of her!"

The dragon blinked.

"You know how to get rid of the witch?" it inquired.

"Um, yes." Calib scrambled to come up with something convincing to say. It wasn't a complete lie, really. He imagined once he got Merlin's treasures into Galahad's hands, it would all work out somehow. His pulse quickened as the dragon's face scrunched up in annoyance.

"Liar," it spat. "And thief! You're not here to help; you're here to take the crystals!"

"We're not lying," Calib insisted. "We're here to help you fight the Saxons! We're from Camelot! Please believe me," he implored. He hoped that whatever Cecily was up to, she'd do it quick. He wasn't sure how much longer he could distract the dragon before he became a mouse-sized snack.

The dragon snarled, then opened its mouth wide. "I don't talk to liars and thieves—I roast them."

The cavern suddenly turned hot, and Calib could feel the heat build in the dragon's chest. Calib flinched, throwing his arms over his face, expecting to turn into blackened char at any second.

Instead, a curtain of water flew at the dragon's face.

The creature tried to dodge it, but it was too slow. Water splashed across its snout . . . and then slowly, the dragon disintegrated.

It crumbled into hundreds of tiny black dots. No, not dots—flying creatures!

In place of the dragon was a squadron of flying armored creatures resembling mice, but with thin, webbed wings where their arms should be. They flew in a tight, coordinated formation, maneuvering as one entity. The slight aftertaste of magic permeated the air. Most of the beasts were in a state of shock. Many of them were drenched from the bucket of water Cecily had splashed on them.

"I knew it!" Cecily said triumphantly, still clutching the miner's bucket she had procured from somewhere. "You're not a dragon at all—you're an illusion. You're just a colony of bats!"

So that's what they were. Calib had never seen bats in real life before. He'd once read about them in *Creatures of the Night* by Sir Tromley Botswell, a knight in his great-grandfather's service who used his insomnia to research other nocturnal animals. Rumor had it, Sir Tromley was practically a bat himself, only without the wings. People started calling him Batswell after he started sleeping upside down in the aviary.

"You lot have some explaining to do!" Cecily said crossly.

"We don't have to explain anything to clumsy ground-beasts!" said one of the bats.

"Excuse me?" Cecily asked, crossing her arms.

"I think he means us," Thomas whispered. "Ground-beasts probably mean any creature who doesn't fly."

"Yes, I got that," snapped Cecily. "Now, listen here, I don't care for your tone—"

"We come from Camelot," Calib interrupted loudly, stepping forward to address the bats. He wondered if perhaps he should have brought a feather offering like they'd once had to do with the owls. Except bats didn't have feathers. He tried to imagine how his father or grandfather might address these creatures in a proper, friendly fashion. "We are here to rid the land of the Saxon scourge!"

"Ech-hem, but not *all* Saxons mind you," Thomas piped up. "Some of us are here against our will."

"Right, not all Saxons," Calib agreed. Again, he addressed the bats. "Surely you wouldn't mind having the mountains back to yourselves again?"

They seemed to confer. After a moment, most of the bats peeled off from the main body, row by row, and flew to their roosts in the cave ceiling. Calib could see that what he'd thought were claw marks in the ceiling were actually little ridges where the bats could grip and dangle.

Two bats, however, flew down to the three adventurers. As they came closer, Calib could see that they wore colorful neck ruffles. They swooped to a low ridge, then hung upside down, putting them at eye level with Calib and the others. The rest of the squadron looked on intently from above.

"If you're from Camelot," one of the bats said, "then tell me this: What is the motto that unites all its creatures?"

"Together in paw and tail, lest divided we fall and fail," Calib said. "Easy."

"What are the qualities of a Camelot knight?"

"Bravery, strength, and wisdom!" Cecily chimed in.

"And who is the rightful ruler of Britain?"

Calib opened his mouth, but found that he did not have an easy answer. He would have said his grandfather, Commander Yvers. But wasn't it Commander Kensington now? Or was it King Arthur? Was it perhaps Galahad? Now that Galahad had Excalibur, didn't that mean he was the new ruler?

"The rightful rulers are the people," Thomas said, shrugging. "At least, that's how it should be."

Calib held his breath, waiting to see if that answer would please the bats. They looked at one another, and then the one with a face framed with graying fur nodded. "Very well. We will hear you speak."

CHAPTER
30

Calib's relief made him almost sag against the wall, but he held himself together as the oldest bat began to speak.

"We apologize about the scare," he said. He bowed deeply, though from Calib's view, it looked like he was doing a sit-up. "We thought you were the witch's spies. I am King Mir Vortigern the Eighth of the Iron Mountains Bats."

"And my name is Horatio Eavesdrip, twelfth of my name. I am the chief listener," said the other, younger black bat in a distinguished, though somewhat snooty, voice.

"Er, nice to meet you," Thomas said, throwing out a paw to shake. "Never seen a winged rodent before."

"We like to keep to ourselves when we can," Horatio said.

"Why are you impersonating dragons?" Calib asked.

"Bats are the guardians of the Iron Mountains. We protect its treasures from being exploited by men," King Mir said. "We use the dragon legend to keep people away. No one had come in many years until the witch."

"You mean Morgan," Calib said.

"If that's what you want to call her," Horatio sniffed. "She is a vile thing."

"How did she find out about this place?" Cecily asked.

King Mir shrugged sadly. "The only Two-Legger who knew about the power buried in this place was Merlin. But I do not think he would betray this information to anyone like her."

"Unlikely," Calib agreed. Though he too wondered how the information had reached Morgan. Had Red found something in his stolen scroll?

"In fact, it was Merlin who first gave us the idea of creating a dragon illusion," Horatio added, seeming to not want to be outdone by King Mir.

"How do you do it?" Thomas asked. "Is it magic?"

King Mir cocked his head. "In a way. Once, long ago, the Iron Mountains used to be volcanoes. The smoke coming from the mountains led people to believe there were dragons in these parts. It doesn't take much convincing when people are ready to believe something."

"Those stories are mostly what keep people away," Horatio added. "But with the help of some illusion spells Merlin provided us, we've made sure to keep the legend alive for generations after us."

Calib's nose grew hot. His mind had also gone to dragons immediately at the first possible hint of them. If someone was ready to believe something, they could make the facts fit their expectations.

"Merlin's final request to us was to protect the last of the magic left in this land," King Mir said.

"So there is no real dragon?" Thomas clarified, sounding much relieved.

"No, but the Saxons don't know that," Horatio harrumphed. "For the past several weeks, we've been practicing, preparing for when we at last will come face-to-face with those parasites."

"I have a question," Cecily said. "What do you eat?"

"We still have pastries in the bag if you want some," Thomas began.

"No, silly," Cecily said, shaking her head. "That's for the others. I've already had a pastry. But what I mean to say is . . . how do you get out of here to get food without the Saxons noticing?"

King Mir and Horatio looked at each other. Horatio

smirked while the king chuckled. "Why, it's easy, mouse-maid. We go up!"

The king launched himself off the perch and began to fly upward, spiraling to the top, where, for the first time, Calib spotted a gray pinprick of light.

He gasped. Was that sky? How had he not noticed before? The night must have only just turned to dawn.

Calib's heart swelled with hope. After days of endless darkness in the tunnels, living in fear, they finally had a way out. A wide grin spread across his face, and he turned back to the bats. "How much are you able to lift?"

"Excuse me?" King Mir asked, clearly disgruntled. "We're bats, not a carrier service!"

"We share the same enemies. We should fight as one." Calib spread out his paws. "Help us free the Darkling and Saxon prisoners, and we could all move against Morgan's army with three times the might that we could muster on our own."

King Mir shook his head.

"Our only command from Merlin was to protect the mountains' crystals, nothing more," King Mir said. "Be you Saxon, Darkling, or from Camelot, all of you stand to be corrupted by greed. All of you are potential enemies. We have nothing to gain by helping you."

Calib felt an old anger throb like a burning coal in his chest. For generations, everyone had lived in suspicion and fear of one another. That was how they got into this mess in the first place. By not working together, they had let a powerful enemy rise and now threaten them all.

Together in paw and tail, lest divided we fall and fail.

That was Camelot's motto, carved on the very doors that once contained the Grail. It was about time they actually lived by those words.

"If Morgan isn't stopped, she will drain these mountains, Camelot—maybe the entire world," Calib said. "You can hide in your caves as much as you want, but as long as she has command over her prisoners, it's only a matter of time before she discovers the crystals. You need us—and we need you."

The bat king was silent for a long while, his face unreadable as he contemplated Calib's words. Everyone looked to King Mir for guidance, but Horatio was the first to speak.

"I agree with the groundbeast," the adviser said softly. "It's true—much of Morgan's plotting has been to divide and weaken Britain's creatures, pit them against one another, so that they never put up a strong enough resistance."

"You know that for certain?" King Mir asked.

Horatio preened back his ears with a flip of his wing. "I'm not the chief listener for nothing."

King Mir scratched his chin with a claw. "What are

you thinking?" he asked Calib, sounding resigned.

Calib smiled, the first one he'd cracked in weeks it seemed. It felt strange on his face, as if he'd accepted a dangerous dare.

CHAPTER
31

Galahad hadn't seen Morgan in many a day—ever since the carp demonstration, in fact. Despite going to the throne room every morning, he found it was always empty . . . though more and more of the rosebushes planted around the throne seemed to have shriveled up.

He had barely seen Red either. The boy had been avoiding him, refusing to look him in the eye whenever they did pass in the hallway. Something was happening, and Galahad had an uneasy feeling deep in the pit of his stomach. In order to not arouse the Saxon guards' suspicions,

Galahad continued to practice his sword routines, but he shied away from trying any magical workings.

The memory of the sapling's pleas echoed through his brain, resounding again and again, never fading. So too did the brief memory of holding the carp's essence—its potential, its life, its magic—in his hands. He had felt so powerful for a moment, for once in charge of Excalibur instead of the other way around.

And still, he could not find the Grail.

The fortress felt like it was nannying him. No matter which twists and turns he took through the corridors, he only ever ended up in the Saxon training arena, where large warrior men honed their skills for an attack on Camelot; in Morgan's spacious throne room; or in his own, cramped bedroom.

After another frustrating day of trying to escape the confines of the three locations, Galahad finally stalked into his room. He felt hot, itchy, and uncomfortable in his own skin. But as he unbuckled Excalibur from his waist, he caught his reflection in the sword's hilt.

A reflection . . .

He hurried to the traveling pack he'd kept under the small bed and pulled out Merlin's Mirror. He hadn't looked at it since arriving to the fortress, not wanting to draw Morgan's attention to it. He had a feeling that maybe she could sense magic even better than Calib's whiskers could.

His heart squeezed. He hoped Calib had found Cecily. Occasionally, he'd used Excalibur to try to find his friend. Most of the times, he'd felt nothing, but sometimes, he'd caught a sense of Calib-ness, deep in the mountains, and his mind had eased a little.

But maybe with the mirror, he'd be able to find Calib—or better yet, the Grail. Holding up the mirror to Excalibur's shining hilt, he tried to look in—and *beyond*. Nothing happened. Disappointment settled over him. It had, perhaps, been foolish to think such objects could work as intended in a sorceress's lair.

That gave Galahad a thought. Again, carefully, he held up the mirror, but this time, he took a look at his surroundings through its reflection.

What he saw made him shiver. Everything in the room, from the walls to the desk, was covered in otherworldly runes. They glowed pale blue, pulsating slowly. They resembled the runes etched onto Excalibur. Only these were roughly drawn, as if someone had painted them by hand. And he had the strange feeling that they were watching him. . . .

Galahad tore his attention away from the reflection and put the mirror facedown on the bed.

"Magic," he murmured. Whatever he was seeing, Morgan had manipulated it just so. Her magic permeated every stone in this part of the fortress.

She was so *powerful*. Galahad wondered what Camelot would be like if King Arthur could draw protective runes around the castle. Maybe Britain would not have been attacked. Maybe the white fever would not have claimed so many lives. Maybe there would have been no need for war at all. . . .

Thinking of the fever and the war, he wondered what Father Walter would have thought of Morgan's training. Father Walter always said healers should try their best. But what if their best was at the cost of another creature?

Galahad removed from under his bed the scroll Father Walter and Bors had given him, then unfurled it. Though he could not read the writing, he recognized a rune in the shape of a familiar cup, with rays shooting from it. It was a symbol he'd seen in Britta's notes as well.

His heartbeat quickening, Galahad stood up, tucking the parchment under his tunic. If he could get to the library, perhaps he could use Britta's decoder to read the scroll. With both Morgan and Red seemingly ignoring him, and dinner long since passed, now would be the perfect time. He just needed to get out of this room first.

But how to break out of the fortress's enchantment?

Unsheathing Excalibur, he tried to focus on the library. After several minutes of concentrating, Galahad thought he felt the slightest of tremors in his hand, guiding him forward. Galahad began to walk, and as he did, the pull grew stronger. The floor changed underneath his feet from stone to wood. His nose tickled as the scent of bound leather and moldy paper filled his nostrils.

"Ha!" Galahad said triumphantly, but then instantly regretted it. Britta was slumped over, head down on a desk, deep in sleep. Tiptoeing as best he could, Galahad got closer.

He glanced down at the documents she was using as a pillow, scanning Britta's notes over her shoulder. To Galahad's surprise, Merlin was recounting his first meeting with a mouse commander named Yvers Christopher. Galahad was stunned at Britta's progress. Everyone at Camelot always had assumed that Merlin's Scrolls were filled with nonsensical ramblings. *We should just burn them all for firewood instead,* Sir Edmund had groused. *Better than letting them take up space in our library.*

And now, here was this Saxon who could barely speak a lick of Gaelic, managing to make sense of it all. Even Bors would be impressed, Galahad thought.

Quickly, he slipped the decoder out from Britta's arm. She startled slightly, and Galahad paused, not wanting to wake her. Slowly, he sank into a nearby chair to wait for her to settle. Referencing Britta's notes, he began to translate the scroll he'd brought with him:

I walk with the wolf and he walks with me. His teeth are mine own as is his hunger. . . .

As Galahad read Merlin's strange ramblings, he

remembered how Father Walter had mentioned seeing a wolf stalk Merlin. Had the wolf eaten him? But that didn't seem right.

The Grail demands life, and I feed it. . . .

Galahad's head began to pound as the spidery writing crawled over the page. He let his head lean on his hand as he continued to translate. He could feel his eyes drooping. If he could just . . . keep . . . going . . .

"Galahad! You did it!"

Galahad woke with a start to see Britta holding a scroll, her curls seeming to spring out in every direction. Ink was smeared over her face from where she'd fallen asleep, but she didn't look tired at all now. In fact, she looked radiant.

And in her hands, was the scroll Father Walter had given him.

"I don't know where I misplaced this scroll," she said triumphantly, "but with it, I can finally make sense of what he's saying. It's a sacrifice!" Britta drew him into a big hug. Her hair made his nose tickle. "The Grail needs a sacrifice!"

Britta let go and ran to the door. "We've discovered the secret to the Grail's powers! We have to tell the queen!"

CHAPTER
32

For the first time in a long time, Calib was hopeful. Looking around the embers of the rebellion campfire, he saw Thomas, Rosy, and Silas snoring softly, while Leftie the lynx personally stood watch over them.

When they had arrived back at camp with the bats and the weasels, there had been a moment when Calib thought everything was about to go wrong. But once Leftie had heard Thomas's story—and met Rosy and Silas—he'd immediately placed all the Saxon weasels under his protection.

"I ignored your words once before, young Christopher,"

Leftie had said. "I swore I would not do so again."

In the early hours of the morning, King Mir of the Iron Mountains and Chieftain Leftie of the Darkling Woods, together with Cecily von Mandrake and Calib Christopher of Camelot, had agreed to a plan. In just a few hours, members of the rebellion would sneak back to the prisoners above and help them find their way to the old abandoned tunnels, where they would be delivered to their freedom by the Dragon of the Iron Mountains.

"We may be few in number and short in stature," Leftie said, "but we are large in courage."

Then, raising his voice, he yowled at the top of his lungs the way only a wildcat can. Creatures shot awake, rubbing the sleep from their eyes.

"There's been a change of plans," Leftie said. "We leave—today."

The rebellion slowly woke, stumbling toward Leftie, stifling yawns. But by the time Leftie had explained everything, they were all wide-awake.

As the rebellion went over the plan to sneak back to the prisoners, a lark named Flora agreed to fly with Horatio and deliver a warning to Camelot. No sooner had she left, however, than she and Horatio came hurtling back, arrowing down headlong through the tunnel.

"Flora! Horatio!" Leftie exclaimed. "Why aren't you on your way?"

"Because," Horatio panted, "we've run into a bit of

trouble—of the magical sort."

"It would be better if you saw it yourself," Flora said sadly.

"You can show us all," King Mir said. "Bring forth the dragon's nose!"

Two of the bigger bats of the group came forward, carrying between them a woven contraption that was shaped like a large lizard's snout, with two rows of sharp rocks lining the edge of the mouth. The bats flipped the mouth open and motioned for Calib and Cecily to sit inside.

"I hope you two are not afraid of heights," Horatio squeaked, and with a rapid flapping of wings, they shot up vertically to the top of the cave and emerged into a cool, starry night.

The bats' wings moved at a frantic pace. Calib's stomach lurched as the basket dipped and swayed. Bats were not built with the sturdy flight patterns of owls or even seagulls. As the ground disappeared underneath them, Calib braced himself against the dragon's head and tried to keep the pastries down.

Calib breathed deep. After days of stifling heat and sulfuric smells, the air was sweet as syrup, cool as a freshwater brook. The stars blinked in and out like thousands of fireflies in the summer sky, and the blue moon shone down like a distant lantern.

The dragon came to a halt just outside, however,

landing abruptly at the top of the Iron Mountains. Calib and the others disembarked uncertainly. Everyone seemed confused as to why the bats had stopped here instead of taking them into the Darkling Woods for safety.

"Watch," Horatio instructed. The bat took off with a pebble in his claw. When he got about three feet into the air, he threw the pebble upward. It ricocheted off an invisible surface just above him and nearly struck Calib's head on the way down.

"There's a magical barrier blocking us from leaving," King Mir observed. "We've never gone much beyond our caves. This whole time, we have been imprisoned too."

"Does it go all the way to the ground?" Cecily asked.

Calib ran to the mountain's edge and threw another pebble. It arched out and got stuck, as if it had landed on an invisible ledge in front of him. Like a punch of strong wind, he could feel the magic surge to push the pebble back, and his whiskers burned. He clapped his paw to his snout, trying to soothe the sharp ache. With a barrier that strong, there would be no way to send a warning to Camelot.

"No!" Cecily shouted. "We didn't just break out of our prison for nothing. We can't release all those crea-tures from their shackles only to be defeated by some big, ridiculous wall!"

Calib winced. It was a *very* strong wall—his whiskers

still burned. They hadn't hurt this badly since he and Galahad broke through the barrier to get into the mountains. But if they'd passed through that one before, they could do it again. All Calib needed was Galahad—assuming he was still in the fortress.

Focusing on the tingle of his whiskers, he thought he felt a slight draft of magic that seemed to belong to Excalibur, and another, slightly stronger breeze that reeked of rosemary and iron. So Morgan was still at the fortress. Surely that meant she still had not solved the mystery of the Grail.

Unless, with the Grail in hand, she was strong enough to conduct battle from here. He shuddered at the thought and hastily turned to King Mir. "Can you fly me to the Two-Legger section of the fortress?"

The king tilted his head. "Of course I am able, but what good would that do us?"

"I know someone who can help us. His name is Galahad du Lac. He's the one who pulled the sword from the stone this past fall."

The bat king's ears twitched. "Another sword in the stone?" he asked. "And tell me . . . does this sword have a name?"

Puzzled, Calib nodded. "Yes. He named it after me. It's called Excalibur."

King Mir let out a thundering hiss while Horatio

looked downright terrified.

"What's wrong?" Calib asked, but the two bats were staring at each other, seeming to have a soundless conversation. Finally, Horatio turned to Calib.

"Some of the mountains' crystals contain powers of prophecy," King Mir growled. "We've been seeing two competing visions in the crystals for many, many years. One deals with the sword called Excalibur."

"But how can that be?" Calib asked. "The sword was named after me—how could you know that a sword by that name would ever exist?"

King Mir shook his head. "Time does not always run straight, young mouse. It twists and turns, doubling back on itself sometimes."

"Er, all right, then," Calib said, though he was still slightly overwhelmed that he appeared to have at least a small part in a prophecy. "What do the prophecies say?"

King Mir fixed his eyes on Calib. "One shows the wielder of Excalibur training under the powers of Avalon and defeating the witch Morgan. The other—"

The king of the bats broke off sharply, as if uncertain whether he wanted to continue. Taking a deep breath, he said, "The other vision says that the wielder of Excalibur will bring Morgan to power—and that they will betray Camelot."

CHAPTER
33

Calib almost laughed out loud.

"That's impossible," Calib said. "Galahad is the most honorable Two-Legger I know. Camelot is his home. His father is Sir Lancelot, one of the greatest knights who ever lived!"

"If you say so," Horatio said, sounding doubtful. "Power has a way of undermining even the most valiant Two-Leggers. They never learned to control their thirst for it. That created the need for the dragon illusion in the first place."

"You don't know Galahad as I do," Calib insisted. "You'll see when you meet him!" His anger was rising now, and he couldn't stop his voice from getting sharp.

"King Mir," Cecily said, stepping between them. "If I may . . . I too had my doubts about Galahad, but he is as Calib says. He is true and loyal and *good*. If it weren't for him, Maman would have died this past spring of white fever."

She took a deep breath before she continued. "If we don't take a chance on trusting one another now, when will we ever? I give you my word as a Von Mandrake that this boy is a friend."

Calib looked at Cecily gratefully, but she kept her gaze steady on the bat king.

At last, King Mir heaved a sigh. "Which of you is lighter? My stamina isn't what it used to be."

With King Mir carrying Cecily on his back, and Horatio bearing Calib, they began to circle the mountains in search of Galahad and Excalibur.

From the outside, most of the fortress windows were boarded up and tightly sealed. Only a handful of windows were lit. One of them might belong to Galahad, or it could belong to the enemy.

They flew due south, peeping into every window they could. Calib closed his eyes and concentrated on Galahad's face. He took a long sniff and wiggled his snout, hoping to get a hint of his familiar scent. A tiny sensation tickled the top right whisker.

"Try flying east." Calib pointed, his eyes still closed. "And higher up!"

"What are you doing?" King Mir asked.

"His whiskers are magically attuned," Cecily explained, as if she were stating the very obvious.

Finally, Calib spotted a thin opening, barely wider than a fissure, running down in jagged edges. An acrid, burned smell met his snout. But underneath, he could sense Excalibur's magic at work. "There! Galahad's in there!"

The bats flew in close so that Calib could hop onto the ledge.

"Wait right here, and be on the lookout," he warned. "I'll get Galahad's attention."

"Don't forget to introduce us properly," Horatio whispered as Calib ventured into the crack. "I'm twelfth of my name."

Calib nodded once, then ran inside. The sooner he could get to Galahad, the sooner they would be free of this wretched place and on their way back to Camelot.

Calib padded along the crevice, getting closer and closer to the source of the magic. Suddenly, the crack sloped down sharply, and the walls widened outward into a large cavern lined with columns, big enough for a small army of Two-Leggers. At the other end of the room stood an empty black throne that looked like it had been carved into the side of the cave wall. Vines of roses covered the back of the throne, but half of them looked dead and dry to the touch.

Galahad was there. He held Excalibur before him, as if he were studying it. His brows were knit in deep concentration, and he was frowning. A Two-Legger girl paced the width of two columns, her energy nervous. Calib had never seen her before. She was as tall as Galahad and about his age, with a mop of hair that reminded Calib of an overused feather duster.

"Morgan said she would make sure Papa and the others would be the first to arrive on the next ship," the girl said, twisting the sleeves of her robe. "Her Highness is so generous. I probably should have told her that Greta is prone to seasickness, though."

Galahad didn't look up from the spell he was working on. "Britta, did you let your family know to expect Morgan?"

"I forgot to send a lark!" Britta clamped a hand to her forehead. "How silly! Of course." She sprinted out of the room, but not before giving Galahad a gigantic hug.

"I'm finally going to see my family!" Britta said, her eyes filled with tears of happiness. "I've waited so long!"

Calib felt a surge of pride for Galahad. His Two-Legger friend was already finding ways to help others.

The girl left the room, and Calib saw his chance.

"Galahad!" Calib cried out, running into the room. "It's me!"

Galahad jolted away with a start, his hand grabbing Excalibur defensively.

"We're here to rescue you so that you can rescue us! We need to—" Calib broke off.

Calib had tried scampering up Galahad's leg, but the boy had stepped back. Something was wrong. Galahad didn't look very pleased or relieved to see him. He had puffy eyes. Had he been crying?

"Are you all right?" Calib climbed up to the armrest of the throne so that he could peer into Galahad's eyes. Maybe the boy was feeling unwell.

"I'm sorry, Calib." Galahad dropped his gaze and shook his head. "But I'm not going to leave."

Galahad's words thudded into Calib's chest, as if they were thrown bricks, and Calib almost slipped off the throne, only managing to catch himself with his tail just in time. "What do you mean?"

"Morgan has discovered something—and she's promised to teach me."

"Is it the Grail?" Calib cried. "We have to stop her!"

"No," Galahad said, shaking his head. "We don't."

Calib was stunned, but Galahad hardly registered it. He continued, "Merlin used magic to put Arthur on the throne, when it rightly belonged to Morgan. She is well within her rights to use magic and take it back."

"She'd take it back for *herself*," Calib said. "She doesn't care about the people or creatures of this realm. She doesn't care that she's killing the land. Or that beasts are getting injured just because she's not the one who hurts. Morgan le Fay would make a terrible ruler!"

"I disagree," Galahad said. "She knows how to make hard choices. And she's the only one who's tried to help me understand my powers."

"You mean," Calib said slowly, "the powers that *we* helped get for you? What about Camelot and King Arthur? What about your *home*?"

"Camelot was never my home," Galahad said softly. "I never wanted to go there in the first place. I never really fit in. The son of Camelot's greatest knight who just wants to be a healer? The wielder of a magic sword who hates fighting? How do I fit into the tales of Camelot's knights?"

"But—"

Galahad pointed Excalibur at Calib. The mouse stepped back, his throat tightening around his words.

"I'm giving you one chance," Galahad said, "because we were once friends. Leave now, before I tell the guards."

"Galahad—"

"I said LEAVE ME!" the boy shouted, swinging his

sword down near Calib's tail. Calib scampered out of sight and back into the crack in the wall, just as the doors swung open.

Red appeared alongside a woman who could only be King Arthur's sister, Morgan le Fay. They shared the same nose and hair color, though Morgan's eyes were a cool gray. A black crown sat atop her tresses. In Morgan's hands was a small wooden box.

"We will need to test Britta's new theory," Morgan said. "In hindsight, I should have guessed it would be so simple. To take is to give is to take. Merlin loved lecturing about the balance that needed to be maintained."

Calib expected Red to make some sort of snide remark about sacrificing Galahad, but the boy remained oddly silent as Morgan opened the wooden box. Inside, a skinny white hare sniffed the air nervously.

Calib held back a gasp. It was Jasper!

"Kill the creature, Galahad," Morgan demanded. "Prove your loyalty to me, once and for all, and I will share with you the Grail's powers."

Calib held his breath, waiting for Galahad to say no, to loudly proclaim that he was a knight of the Round Table and would never murder an innocent life.

But Galahad remained silent and unmoving.

Morgan narrowed her eyes. From the darkness, a golden hawk flew to perch on her shoulder. It ruffled its feathers, but it was very careful to not let its claws dig too deeply into its master's shoulders.

"I need to know if you are ready," she said. "Will you allow a weak king like my brother to continue to lead the people of Britain astray? Or will you help me issue law and order so that the fight between Saxony and Britain may finally be over?"

Galahad stayed silent, unable to answer. The poor hare was trembling tail to ears, his head bobbing up and down. Calib desperately looked around for some way to intercede on Jasper's behalf, but there were too many of them.

"The time has finally come," Morgan continued, "to march on Camelot. I only want the strongest and the smartest with me."

She turned to Galahad.

"Will you join us?"

For one last moment, all was well. Galahad sheathed Excalibur at his side, and Calib breathed a sigh of relief that Jasper would live. And then, with one swift motion, Galahad reached for a dagger that had been tucked into his belt, then lunged and pierced the blade's tip into Jasper's heart.

Calib cried out in shock, but the noise was drowned out by the sound of the dagger clattering to the floor. Galahad picked the hare out from the box, and Jasper lay in his arms, limp and lifeless. Bright-red shocks of blood were splattered in stark contrast to his white fur.

"It's dead," Galahad proclaimed, holding the hare out for everyone to see.

Deep horror twisted into Calib, as if the dagger had pierced him instead. Even Red looked a little queasy. Morgan le Fay's expression, on the other hand, was completely unmoved.

"Let the blood flow into the Grail," she commanded. She materialized the Grail out of thin air and held it before Galahad. He walked over to the wooden cup and let the blood drops fall in.

Rays of yellow light shot up from the bowl, shining golden upon Morgan's triumphant face.

"It works!" Red murmured in complete awe.

Calib fell back onto his haunches, feeling faint. His vision swam with tears. How could Galahad have betrayed them so brutally? Against Calib's best efforts, the secrets of the Grail had been revealed to Camelot's greatest enemy. And it was his best friend who'd helped them.

Morgan waved a hand over the light. Then, taking the dagger that Galahad had dropped, she ruthlessly stabbed the blade through her hand. All who watched flinched as the knife went clean through her palm. Unblinking, she pulled it out again. The knife had left no mark.

"You're invincible now," Britta whispered. She had just returned from her letter writing to witness Morgan's feat.

Britta's voice was full of awe and tinged with fear as she eyed the dead hare in Galahad's clutches. "My theory actually worked!"

Morgan was smiling. Her face contorted into a mask of vengeance and contempt.

"Brava, my brilliant Britta," she said, smooth as a fox. "Your family would be proud of you. When they arrive, we shall have a celebratory feast in your honor."

"Thank you, Your Majesty."

Red reached out a tentative hand to the Grail, but Morgan quickly pulled the treasure away from her son's grasp.

"No. You have done nothing to deserve it," Morgan said.

Red looked as if he'd been physically struck by her harsh words.

"You have been a complete failure at every turn," Morgan continued. "I've had to clean up your messes over and over. The Grail is not your plaything."

"But, Mother," Red said, and for the first time, Calib felt a little sorry for the sorceress's son, "I was the one who brought back Merlin's Scrolls."

Calib's sympathy vanished.

"The wrong ones," Mogan replied coldly. "The one that held the answer was delivered to us by Galahad. The one that Britta translated. I've had enough of your petulance.

Go to your room, Red, and await further instructions. You are no longer needed here."

After a few seconds of dreadful silence, Red stormed away, his footsteps echoing in the vast throne room. Morgan turned her attention back to Galahad and Britta.

"Our ships will depart this evening," she said. "Galahad, you will accompany me. Britta, you will remain here and prepare the rooms for your family."

And as Galahad—a knight of the Round Table—bowed to Morgan, Calib's heart shattered.

The Two-Legger in front of him looked like Galahad, even smelled like him, but this was not his friend. This was a stranger. This—Calib almost choked—was a traitor.

CHAPTER
34

alib sprinted back up the ledge to the safety of the sill, his instinct and training kicking in and overriding the other feelings that threatened to overwhelm him. It felt like something large and ugly was clawing at his chest.

"Where's the boy?" King Mir asked when Calib appeared. "Where is he who bears Excalibur?"

"Fly," Calib said gruffly as he clambered onto King Mir's back. "We cannot rely on Galahad any longer. We've lost Excalibur and the Grail to Morgan le Fay."

Calib tearfully recapped what had happened, including the murder of Jasper.

"Two-Leggers were always weak creatures," King Mir called to Calib as he dipped around the mountains. "For all their size and strength, they are too easily corrupted and will turn on you in an instant."

Calib glanced to his side, where he could see Cecily gripping on to Horatio's neck ruff, tears silently whipping off her face as they flew. He didn't know what to say, so he stayed silent, lost in his thoughts. Had he somehow caused his friend to turn? He thought of the Lady of the Lake and how disappointed she'd been that Calib hadn't brought Galahad. If Galahad had gone to Avalon, the Lady could have trained him, and then maybe he wouldn't be under Morgan's spell—or whatever it was—now. Maybe this *was* all Calib's fault.

Just like Valentina's burned wings.

Just like the fact that Camelot's greatest enemy now had the Grail.

His fault.

"It's not your fault," Mir said kindly, and Calib was startled to realize he must have spoken out loud. "Men cannot be trusted. It's becoming clear to me that Two-Leggers aren't going to be able to save themselves from this mess. Where to, Calib Christopher?"

Calib tried to collect his thoughts. What hope could

they possibly have with Excalibur and the Grail gone? Then it struck him—the remaining treasure.

"We need to steal Merlin's Mirror back!" He looked at King Mir.

"I have an idea of where the magical mirror might be," Mir said. "I'll take you to where we've overheard most of Morgan's plots."

Calib clung tightly as Mir swooped left. The bats maneuvered to the other side of the mountains, toward the pink dawn that was just starting to peek over the horizon. Calib's eyeballs throbbed with sorrow, but he found there were no more tears left to cry. He thought about what he would have to say to Commander Kensington—that he lost their strongest Two-Legger ally to Morgan's influence.

Horatio and King Mir delivered the mice to a tall window in a turret that faced east, back toward Camelot. They alighted on a small balcony just as the sun began to rise.

"Be very careful. Next to Merlin, she is the strongest Two-Legger I have ever encountered," Horatio whispered.

Calib thought about Queen Guinevere defending her castle with her ladies-in-waiting at the Battle of the Bear. "I know stronger."

Calib and Cecily squeezed inside between the alabaster-lined windows and made their way down to the landing that led to the balcony doors. Calib concentrated on sensing for any magical traps or snares, but the place was empty of the running blue marks he had come to associate with protection spells. The smell of darker, rawer magic, however, was overpowering. Inside the rounded room where they found themselves, mirrors lined every square inch from floor to ceiling.

They were in different frames and shapes—some as tall as Two-Leggers, others as small as their palms. None of them were Merlin's Mirror, and yet they were clearly magical. Their reflections showed strange, fleeting scenes that came in and out of focus. One seemed to hover over a wooded section of the road to St. Gertrude. Another showed a cave at a beach's mouth.

All the landscapes seemed to strain against the glasses that contained them. Calib feared that at any second, the mirrors would come crashing down.

"We need to be careful." Cecily sniffed the air, and Calib thought for a moment that the magic must be so powerful here, even normal whiskers could detect it. "Something's not right."

Calib studied one of the reflections. It seemed to flip between a sandy, unfamiliar beach and a cave mouth that resembled the one they'd entered to reach Morgan's fortress. Saxon ships poured out of the cave like marching ants. The army was on the move.

Another mirror seemed to hover near the craterous top

of the Iron Mountains. Cecily's eyes widened at something behind Calib.

"Look, there it is!" she cried out, pointing at one of the mirrors near the ground, a small oval one with a silver frame. In the reflection, Camelot stood shining and whole.

Calib placed a paw on the glass that separated them from the castle. The glass shimmered, and his paw went straight past the surface of the glass, as if it were water. Calib felt a cool tickle crawl up his paw.

"I think these are portals, like the one the Lady of the Lake created on Avalon." Calib realized he was whispering, awed by Morgan's powerful command of her magic.

Slowly, he reached out to Camelot. If this was truly a portal, and he could walk through right then and there, he'd be able to warn Commander Kensington in a heartbeat. All he had to do was summon the courage to take the first step.

From behind him, Cecily let out a startled squeak. Calib turned just in time to see a shadow appear at the balcony door.

Calib's stomach lurched as Sir Percival Vole stepped forward, brandishing a sword against Cecily's throat.

"Stay where you are," the vole snarled, dragging Cecily to the balcony's railing, "if you value your life."

"Get your filthy paws off my friend!" Calib shouted, heat in his chest.

"You don't get to make the demands here," Percival growled. "The Christophers have been in power long enough. Bossiness must run in the family."

"Whatever grudge you have against my family, it doesn't involve Cecily," Calib said. "Face me."

"The destruction of all that your family holds dear has been my only goal." Percival dangled Cecily over the edge of the balcony. "I don't care who is collateral damage."

With a flick of his wrists, Percival dropped Cecily off the ledge.

"Cecily!" Calib screamed, running toward where the mouse-maid had fallen.

The vole blocked his path with a parry aimed at his gut. Out of instinct, Calib dodged, trying to remember what he had been taught about dueling from his training. One-on-one dueling was a game of strategy, of mind over might, speed over strength. He needed to plan his moves five steps in advance.

Calib waited until Percival's sword was just about to strike again, and then twisted to the left. He delivered a cracking blow to the side of Sir Percival's jaw.

Sir Percival yelped, but recovered his footing fast enough to pivot direction. A flash of steel whirled by, missing Calib's snout by millimeters.

Sir Percival tried twice more to skewer Calib. His attacks were sloppy and frantic, but they were faster than Calib would've expected. With each slash, Calib narrowly jumped out of the way, trying to channel Cecily's ability to move at the last possible moment.

Behind him, he heard Cecily's voice from the balcony, as if his thought had summoned her. Horatio must have caught her!

Relieved though he was, the distraction cost him. Percival nicked Calib on his ear and split it open. Calib muffled a yowl of pain and backed away, nearly falling into one of the mirrors. He looked through to the tundra on the other side. A heavy snowstorm swirled around a plain of ice.

It gave him an idea.

"Get back here!" Sir Percival huffed. It was clear he hadn't gotten this much exercise in years.

"Come and get me," Calib taunted. "The last Christopher still stands!"

The vole charged again, this time slower.

Calib dodged his sword and hopped to the side. Percival wheeled around to face him, but lost his balance, and Calib delivered a sweeping kick to one of Sir Percival's knees. The knight lost his balance and toppled into the surface of the magic mirror.

"No!" Percival shrieked as he let go of his sword. It fell out of his paws and skittered across the floor, catching the light as it did so. It was Lightbringer! Calib thought he had lost it forever.

Calib ran for the sword and grabbed it. Turning around,

he saw that Percival was hanging on to the edge of the frame with just the tips of his paws.

"My vengeance . . ." he began through clenched teeth. Now he hung on to the ledge by only one paw.

"Will not keep you warm," Calib finished.

Sir Percival slipped and disappeared into the blizzard.

CHAPTER
35

Calib brought his sword down on the mirror's wooden frame, hacking it clean through. The mirror froze over, as if it were the surface of a winter lake, and then shattered like ice. He turned to tell Cecily that everything was all right, that Percival was gone, when—

Thwack!

Something hard and feathery slammed into him from behind, sending him flying across the floor. Calib felt a sharp talon scrape down his side. He rolled away, skidding to a stop before he nearly fell through a mirror that showed a rocky island shore.

He clutched at his injury, and his paw came away red. He looked up and stared right into the cruel, hooked beak of Theodora the hawk. In her taloned claw was Cecily, struggling to wriggle free.

The hawk screeched loud and triumphant, "Gotch-aaa!"

"You'll pay for hurting my friends!" Cecily shouted. "Horatio won't be down for long!"

"Now, now, Theodora, I know you're excited to see your old friends again," said an oily voice. "But that's no excuse for poor manners."

At the sound, Calib felt his entire being sag. He'd been foolish. The fight between good and bad was *never* over. He choked back a cry as the Manderlean emerged from a mirror on the far side of the room, stepping through the glass as easily as if it were fog. He wore a gold, fox-like mask that shimmered beneath a bloodred hood.

The Manderlean held out his gloved paws in a mock welcome. "Even under the layers of grime and dirt, I can still smell a Christopher from a league away."

His eyes flashed like a hungry predator's, but there was also a weariness behind them. The scent of raw magic, like fresh tar, rolled off the beast, so strong it made Calib choke. Whatever the Manderlean had just done, he had more magic than Calib had ever encountered.

"You don't smell so great, either," Calib said, holding back a gag.

"The price paid for powers such as mine require more than you can fathom, little beast." The Manderlean strode forward, moving his paws in a continuous circular motion, like he was trying to contain something slippery.

A glowing red fireball formed in the space between his paws, pulsing and crackling.

"The only cowards I see are you and your vermin army hiding away in these caves," Cecily spat. She was still pinned to the ground by Theodora.

The Manderlean turned his golden face toward Cecily, and though Calib could not see the creature's expression, he could feel disdain dripping from the creature like a leaky cauldron. "Big words from such a small mouse. But we have no more reason to hide, now that Galahad has joined our side."

The memory of bright-red blood flashed in Calib's head, but he banished it quickly.

"I don't know what you did to him," Calib said shakily, "but we're going to break whatever spell you put him under!"

At that moment, Cecily managed to free one of her arms, and she bit right into the hawk's right foot. Theodora squawked and flew up in surprise. Cecily sprang to her feet and charged at the Manderlean at full tilt.

The Manderlean tried to dodge, but Cecily was too fast.

"Show us your true face!" she shouted, and then ripped the Manderlean's mask off.

Where Cecily had expected a creature's face, there was nothing. Just empty space.

The Manderlean collapsed into a pile of clothes.

Calib had known fear before, but never like this. His insides turned to liquid; his blood turned to ice. A disembodied voice began to giggle.

The spectral laughter surrounded them on all sides, reverberating from every mirror. Calib pulled his ears flat to his head—the sound was making him dizzy. Then slowly, the voice began to change and concentrate to one area.

The Manderlean's cloak shot up from the ground and hovered above their heads, expanding and changing into a long curtain of red hair. A Two-Legger body began to emerge from the hair, clad in a velvet dress the color of midnight. With a screech, the hawk came to perch on her shoulder, its talons still dripping Calib's blood onto the floor.

"Wish granted," the woman said in a cruel voice as Calib stumbled back with recognition.

The Manderlean had been Morgan le Fay all along.

CHAPTER
36

Suddenly, it all made sense.

How easily the Manderlean had traveled from place to place and how quickly Morgan was able to organize animals to do her bidding. She was a shapeshifter like Merlin, who was able to turn into Howell, the great white wolf. But at the same time, she was *nothing* like the kind wizard who'd helped Calib before.

"My dear little mice," Morgan said. "Merlin was a fool to trust in your kind." She cast her blue eyes at Calib, which were so much like King Arthur's, but colder and harder. "But the old man was never much of a critical thinker. At the end of the day, your earnestness betrays you."

"Merlin knew better than to trust you with anything," Calib said.

Morgan stopped smiling. "Did you truly believe I would let you walk in here unchallenged? I can see everything happening in this fortress from my hall of mirrors," she said. "I even saw your desperate plea to sway Galahad to your losing cause. There are no surprises in my fortress!"

Suddenly, the hawk was knocked off the Manderlean's shoulder with a surprised squawk. It had been struck by a candlestick. Theodora lost her grip on Cecily.

"There is at least *one* surprise," Galahad said as he appeared from one of the mirrors. He ran between the mice and Morgan. He pointed Excalibur right at Morgan's heart. His left hand was bandaged roughly with a torn piece of cloth.

"Indeed," Morgan said quietly. Her face was pale with anger. "I must admit this is disappointing. I had high hopes for you. . . ."

"And you call the mice fools," Galahad said. "Here I am with a sword to your chest."

Morgan sighed. "So much power in the hands of such children. *Oppilo.*"

The sorceress waved her hand from underneath her

sleeves. The boy froze, and Calib felt his body stop in place too. He tried to run toward Morgan to stop her, but his paws no longer obeyed him. He ground to a halt and fell forward. His limbs were frozen in place.

"Now you'll all stay here until I come back as the Empress Morgan le Fay of Saxony and Conqueror of Camelot."

And with one fluid movement, the sorceress snatched up Theodora and dove into the small mirror Calib had nearly entered himself—the one that showed Camelot.

Before Calib could even let out a cry of surprise, the glass froze over and shattered behind her. There was no way to follow the sorceress now.

He turned his attention back to Galahad.

"Whose side do you stand on?" Calib asked. Lightbringer was still unsheathed in his paw, but he could not swing his arm any more than he could move a mountain. Next to him, he heard Cecily trying to break the spell, but she remained in place too.

Galahad looked hurt. "I'm sorry for what I said," he said softly. "I knew Morgan would be back any second, and I knew that was the only chance to learn how the Grail worked."

"You betrayed yourself and Camelot!" Calib shouted, the horror of the scene again bearing down upon him. "You hurt an innocent creature—you *killed* Jasper!"

"Oh, you mean me?"

If Calib had not already been petrified, he would have been stunned, as first one ear, then another, emerged from under Galahad's tunic, followed by one very disgruntled hare.

"But I saw the blood! You're dead!" Calib cried.

"News to me," Jasper said as he wiggled out and hopped onto the floor. Morgan, not knowing that the hare still lived, had not included him in her spell. "That Two-Legger over there"—he pointed his ear in Galahad's direction—"can speak with animals, and he told me to pretend to be dead."

"But the blood—"

"Was mine," Galahad said, wincing slightly. "I cut my hand, but the wound grew bigger when Morgan stabbed herself."

Calib looked at Galahad's frozen fist and saw blood slowly leaking out. He scrutinized Galahad's face, looking for any hint that his Two-Legger friend might be hiding something or still under the influence of a spell. There was a pain in his eyes, and an anxiousness Calib had not noticed before. Galahad looked older—and he looked *tired*—but he did not look like a liar.

"I'm sorry, Calib," Galahad said. "It seems we ended up stuck in a sticky situation regardless."

"Now, isn't this interesting?" A new Two-Legger voice

joined the fray—one that made Calib want to bare his teeth.

Red stepped out from one of the mirrors. "But maybe I can help."

CHAPTER
37

Galahad's stomach lurched at the sight of his nemesis, now free of the room he'd locked him in. He commanded his arm to move, to swing Excalibur and protect his friends, but there was nothing he could do. Morgan's spell held fast.

"Ow!" Red exclaimed, suddenly hopping on one foot. "That hurt!"

Looking down, Galahad saw that Jasper had kicked Red, right in the shins.

"Call off your animals, Du Lac!" Red howled. "I'm here to call a truce!" Red held up his empty hands. "Your command of magic may be better than mine, but I *know* more. And I'm done trying to be someone I'm not."

Galahad felt as though Red had sprouted another head—except that would have been less strange than this conversation. "Why should we trust you?" he asked. "How do I know you're not a spy?"

"For one, I'm helping you get loose." Red held up both his hands and intoned in a loud voice, *"Dissolvo."*

Galahad felt the rigid tensions of Morgan's spell suddenly melt away, and he saw Cecily immediately run up to Red's side with her sword brandished.

"What do you want, traitor?" she demanded, seething.

"You don't have to trust me. I know I haven't earned it," Red said, keeping his eyes steady on Galahad. "But perhaps I can prove myself by helping you stop my mother—and in exchange, I want amnesty."

"I don't know I can promise that," Galahad said. "You tried to kill King Arthur, remember?"

Red looked down, and Galahad was surprised to see something like shame on his face. "Yes, well, I'm sure the hero of Camelot could put in a good word."

Galahad hesitated. His hand wavered. Something about Red's tone of voice made him curious despite his better judgment.

"One last question," Galahad said. "Why would you turn on your mother?" he asked.

Red looked uncertain. "That day with the carp. You

had somehow transferred its pain into me. It felt awful. I never knew that's what my mother's magic felt like to living beings. . . ." His voice trailed off, and his eyes held a faraway expression, as if he were reliving that moment.

Slowly, he shook himself, then continued, "Mother is brilliant. But she should never be in power. She has only ever thought of vengeance her entire life—of taking back what's hers. Her heart has no room for anything else—not even me."

Red's eyes were bright, and his jaw tightened. Galahad saw much of himself in Red at that moment. He also knew what it felt like to be seen as a tool for someone else's war. Still, Galahad didn't fully trust Red. He could sense from Excalibur that Calib was wary as well.

A clacking from the direction of the balcony made them jump and turn. Two bats were perched outside. One wore a crown askew while the other wore a neck ruff and nursed a small rip in his right wing. Sensing their distress, Galahad ran to help them.

"Close the window," the crowned bat gasped. "Quickly! Before the infernal hawk finds us again." Galahad obeyed, but before he could tell them that the hawk was gone, along with Morgan, the two bats started attacking him and Red.

"Away, you two-faced Two-Legger!" the second bat wheezed, still out of breath. The crowned bat, meanwhile, had a chunk of blond hair in his mouth and was pulling—hard.

"Stop!" Calib yelled to the bats. "King Mir—it's all right! Galahad and Red are on our side!"

The bats stopped midsqueak. "Are you sure?" the bat king panted.

"My apologies, King Mir," Galahad began, "but I—"

"Ahem?"

Startled, Galahad, Red, and all the creatures turned around to see Britta standing in the hallway, tugging on a curl as she took in the room. "I was coming to show the queen the final scroll when I heard shrieks," she said.

She looked a little pale. "I ran here as fast as I could, but then you—he—I mean . . . Are you talking to the animals?"

"Yes," Galahad said. There was no point in denying it.

"How *fascinating*," Britta said, her eyes growing wide as she took in the bats and mice. "Have you always been able to do that? Did Morgan, with her new powers, give you that ability?" Britta paused and took in everyone's injuries. "Galahad, where is Queen Morgan?"

"She is launching her attack on Camelot," Galahad said. "And we must hurry to stop her."

Britta's expression went from confusion to anger.

"No," Britta said. She unsheathed a short sword, which hung on her belt, next to her quills. She brandished it dangerously. "I've worked too long on those translations.

And just when Morgan promises to bring my family over, you're going to ruin that for me?"

Britta looked ferocious, and so Galahad again raised Excalibur, just in case she attacked. "Britta, there's something I have to tell you. Morgan hasn't been saving Saxony—she's the one who caused the drought."

Britta shook her head, her curls bouncing. "That's not possible. Saxony has been in decline since long before Morgan arrived."

"Maybe Mother did not start the drought," Red said, stepping forward, "but I'm sure she pushed it along, both for her own magic and to have the Saxons turn to her in their time of need." His face grew stormy. "She used you. She lied to you, like she lies to everyone!"

"Red's right," Galahad said, hardly believing that he would ever utter such words. "Morgan won't stop. So many will suffer if we let her win. The only person she really cares about is herself."

"But Papa and my sisters . . ." Britta's sword tip lowered as she lost her resolve. "She promised me she would bring them here! This is their only hope."

"No, not their only hope," Galahad said.

As quickly as he could, Galahad told Britta everything, including his plan to vouch for Britta and Red and her family. Cecily and Calib nodded along on his shoulders. When he'd finished, Britta looked as if she might faint.

"If this is all true," she said, "then the queen—I mean, Morgan—shouldn't have this." She pulled out the scroll she had brought and unfurled it like a treasure map. The parchment was covered in an old cipher, different than the others—one that Galahad had never seen before. He couldn't understand any of the words except the title, which was written in big, swirling letters across the top:

Merlin's Last Quest.

CHAPTER
38

"What's this?" Galahad asked.

"The only scroll of Merlin's I've been unable to decipher," Britta said. "Before you brought the scroll from Camelot, I thought that this would hold the key to using the Grail. When the ritual worked without the secrets of this scroll, I was relieved—even if I hated to see the pain caused to that poor bunny."

"I'm a *hare*," Galahad heard Jasper whisper indignantly.

Galahad smiled. "The hare is just fine. He only pretended to be dead—and quite melodramatically, too."

"What's your point, Britta?" Red said, crossing his arms. "You and I have both cross-referenced that scroll with the decoder and with every language known to man. It's completely illegible."

She looked at the animals, who seemed to understand what she was saying.

"But that's what the rabbit made me realize. Maybe this scroll wasn't meant for man," Britta said, looking at the mice on Galahad's shoulders and the bats hanging on the rafters, their ears swiveled in her direction. "Maybe Merlin meant for one of these creatures to read it."

Galahad squatted down for a closer inspection. "Calib, what do you think? Can any of you read it?"

And though both the bats and mice took a look, none of them knew the language.

"Either way, it doesn't matter now, we have a more important task at hand," Cecily said. "Morgan's made off with the Grail now, and we still have an entire mountain range full of prisoners to evacuate."

Galahad shared a look with Calib. "I can't believe I'm asking this, but, Red, do you have any ideas on getting out of here?"

Red pointed to one of the largest mirrors; a framed masterpiece displayed a large gray mountain with a crown of fog. A formation of bats circled the highest peak, still trapped underneath Morgan's spell.

"These mirrors allow Mother to be in many different places very quickly," Red added.

"Dose she have a portal near Camelot?" Britta asked.

"She did," Galahad said glumly, pointing to the shattered mirror on the floor.

"It's true, we can no longer use the direct portal, but I can at least get you out of this fortress. Come with me." Red stepped through the portal that opened onto the top of the mountain.

"I don't believe him," the bat wearing a neck ruff said. "We should shove him off a cliff the earliest chance we get."

"What do you think?" Galahad asked Calib and Cecily.

Calib scrunched his snout and rubbed his black whiskers in deep concentration. He looked back at Galahad with anxious eyes. "I think we need as much help as we can get."

"We'll be on our guard just in case he tries anything, though," Cecily added.

"Ready?" Galahad asked the creatures. Cecily and Calib ran up his pant leg and settled on his shoulder without a second thought. A moment later, the bats fluttered to his back and hooked their claws into the fabric of his tunic.

Galahad took a deep breath and stepped through the mirror.

He felt a cold tickle go up his spine again. There was

a moment of vertigo as the sensation suddenly changed from falling down to falling up. His whole world spun. Galahad was suspended in the air for a brief second before plummeting down onto the cold, rocky surface of the mountain's crater.

He was momentarily winded, but gradually, he became aware of snarls and growls and one very panicked voice.

"Get off me!" Red yelped as an onslaught of escaped prisoners swarmed him.

"I'm here to *help!*" Britta clutched her hair to keep the bats from clawing at it.

"Pull out his hair," demanded a weasel. "Make him *furless!*" Two little weasels bared their canines in agreement.

"No one is becoming bald today," Galahad said loudly. "And we need to have Red's vision at its best since he's going to help us."

Immediately, the frenzied commotion stopped as all eyes turned to Galahad—the Two-Legger who had clearly understood animal speech.

Quickly, Calib addressed the crowd. "This is Galahad," he said, pointing his tail to Galahad's nose. "And that, as you know, is Red. But both are here to help break the barrier!"

"Two-Leggers!" a bat called out. "You can't be serious!"

"Galahad is a good one!" Jasper the hare ran forward

from the crowd. "I will vouch for this Two-Legger—he saved my life. Warren can attest to it."

Galahad gave Calib a quizzical look. "Warren?"

"Er." Calib tugged his ear. "It's a long story. But, Galahad, the mirror! Show them!"

A shadow prowled around Galahad's boots. "What mirror?" a large lynx growled, his bobbed tail twitching angrily. This, he supposed, was Leftie the lynx, chieftain of the Darkling Woods. Hastily, Galahad reached into his pack to produce Merlin's Mirror. Carefully, he lowered it to the one-eyed wildcat.

The lynx's yellow eye widened, and his pupil dilated.

"Shave my whiskers," Leftie breathed, and his big velvety paw snatched it from Galahad. "I *know* that mirror!" He turned it over, the handle fitting his paw perfectly, and Leftie practically purred in delight. "I thought it had smashed to smithereens!"

Leftie clutched the mirror, as if he would never let it out of his sight again. "At last, with the help of this mirror, we will be able to plan for the seasons again."

"No more raiding to survive!" a big badger added.

"Aye! Peace, perhaps, at last," the wildcat agreed.

Galahad smiled before glancing back to check on Britta and Red. Britta had pulled a quill out of her curly hair and was rapidly recording everything she saw in her notebook.

"Normally, I would say this kind of magic is impossible.

How could you be talking to these animals, Galahad, without drawing your magic *from* something? I've since been working on a new theory about magic," she said.

"No more theories from you," Red said, only half jokingly. "You're too good at them."

Britta ignored him. "Morgan was always saying that Merlin had taught her how magic is about balance. To do something, you have to take from something else. Well, I've been translating those scrolls for months, and I think she is missing something important."

Britta's voice rose in excitement as she laid out her new theory.

"I think magic can also be powered from within. I think it's true that Morgan can manage such big magic because she's taking power from others. If she were to give only of herself, she would surely die from the exhaustion. But I think, taken in smaller quantities, a person can power his own spells, as Galahad does."

Red stood still, staring at the ragged animals gathered around them. Many of them bore bandages from injuries sustained in the forges and mines. All of them were underfed and dirty. The boy paled, his face white under his shock of red hair.

"I think enough has been taken from others," he said. Red turned to face the crowd of gathered animals. "I'm sorry. This is my fault as much as it is my mother's. I cannot give you back the time you lost and the suffering you have endured. For that, I am truly sorry."

Red looked at Galahad grimly. "On my mark, strike your sword against the sky."

Galahad nodded while Red raised both his hands. The older boy began chanting in the words of old magic. His fingers moved in complicated gestures, and slowly, a thin dome appeared above them, wavering with blue currents of magic. It arched all the way down to the ground. Morgan had trapped them like bugs in a jar.

Well, she'd be very sorry that she'd ever trapped *this* bug. Galahad would make sure of it.

"Do it now," Red called to Galahad through gritted teeth. He was sweating now. As he continued to chant, tendrils of magic poured down from his fingertips. The dome seemed to sag as a result. "Break the shell!"

Using all his energy, Galahad jumped and sliced Excalibur through the translucent membrane. It felt as though he were trying to slice through thick cloth.

There was immense resistance, but then it began to tear. Galahad's heart leaped. The plan was working! But almost as soon as he thought it, he heard a groan from Calib, who was looking at where he'd made his tear. Galahad's heart lurched when he realized the rip was no longer there.

The barrier seemed to have immediately healed itself.

It was as smooth as ever—not even a nick remained where Excalibur had sliced through.

Suddenly, Red dropped to all fours, panting for breath. "It's too strong," he gasped. "I can't do it. Excalibur isn't enough." He locked eyes with Galahad. "We're not strong enough."

And at his words, the blue glow of the dome faded into nothingness, leaving them exactly where they had been before.

Trapped . . . and hopeless.

CHAPTER
39

Calib felt a frustrated sob rise in his throat, but he swallowed it back. There had to be a way out—there just *had* to!

"Morgan le Fay cannot be stronger than us," Cecily cried. "She's just one Two-Legger, but among all of us, we know so much! The moles know how to dig, the bats how to navigate the dark, the Saxons know how to read the runes. Surely there has to be a way out of here!"

"Morgan knows how to manipulate real magic. Magic older than Earth itself," Horatio murmured. "Unless you can somehow use something she's already built against her, there's very little we could do."

Red prodded Galahad in the ribs. "This is annoying," he said while Britta stood behind, rapidly nodding her head in agreement. "What are they all saying?"

Quickly, Galahad filled in Red and Britta. When he had finished, a thoughtful expression crossed Red's face.

"What is a mirror but a reflection that can be turned into a portal? None of my mother's mirrors are strong enough to get everyone out, but we do have the underground lakes and the water gate!"

"Have you ever created one?" Galahad asked as Calib thought again of the Lady of the Lake. She had turned Avalon's lake into a portal to send Cecily and Calib home.

"No, not on this scale." Red rubbed his forehead in fierce thought. "Mother couldn't either, or else she would have sent her entire army over to Camelot that way. She was only able to get herself across, and usually, only in her ferret form. This was why she always needed more magic. She was convinced there was untapped raw magic buried somewhere in this mountain."

Hope thundered back into Calib. "Your Majesty," he said, catching King Mir's eye. "Do you think . . . ?"

King Mir let out a gusty sigh. "Follow me, please, to the dragon's lair, where we will get you your crystals."

* * *

Two days passed as they painstakingly unearthed the crystals with help from the rest of the prisoners. Red, pretending to act on behalf of his mother, was quickly able to trick the few remaining guards to disarm. Once they did, Red put them under a sleeping spell. Thomas, the weasel, and Britta went about convincing the rest of the Saxons to join their side.

One by one, the animals arranged the crystals in a circle around the circumference of the lake. Per Britta's instructions, they placed them about two feet apart. With each passing hour, Calib grew more and more antsy. The Saxons must have arrived at Camelot by now. A siege could be underway.

Finally, the animals all crowded around the lake, armed with the secret stash of weapons they'd stolen from the forges. They were ready to rescue Camelot—as soon as they could get out. To Calib, it looked as though they had formed their own kind of Round Table—Saxons stood alongside the bats, Darklings alongside Camelot.

This was how it should be, the mouse thought—a land united.

He looked to the middle of the lake, where Galahad and Red were seated in a small boat. The older boy looked tired but determined.

After a few deep breaths, Red began to chant, tendrils of magic pooling out from his hands and into the water.

The crystals responded to the magic and began to shoot forth light into the lake.

"I need you to channel Excalibur into the lake as well," Red said as the surface of the water begin to glow blue. "Every bit of power is needed. The portal will last only for a few seconds. When I say 'jump,' all the animals will have to go at once."

"I will remain behind to close the portal," Britta called from the shore. "Don't forget your promise to me, Galahad."

"I swear it." Galahad nodded. "Your family will have a home in Camelot after all this is over."

Galahad dipped the tip of his sword into the lake. The surface of the water began to change colors, slowly swirling to form a river scene—a hillock that Calib knew stood only half a league away from the castle.

"This is as close as I can get us," Red said, his hands shaking to keep the spell intact. The boat was starting to sink.

The animals began to mutter among one another. "I'm not stepping in there until I see someone else do it first. . . ."

Calib's old fear of swimming reared its head. What if Red was lying? What if he dumped them all in the sea or . . .

"*Go!*" Red shouted.

"FOR CAMELOT!" Calib yelled, then, taking a deep breath, he jumped. He splashed into the water and immediately felt a magical force yank him down below the surface. Before he had a chance to cry out, he found himself falling through air instead of water. He somersaulted a few times and landed on a soft cluster of weeds, tumbling to a stop on a mossy glen.

Cecily, Ginny, Thomas, and Thomas's siblings fell through the air right after him, followed by the prisoners of the Iron Mountains. For a solid five minutes, it was quite literally raining animals. Finally, a wooden boat bearing two boys appeared, hovering in midair.

The boat jerked around violently, as if struggling with the physics of gravity, before falling. It hit the ground with a large *crack*. The boat splintered into pieces.

"Whew," Thomas said, shaking his head. The weasel looked somewhat dazed. "That was some ride."

Calib ran to make sure Galahad was okay. The boys were lying on the ground, winded from the fall.

Red smiled wanly. He was deadly pale and looked in need of a long nap, but he seemed unharmed. "That was some magic," he murmured. "But Britta was right; it came from within."

"We made it!" Galahad shouted with glee. He stood up, wobbled some, but regained his balance. He pointed to the west. They had arrived on a hill overlooking Camelot.

A warm, orange light seemed to make the towers and turrets of their home glow.

The plan worked! For a moment, Calib felt invincible. But in the last rays of the setting sun, Calib's eye caught something that made his heart stop.

"Oh no," Cecily whispered from his side, for she saw the same thing.

At the top of Camelot's turrets hung not the sigil of King Arthur—three crowns against a background of blue. Saxon flags flew above every tower, the red stripes on white banners rippling against the evening wind. Warships—both Two-Legger and animal—clogged the river leading to the town.

They were too late. Camelot had already fallen.

CHAPTER
40

Calib stood numbly, unsure if he wanted to scream or cry, hit something or go hide. His home had been attacked, and he'd not been there to protect it.

Suddenly, there was a soft *whissh* through the air, followed by a hard *thwack* as a creature-sized arrow narrowly missed Galahad's boot and buried itself into the ground.

"That was a warning shot!" said a voice from the trees. "Who goes there?"

"Macie!" Calib cried out. "It's me! It's *us*!"

The red squirrel's face popped out above the tree branches. "Calib?" Her eyes widened. *"Cecily!"* Quick as a flash, Macie ran straight down the trunk of the tree and wrapped Cecily in her arms. "Thank goodness you're all right!"

"I'm fine," Cecily said, hugging her friend back. "But you're clearly not." Cecily was right. A white bandage was looped lopsidedly around Macie's left ear, and a scrap of cloth had hastily been tied around her forearm.

"What happened?" Calib asked. "Where's Commander Kensington? Where are the others?"

Macie's smile fell off her face. "Most of them are still in the castle," she said, her voice strained. She drew up her bow again. "And some are behind you!"

"I know," Calib said, and was aware of Thomas shuffling farther back into the crowd, sweeping Rosy and Silas back with him.

"But I promise," Calib continued, "these are friendly ones. They have been hurt by the Saxon army and Morgan—er, the Manderlean—just as badly as us."

"Speaking of," Cecily interrupted, "Macie, what happened? Is Maman all right?"

Macie threw one last suspicious glance at the mishmash of animals behind Calib before looking at Cecily. "For now," she said cautiously, "Viviana is hiding with some others in the caves. It all happened so quick!"

"What did?" Leftie growled as he made his way to the front.

"Leftie!" Macie cried. "Where? How?" But she seemed at a loss at what to say first. Finally, she seemed to settle on the most obvious truth. "I'm so glad you're here!"

Leftie tapped his paw on the ground. "I expected more precise reporting from Camelot's chief scout," he chided. "Report!"

"Yes, sir." Macie saluted with tail to forehead. "The invaders took the castle by surprise. We think that Morgan cast a sleeping spell that put all the sentries into a slumber, because she rode into the courtyard on a jet-black stallion with no one raising so much as a hiccup." Macie shut her eyes briefly before continuing. "It wasn't until she had King Arthur and Queen Guinevere at swordpoint that anyone realized what had happened. Commander Kensington is still trapped in the castle with most of the others, held hostage by Saxon weasels."

"And how did you escape?" Galahad asked, kneeling down into the dirt. To Calib's surprise, Macie didn't look the least bit startled when Galahad addressed her. Man and beast were getting better at conversing—at listening.

"Commander Kensington and most of the mouse-knights were set upon in a similar way," Macie said. "We were only able to get out because Warren knew about the secret tunnel leading out to the beach."

"I knew it!" Red said, stepping out from behind Gala-had, who must have been translating for him. "I *knew* those passageways under Camelot had to lead to some-where."

Before Calib could even blink, Macie had notched her arrow and let it fly loose.

"Ow!" Red yelped as suddenly as the arrow dug into his calf. "You know, you animals are making it very hard to want to help you!"

"You deserved it," Cecily snapped while Macie quickly notched another arrow.

"Peace, squirrel," Leftie said. "That Two-Legger is helping us."

Surprised, Macie's bow dipped slightly. "Isn't that Mor-dred? Morgan's son who just last season attacked King Arthur?"

"Er, yes," Calib said. "It's a long story, but we trust him. For now. You keep saying 'we'—who else is here?"

Hesitantly, Macie lowered her bow all the way, but she still kept the arrow in her paw. "Follow me," she said. "I'll show you."

As silently as they could, the procession from the Iron Mountains wound themselves through the trees. Soon, Calib heard the sound of water, and a few minutes later, saw the river. Anchored near the tangled roots of a willow, there floated a rodent-sized ship with black sails.

Galahad moved his hand to Excalibur, but Calib immediately recognized the ship as *The Salty Pup*—the very same vessel that had taken them to Avalon. At that moment, the head of a plump mouse popped up over the prow of the ship.

"My friends! At last!" Barnaby's face lit up in a gigantic grin, and a few minutes later, the brown mouse was joined on deck by even more familiar faces: Warren, Devrin, Sir Alric, and Dandelion.

"Admiral Barnaby," Macie called out, "permission to board?"

"Granted!"

"Oh, so you're an *admiral* now!" Ginny teased once they'd clambered on deck. "I must have missed that!"

"Ginny!" Barnaby cried, his whiskers curling in delight. "Your letters stopped coming! I thought the worst had happened!"

Ginny ran up and planted a big kiss on his snout. "Well, it wasn't great, I'll tell you that."

Suddenly conscious of everyone watching, Barnaby quickly composed himself.

"Er, yes, Tristan decided he wanted to settle on some island he found far north of here. He's given *The Salty Pup* to me to run for those of his crew uninterested in farming."

The crew of *The Salty Pup* was hurrying around,

handing out blankets and hanging up extra bunks for the unexpected number of guests. The larger animals, like the foxes and badgers, were handed spare sails to wrap themselves in as they settled along the grassy banks. Leftie organized the older animals into sentry shifts.

"How did you get here so fast, Barnaby?" Cecily asked. She was sitting comfortably between Devrin and Dandelion, and she had wrapped her arm around Dandelion, who couldn't seem to stop trembling. Warren stood stiffly to the side on account of a bandaged tail.

Barnaby walked over and handed each of them a piece of hardtack. "After Ginny's messages stopped arriving at my ports of call, I began to get worried. So I sailed back as quick as I could. We arrived just as the Saxons had broken through the main castle gate. I managed to smuggle everyone I could out through the secret tunnel that leads to the beach."

With an eye on the shivering Dandelion, Calib leaned over and whispered into Barnaby's ear, "What happened to her?"

Barnaby shook his head, eyes sad. "She's been like that ever since we got word of Morgan's plan."

"The Saxons will execute King Arthur and Queen Guinevere in the morning."

"We have to stop them!" Calib cried out.

"Yes," Cecily said grimly. "We need a war council."

CHAPTER
41

While Galahad and Red snuck their way into town
to find anyone who might be able and willing to
help, the allied animals of Camelot, the Darkling Woods, the Iron Mountains, and Saxony were hard
at work executing the plan decided on by the war council.

Squirrels hacked away at the willow branches that lined
Rickonback River. Hares hopped along the ground, gathering fallen branches, while mice and weasels lashed them
together with vines braided by the shrews.

Calib hoped his idea would work.

Taking a break from building, Calib grabbed a walnut shell to fetch water for the other thirsty creatures. The mouse walked until the sounds of the camp faded away. He let the burbling of Rickonback River quiet his thoughts down to just one:

This was where his father died.

Your heroes are not the perfect mice you think they are! Sir Percival's accusations lashed out from the past like a mental barb. Calib closed his eyes and tried to banish the memory. He leaned over to splash water from the river on his snout, as if that might wash away Percival's influence.

The vole was a known liar. Nothing he said could be trusted. However, Calib simply did not know enough about the circumstances concerning Sir Trenton's death to have a defense.

Perhaps that's why he had walked all the way here to the river—to look for any evidence he could use to prove his father's honor.

He looked at his reflection in the water. For a moment, he could almost see the ghost of the mouse he only knew from a tapestry.

He remembered what Red had said back on the mountain.

What is a mirror but a reflection that can be turned into a portal?

A cool tingle traveled down Calib's spine. All along, Merlin had ensured that any Two-Legger treasure could not be attained without the cooperation of the woodland folk, be they from the Darkling Woods or Camelot. Merlin's Crystal unlocked Excalibur. Perhaps Merlin's Mirror unlocked something else?

Leaving the quiet of the river, he quickly ran back to camp to find Leftie assisting Rosy and Silas with their painting.

"I'm not quite sure I understand what you're getting at," the wildcat grunted as he pulled out the mirror for Calib. The Darkling leader now carried the mirror by him at all times. He was determined not to lose it again.

"I think the mirror isn't just for fortune-telling." Calib unfurled the scroll that read "Merlin's Last Quest." The runes were still as mysterious as ever. "I think it might be a portal, too—one that only a creature of small size can go through. It just has to reflect the correct object."

Calib tilted the mirror toward the page and looked at its reflection. At first, nothing happened. He felt foolish. He thought for sure he had figured out what Merlin's secret was.

But then suddenly, the parchment in the mirror swirled, and words began to appear like a running river of blue on the scroll. Too fast to read. Calib realized that everything had ceased to move around him. The scene reflecting in the mirror was not a blank page, but a full and vibrant valley, with a mouse that looked very much like an older version of Calib.

This mouse was trying to say something to them.

Calib leaned in to listen, but as his snout touched the glass surface, he was pulled into the mirror.

"We should camp here for the night. The water at Rickonback is fresh and clean. It will be our last chance to replenish before entering Fellwater Swamps."

Calib knew this voice, even though he had no true memory of hearing it before. He recognized it as clear as his own, having spent many years wondering how this voice might sound in his ears. As his vision cleared, Calib's ribs tightened like a screw.

Before him crouched a tall, proud-looking mouse-knight with tawny fur and kind eyes. A white patch of fur marked his right ear. He wore colors of rich burgundy and gold, all hidden underneath a green cloak camouflaged with leaves.

"Father?" Calib's voice came out like a croak.

Sir Trenton sniffed the air, as if sensing a change in the winds, but he did not see Calib, who stood a mere arm's length away.

"Owen, would you mind checking the wheels? I think some mud might be stuck in the axel from when we forded the river."

Calib turned, and he was surprised to see a burly black mouse emerge from the banks of the river. He knew Sir Owen as a grizzled old soldier with only one whisker, which he groomed meticulously. And yet, here he was, sporting the biggest cluster of fine hairs that Calib had ever seen on a mouse. It was practically a Two-Legger beard.

Was he in a memory or a vision? Calib could not tell. Or perhaps he had traveled back in time?

"Hello! Father!" Calib jumped up and down and waved his paws in front of Sir Trenton's face. But he was invisible to the knight. Sir Trenton walked right through Calib, sending a jolt of emotions through the mouse. Calib sensed that his father was worried and upset about something.

Calib followed his father and Sir Owen as they walked past at least twenty soldiers setting up camp along Rickonback. They were all guarding a small wagon covered by a canvas tarp. Calib didn't even have to look; he knew what was underneath it the moment Trenton walked through him: The Grail was strapped down inside the wagon.

Sir Trenton and Sir Owen set to cleaning the mud off the wheels so the wagon would roll more smoothly.

"*Trenton!*" Another familiar voice reached Calib's ears, but this one filled him with venom. "*I've scouted ahead.*

We're all clear for the next few leagues. No Darklings to be found."

Calib's blood ran hot as a young Percival Vole emerged from the far side of the wooded clearing. The vole was less portly, and when he smiled toothily, Calib saw that he still had most of his teeth.

"Thank you, Percy!" Trenton waved and smiled back. "Please make a note of your scouting in the commander's log."

Percival saluted and retreated to the largest tent set up by the river.

"Commander Yvers wanted this delivered to General Thaddeus for safekeeping by nightfall," Sir Owen whispered under his breath, patting the top of the wagon reverently. "Are you sure we should camp overnight?"

"The owls will meet us here tonight and carry it back by air," Sir Trenton said in a voice barely above a whisper.

Sir Owen looked confused. "But you just sent Percival on a scouting trip. . . ."

"I know what I told Percy," Sir Trenton said. "And there's a reason for that which I will not speak of here."

Calib's jaw fell open. His father had suspected Percival Vole was a traitor from the beginning! But then why did he never tell anyone? The answer came quickly: because he would never get the chance to tell anyone. This must be Sir Trenton's last day—the day of the Battle of Rickonback River.

Calib's eyes smarted from unshed tears, and his throat closed up. He felt sorrow from deep inside his gut. Still, he forced himself to watch Percival disappear into the tent, and he followed him as he snuck back into the woods to leave a note in a trunk.

Calib read over Percival's shoulder: *Grail is in the wagon. Remember to wear the Darkling colors.*

Calib balled his paws into fists. So Howell *was* telling the truth after all. Sir Trenton was never murdered by Darklings, as the stories said. It had been the Saxons all along, tipped off by Sir Percival. The entire Darkling war of his grandfather's was based on a lie. The Saxons had tricked both sides into thinking the worst of the other. They had spent years fighting for no reason.

Time sped forward, and the sunlight fell away like a dying candle. Calib could see the Saxons slipping silently forward out of the darkness as the moon hung low in the sky. With a wild whoop that mimicked Leftie's war cries, the Saxon raiders fell upon the group, taking many of the knights by surprise.

Trenton and his knights fought viciously on the banks of the river. Sirs Owen and Trenton stood back-to-back in a way that reminded Calib of fighting alongside War-ren or Cecily. He couldn't stand to watch, knowing that at any moment, an arrow or a sword slash would kill his father.

He couldn't look away, either.

Trenton kept casting desperate glances up at the sky. The owls had not arrived yet. The Saxon raiding party outnumbered them five to one. A number of them had fought their way to the wagon.

Sir Trenton and Sir Owen rushed forward to wrest the treasure out of their grasps.

The Grail fell out of the wagon and cracked on the rocks of the river.

Bending down, Trenton placed a paw on the Grail and muttered something Calib could not quite catch above the din of shouts and clanging metal. The Grail suddenly began to glow.

"What are you doing?" cried Sir Owen. His snout was bloody, and most of his whiskers were now missing.

"Send my love to Clara," Trenton said apologetically to his friend. *"Tell her I'm sorry, but I know she is strong. And give this to Calib when he is ready."*

Trenton handed Sir Owen his sword, the one called Darkslayer. The same one that Kensington had eventually given to Calib before he went questing for Avalon. And the same one that Calib sacrificed to the lake to learn the cure for Camelot.

The golden light of the Grail grew blinding, and it consumed Trenton in that instant in a bright wall of illumination. The Grail's light then shot up into the night sky, and in an arc, poured onto the remaining ten Camelot knights still standing, including Sir Owen.

Golden armor formed around their bodies, and they suddenly moved with increased energy and speed. Calib's eyes widened at this transformation.

Sir Owen fought as if he were not one creature, but twenty—fighting off the Saxon attackers with two swords in his paws, his own and Sir Trenton's.

Calib rubbed his eyes. The power demonstrated here by the Grail was so much more than what Morgan and Galahad had been able to achieve. Compared to his father's army, Morgan's feat was a mere parlor trick. What could be making the difference?

The harsh screech of owls broke through the noise of battle. Calib looked up to see a cluster of wingspans blotting out the moon. General Thaddeus and his owl regiment had finally arrived. A number of his group began dive-bombing from the sky, hacking and slashing with their claws.

The Saxons booked a hasty retreat to the cover of darkness. One of them pocketed the piece of the Grail that had broken off. Calib knew that would be the piece that Morgan would eventually fashion into a cursed ring, corrupting its magic to spread the mysterious white fever to Camelot.

"Our plans have been betrayed. The owls cannot harbor this treasure. Take the Grail back to Camelot, and tell Merlin and

Yvers—" Thaddeus looked around for Sir Trenton. *"Where is Trenton?"*

Calib was stunned by what he had just witnessed. His father had not been killed. He had willingly sacrificed *himself* to activate the Grail's powers.

The Grail did not just require a sacrifice—it required *self*-sacrifice.

Which meant Morgan didn't know how to unlock the Grail after all; she assumed she could it operate it out of greed. Like Britta had said, her fundamental misunderstanding of magic was that she assumed you must take from others to create your own. Little did Morgan know the opposite was true: to power the Grail—the most powerful magical artifact of all—you had to give it something of yourself.

"Now you know."

Calib turned, sure that the voice must be addressing someone else.

A white wolf stood among the trees, looking straight at him with one green eye and one blue eye. Merlin. Howell. One and the same.

"You can see me?" Calib said.

"As sure as you can see me," Howell replied. "In a way, this is just an echo I've left of myself in this memory, in case it was ever needed."

"You *are* needed, Howell!" Calib said. "Morgan has defeated Camelot."

"I'm afraid my time on this Earth is quite long past. This account of Rickonback River was only to reveal the truth to you when you were ready. Do you now understand what your father did?"

Calib nodded. "Yes, he sacrificed himself to save others. To save Camelot. Is that how the Grail truly works?"

Howell nodded once. "The Grail possesses the most powerful magic of all: magic that is only given when you give of yourself. That kind of power, self-sacrifice—it can change the world."

"But if King Arthur uses it," Calib said, the consequence of their earlier plot now dawning on him, "we'll have no king at all!"

"The time of kings cannot last forever," Howell began, but Calib was barely listening. "Camelot itself cannot last. . . ."

"I have to go back and warn Galahad about how the Grail truly works!" he exclaimed.

"Very well, Calib Christopher," Howell said, sighing. "Perhaps this is a lesson better experienced than told."

The wolf held up one paw and traced a circle in the air. The circle turned into the shape of the mirror. It showed Leftie's concerned face.

"I think the mirror ate Calib!" Leftie's voice warbled,

as if he were speaking underwater and from a great distance. "We can't attack today without him!"

"Go back to your home, Calib," Howell said. "You will need all you have learned here to guide you."

CHAPTER
42

The sun rose that morning cooler than it had been. The beginning of autumn was undeniably in the air. The moss that grew on the birches had been thick that summer. That meant there would be an early frost. Galahad remembered this from Father Walter's teachings. He took this as a sign of positive changes to come as he tiptoed through the thick brush, making his way anonymously onto the castle grounds.

In his brown, hooded cloak, Galahad blended in with the crowds that were gathering in the castle courtyard. He knew Red was hiding somewhere nearby too.

Galahad followed the number of raised and angry voices back to a hastily built platform by the stables. Kneeling on the dais were two rows of prisoners from the castle, each shackled hand and foot. He saw that Malcolm, Bors, and most of the knights, including his father, were among them.

They all bore the marks of a struggle. Sir Lancelot still had a bleeding cut on his cheek. No sign of the king and queen, though.

The crowd of townsfolk looked tense and wary. Saxon guards surrounded all sides of the courtyard, swords at the ready. There were two to every villager.

Galahad reached under his cloak, feeling for Excalibur. He couldn't help but notice that it was an off-tune feeling now, like the sword sensed that something dangerous was about to occur. He would have to move fast. As soon as Red was able to complete his spell and break the chains of those trapped inside the castle, it would be up to Galahad to seek the king and queen immediately.

From out of the corner of his eye, Galahad could see subtle movements from small shadows at people's feet. Leftie and his Darklings were moving into position.

The sound of half-hearted trumpets made Galahad jump. His eyes went to the stage as Morgan stepped out with her hawk, Theodora. The bird preened on Morgan's shoulder, as the woman looked over the crowd trium-phantly.

By the looks of it, Morgan had raided Queen Guinev-ere's wardrobe and put on her most lavish evening dress: a plum velvet number with silver larks embroidered in intri-cate detail. Over it, however, she wore a sturdy chestplate. No matter how much she wanted to show who was queen now, she still didn't trust those around her.

On her head, she wore King Arthur's golden crown. The crowd murmured their displeasure but was quickly silenced by the threatening Saxon soldiers.

"Today you will have the pleasure of seeing true power rise to the throne," she said, as prideful as ever. "Too long have you had to live with an imposter king. One who has let magic slip away from his grasp like a child. I am here to remedy that."

"You lie!" yelled out an old cobbler.

Morgan glared as two guards apprehended the man. Only the Saxons in the crowd cheered as the old cobbler was escorted to the dungeons. Morgan smiled serenely and resumed her speech, reciting the many reasons King Arthur made a poor king.

"You may all think the Round Table is a noble con-cept. But it has always been Arthur's excuse to shirk the responsibilities of true leadership. A real king does not rule by committee!"

As the crowd around him became more outraged, Galahad grew anxious. Where were King Arthur and Queen Guinevere? Why hadn't they been brought out yet? Were they already dead?

Morgan kept rambling on about her vision of a kingdom ruled by magic. "On the other hand, if you place magic in the hands of someone who knows how to wield it with precision . . . why, I could make Camelot the most feared kingdom of all. There would be no more war."

But the crowd was no longer paying attention. All faces were turned upward, at a dark speck in the sky that had suddenly blotted out the morning sun. Slowly, it grew bigger and bigger, until . . .

"IT'S A DRAGON!" someone shrieked.

Choruses of panicked shouts pierced the air. Morgan went silent, and her expression turned livid.

A cold sweat broke down Galahad's back as he saw the shadow of the winged dragon. Calib was far, *far* too early with his distraction—Camelot's humans were still in chains, unable to help.

The chains that were holding the hostages began to glow blue: Red's doing. At last, the chains broke in half and fell at the prisoners' feet with a collective *clang*.

Sir Lancelot leaped to his feet. "For Camelot!" he bellowed. "For King Arthur!"

The other freed prisoners—Sir Edmund, Sir Kay, Bors,

Malcolm, Father Walter, lords and ladies, members of the castle kitchens all the way to the gardeners—joined in with Sir Lancelot:

"FOR KING ARTHUR!"

Suddenly, Theodora froze in place with an alarmed squawk. She fell off Morgan's shoulder like a rock. Red's stun spell had missed his mother, hitting the hawk instead.

Morgan recognized the magic. "Mordred le Fay! You insolent boy!"

There was a *crack* as her spell lifted Red out from his hiding place beneath the platform. He was suspended in the air, as if held up by invisible talons.

"You can't keep using others, Mother!" Red shouted, twisting. "Stop this now, and maybe it can all end without any more harm—to any man or beast or you!"

"You are weak, Mordred," Morgan retorted, seething.

Morgan's hands formed into claws, and she made a slashing motion in the direction of Red. Bright daggers of light shot forth and struck Red, square in the face, and he dropped to the ground with a thud. He curled on his side, clutching his eyes.

Morgan, meanwhile, had vanished.

"Red!" Galahad shouted, running to the injured boy's side, but Red pushed him away gruffly.

"It's just a blinding spell," Red said, the heels of his palms covering his eyes. Galahad saw tears leaking out, but he didn't think it was all the spell's fault. "The curse will wear off, but she's transformed again. Probably back into that ferret form she loves so much!"

Leftie and his Darklings sprang into action. They were now gnawing at ankles, clawing at toes, and tripping the Two-Legger Saxons. Hidden Saxon creatures streamed out from the platform, ready to counter them.

Someone began to ring the chapel bells. Hidden villagers charged out of the chapel, armed with candlesticks, broken glass, and chairs for weapons. The town blacksmith swung two of his massive hammers, smashing in breastplates, shields, and helmets of any Saxon who came within arm's reach.

The villagers were not skilled at battle, and they were badly outnumbered, but this was their home. They knew every nook and corner of the town, and they used that knowledge to their advantage. If they ran into a Saxon force too large to handle, they could scatter down back alleyways and onto rooftops, melting away only to regroup one street over.

The sound of high-pitched screeching filled the air. Above, an army of larks, crows, and owls had appeared from the south to join the battle. They dive-bombed the Saxons while squirrels and hares and otters fought them on the ground.

And above them all flew the dragon, spitting flames

and growling with a voice that sounded very much like Thomas the weasel.

In the ensuing chaos, Galahad snuck behind the platform and ran into the castle. Most of the Saxons had emptied out of the hallways. They were outside trying to quell the revolt. The halls were eerily quiet. Galahad was stumped. King Arthur and Queen Guinevere could be held anywhere—in a tower, in the dungeons.

Galahad paused and tried to see the world through Morgan's eyes. In all the training she'd given him, what was the one thing she always stressed? Magic was balance. If Morgan needed to perform any magic, she always needed a life force to draw it from, usually a green and growing thing.

There were many gardens, but only one garden that connected to Morgan's childhood rooms: Guinevere's cliffside garden.

Galahad began to sprint in the direction of the throne room. It was thankfully empty, though Galahad noticed with annoyance that Morgan had already carved a giant *M* onto the back of Arthur's throne. Galahad climbed on to the Round Table and did a running leap through the stained-glass window; thankfully, it hadn't yet been fixed from his and Red's duel months ago.

Galahad caught his fall on a bramble of bushes. Ignoring the cuts and scrapes on his knees and palms, he took off running down the moss-covered hedges and overgrown fruit trees.

"King Arthur! Queen Guinevere!" he called out to the vegetation.

"Over here!"

Galahad's pulse raced and he ran even faster. He found the king and queen lashed against an old willow whose branches hung precariously over the stone wall that overlooked the cliffside.

"Galahad!" King Arthur cried. "You found us!"

"What is happening in the village?" Guinevere asked anxiously. "All we hear are shouts and screams!"

"Not to worry, Your Majesties. We're taking the castle back," Galahad said confidently. Using Excalibur, he sliced their bindings.

King Arthur rubbed his wrists. "Where's my sister?"

"Morgan has the Grail," Galahad blurted out. "She carries it with her."

"The Grail?" King Arthur's eyes widened in shock. "But how? I've spent years looking for it!"

His words caught Galahad off guard. "You believe in its powers? But you forbade anyone from seeking it!"

King Arthur bowed his head. "I have searched for it many times these long years—that's why your father and I have so often been gone from the kingdom. But when last I left searching for it, the Saxons attacked, and I realized that I needed to stop hoping for magic to save us. That perhaps peace was truly impossible. So I prepared for war."

Queen Guinevere patted the king's shoulder and said, "Arthur has always taken each misfortune to Camelot as his own fault, and he sometimes forgets that the burden of ruling should fall to a group so that we may all support one another."

Arthur nodded. "Indeed. I had forgotten. I thought Merlin had abandoned us, but I see now that Merlin's intent was for the power to be shared."

"Somehow," Galahad said grimly as the sound of battle rose in his ears, "I don't think Morgan shares the same philosophy."

"Then I have a meeting with my sister," King Arthur said. "Come, Galahad. Let us end this."

CHAPTER
43

Calib saw Camelot's spires from a dragon's point of view. He sat squarely in the glass bowl that served as the dragon's left eye. The dragon that he and all the creatures had created together for a distraction. Unfortunately, things hadn't gone as planned.

And now, if Arthur used the Grail as the plan intended, he would die!

"To the left! The main battle is gathering on the cliffside!" he shouted into a hollow tube that relayed his message to the owls and crows manipulating the recently crafted dragon's winged movements.

"Understood," the owl general, Gaius Thornfeather, said, his words traveling down to Calib's ear from Sir Alric's contraption. The entire body of the dragon groaned and shifted against the wind.

Exhilaration chased away Calib's exhaustion. He looked down at the Two-Leggers far below, moving in ant-like formations. All of them had paused to stare up in wonder and fear as the dragon blotted out the sunlight. Occasionally, an unnerved soldier would peel away from the chaos to run into the woods.

Calib and the rest of the free animals of Camelot and the Darkling Woods had spent the whole night working in the forest to construct this dragon. It had to be lightweight enough for the owls, crows, and bats to hold aloft a great distance. So far, the willow branches were holding steady. Time would tell if the reinforced wings made out of *The Salty Pup*'s sails would be strong enough to withstand arrows. To fill the body, they had molded papier-mâché and scraps of linen over the wooden framework. Ginny had the brilliant idea of using a glue-like substance made from the thistle weed. Dandelion had chosen the metallic-gray paint, created with flour and ash. Finally, with a few of King Mir's illusion spells thrown here and there, they had a functional dragon.

"Rawwwwrgh, I'm hungry for Two-Legger meat!"

Thomas bellowed into the instrument. The Saxon weasel was having the time of his life.

Calib motioned to Cecily, who sat in the dragon's right eye. She nodded. "Get the fire powder ready!" she shouted into her tube. "Let's give them a show, boys!"

Calib held his breath—this would be the biggest test.

Sir Alric's trumpet served the dual purpose of spewing the fire powder they'd brought from the Iron Mountains. They'd have just enough for three displays of fire breathing.

As the dragon rose up alongside the bluff, Calib took heart in seeing their hard work already paying off in the frightened faces of their Saxon enemies. Thomas continued to roar nonsense into the sound amplifier.

"Taste our fury!"

At that moment, Devrin and Warren set off a great fan of flames from the dragon's snout, showering their enemies below with ash and sparks.

That seemed to do the trick perfectly. The Saxons were panicking and abandoning their posts. With the sun high above them, the dragon must have looked like it was turning red for another attack. Pure chaos ensued down below.

"I think this is going to work!" Thomas shouted. "These Two-Leggers are running like cats out of water!"

"Now we just have to find Galahad and King Arthur," Cecily said.

Calib had told the animals the truth of how the Grail worked as soon as he'd returned from the mirror. But Galahad had already left for his part of the rescue mission. All the creatures agreed that the Two-Leggers did not know what they were dealing with. The animals had to retrieve the Grail before anyone got hurt.

Cecily pivoted her telescope to scan the crowd. "Wait, I think I see Galahad!" she exclaimed, pointing off into the distance. "He's with Arthur already. By the cliffs in Guinevere's garden!"

The dragon groaned and shuddered as the orders were relayed. The body slowly tilted to glide toward where Cecily had indicated.

They were going to pass above King Arthur and Galahad, but Calib could already tell they would be too high off the ground for him to jump out.

"We need to get lower!" Calib shouted. "I can't land safely from here."

"This thing was not built for speed or maneuverability," Sir Alric complained to them from above. "If we get too close to the ground, we could crash! This is the best I can do!"

"Looks like you need some more nimble wings," a crow's voice cawed brightly.

"Valentina!" Calib could not believe his eyes and stared at the healthy-looking crow who had joined him in the bowl. "You're all healed!"

"I couldn't miss out on another big adventure, could I?" the crow declared with a wink.

"I . . . don't know what to say," Calib said, tears in his eyes. For weeks, he thought he might have crippled Valentina. "I'm so sorry for not listening to you that night in the storm. . . ."

Valentina ruffled Calib's fur. "Save your tears until after we save Camelot. Come, I'll give you a ride to Galahad!"

Calib brushed away his tears and nodded. He jumped onto Valentina's back, and the crow took a running leap from the dragon. They took to the air and banked back toward a flash of white-blond hair. Galahad stood waiting to give the signal to the vanguard of the Camelot forces. They were about to charge the encroaching Saxons.

"There! Off to the side!"

Valentina maneuvered closer in, landing on Galahad's head.

Galahad shouted in surprise. "Calib, why aren't you on the dragon?"

"The Grail's powers aren't what Arthur thinks!" Calib gasped, out of breath from his sprint. He climbed down to Galahad's shoulder. "It cannot be used for selfish reasons. It only truly works if a great *personal* sacrifice is made in exchange."

"What do you mean?"

"For the Grail to truly work, King Arthur would have to give up *his* life."

Calib quickly recounted all he had seen in the mirror, including how his father's death had woken the Grail. Galahad's eyes widened. "I wonder if that would explain Merlin," he said. "If he gave up his human life for the castle. He wasn't eaten by a wolf—he turned into the wolf."

"We need to tell King Arthur," Calib said. They began to push forward to where the king stood. "We need to warn him!"

"Your Majesty!" Galahad tried to shout above the noise. But the soldiers mistook Galahad's movements as a signal to advance. The boy and the mouse were swept away from the king in a rush of bodies.

The Saxons had divided their forces in two, splitting them on both sides in a pincer movement. In between them stood Arthur's men, in the last stand of Camelot. At the very front, King Arthur was fighting his way to Morgan.

The sound of the Two-Legger armies was the most terrible sound Calib had ever heard—the smashing of metal, frightened horses, and angry shouting. Galahad and Calib were surrounded on all sides by flailing limbs and sharp edges.

Galahad pressed on. Frantically, the two made their way to King Arthur as arrows rained down, thudding against the shield that Galahad held high over his head.

"The king!" someone screamed, and, as if there were magic at work, the soldiers suddenly parted, allowing Calib and Galahad to see Arthur, just as he crumpled to his knees, an arrow protruding from his side.

Morgan le Fay lowered her bow and smiled with smug satisfaction.

CHAPTER
44

"*A rthur!*" Queen Guinevere's panicked shouts cut through the ensuing battle cries.

Morgan, sensing the others coming to the king's rescue, raised both her arms toward the chapel. A giant cracking sound shook the ground beneath their feet. The chapel bells jangled as the entire building was lifted from the ground, rising at least ten feet into the air. The grass around Morgan dried to dust as she worked this magical feat.

Galahad saw that Morgan meant to use the building

to separate Arthur from his rescuers. He began to sprint toward where Arthur had fallen. He withdrew Excalibur and willed his feet to move faster.

As it moved through the air, the chapel crumbled into rubble and reformed into a giant wall of debris, threatening to ford the river and block his path to Arthur. Morgan made a throwing motion, and the wall came crashing down.

Galahad slid under the falling barrier just in time. One of the bells nearly took off his head, but he had cleared the wall. Bruised, his ears ringing, he got up and continued to run after Morgan. She was already at the riverbank now, stooped over the figure of King Arthur. She cruelly wrenched the arrow from her brother's side.

The paper dragon swooped in and intervened.

"Not another move, witch!" the dragon shouted.

The dragon's chest grew fiery red as the dragon prepared another fire blast from its mouth. But before it could fire, Morgan raised her arms again. A gale-force wind suddenly caught the dragon's wings like two kites and pinned the whole construct against the wall that had recently been the chapel. Unable to release the fire powder, the dragon's chest caught aflame.

The witch grinned with wicked satisfaction and sent the burning structure high up into the sky. All the trees that surrounded King Arthur turned gray and ashen as Morgan brought the dragon careening back to the ground.

The dragon deflated as the birds and bats who had powered it flew out of the burning carcass.

Morgan was breathing heavily now. Her recent acts of magic had taken a toll on her, and the garden that had once grown in this place had turned to dried bits of bramble and weeds.

She was moving in for the finishing blow.

Morgan unsheathed a wicked-looking blade that glowed with a black aura around it. The scent of it smelled like death itself. This would bring about the final blow that would kill Arthur.

"You should have listened to the old man, little brother," she said to Arthur, with a triumphant sneer. She was only a few feet from the incapacitated king. "Merlin always told you not to trust me. But you always had a soft spot for your family, didn't you?"

"Blood is blood," Arthur said, spitting out some of the blood that was in his mouth. He put his arm up as if to shield himself from the next blow with his own bare hands. "But yours was always bad, Morgan."

Morgan waved her hand in the air, and the next moment, the Grail appeared in her hand. "Good thing, then, that you have plenty to give."

Taking some of Arthur's blood from the arrow, she smeared it inside the Grail.

Nothing happened. Her armies did not gain speed.

They did not gain strength. With a start, Galahad realized that the only reason she had gained some invincibility last time must have been that Galahad had sacrificed his own blood for the hare.

Morgan had been able to see right away that the Grail wasn't working. In her confusion, she hardly seemed to notice Galahad as he ran to stand between her and King Arthur.

"You again," Morgan sneered. "It seems the Grail is picky about its blood. It craves *yours*." Without warning, Morgan came at Galahad with her sword, but after weeks of combat training with Red, Galahad dodged it easily.

Galahad moved with precision and confidence that he hadn't possessed when he'd first arrived at Camelot. His powers and command of magic were more advanced too. Now that the witch had overextended her powers, Galahad realized he could defeat Morgan on his own, once and for all.

Spells flew back and forth between the two. Galahad shot wild, lightning-bright bursts of energy from Excalibur, fueled by his anger. Morgan responded with lashes of black magic that whipped out and tried to entangle Galahad's limbs. The grass around them turned black and crispy, crunching underneath Galahad's feet. They couldn't do this indefinitely; they'd turn the entire cliffside into sand.

The time to act was now or never.

Galahad began to pull all the magic he could muster from Excalibur—through himself. It traveled from his fingertips, up his arm, and filled his body like an electric current. Every joint and muscle seemed to twist in pain.

Galahad grit his teeth and reached out with his free hand, willing the magic out of his sword and toward the Grail. His hands began to tremble.

Finally, when it seemed like he might reach his breaking point and explode into nothingness, the Grail flew out of Morgan's hand and into his. The cup felt heavier than it should, like it was already filled to the brim with some unseen liquid. The grainy pattern in the wood of the Grail began to swirl. Everything moved in slow motion now, as if Galahad had fallen out of step with time itself. Morgan raised her blade over her head, her face twisted with fury.

An otherworldly voice sounded in Galahad's mind. It was a voice that he imagined might have belonged to a god.

What is it that you wish?

There was no other choice. King Arthur was unconscious, and no one else besides Galahad knew the secret of the Grail. Morgan, he knew now, would stop at nothing to become queen.

She would rather see Calib, Cecily, and all the others die than lose. She would kill her own brother; her own son.

She would rather have war than peace. And Galahad knew that his home at Camelot would never truly be a home until peace reigned.

"I wish to trade my life for Camelot," Galahad whispered.

The Grail answered Galahad's plea with a blinding ray of light.

CHAPTER
45

A searing golden beam of light shot out from the Grail. It unfurled just like it had always been depicted on the Christopher crest.

Calib squinted against the light. He could see the silhouette of Galahad dropping Excalibur to place both his hands on the Grail's stem. Galahad's arms shook as he tried to maintain control of the Grail's power.

The light shot into the sky and arced like a rainbow across the battlefield. Where it traveled, drops of iridescence fell onto Camelot's armies, both human and animal.

It spread and formed an armor of light around their bodies. Camelot's forces suddenly seemed reenergized. A rallying roar sprang up through the ranks as the troops regrouped for a final showdown.

Calib felt a drop of something on his head and then his snout. It tingled as it ran down his fur, and his mind became calmer and more alert. Looking down at his torso, Calib could see a near-invisible layer of armor wrapping him like a glove.

"Give it to me!" Morgan's expression was a mixture of fear and jealousy as she charged toward Galahad. "You can't control it. Let me teach you, Galahad. I will never abandon you the way your mother and father have. Come, become my new son, and we will rule Camelot together."

Surprised, Galahad directed the Grail's ray right at Morgan.

It froze Morgan to the spot. She let out a bloodcurdling shriek, and then suddenly, she disappeared. King Arthur's crown fell onto the heap of clothing left in her place.

A surprised-looking ferret crawled out of the clothing pile. *The Manderlean.*

The ferret that was both the Manderlean and Morgan looked dazed for a moment, but then her eyes fell on Calib. With a vicious hiss, she charged at him.

"You! This is all your fault."

Calib barely had time to draw his sword before Morgan was upon him. She did not break stride but lowered her shoulder as she slammed into Calib.

His magical armor absorbed most of the impact, but the hit was enough to send Lightbringer flying from his grip. Calib scrambled up, almost losing his balance on the slick moss that covered the rocks. He turned to face Morgan, but she was nearly on top of him.

He scampered backward, trying to put as much distance between himself and the ferret as he could. The ferret hissed and lunged after him.

"Oh no you don't!" Devrin jumped down from a muddy embankment, twirling a length of rope knotted into a lasso over her head. On her heels were Barnaby and Cecily. Morgan kept running straight for Calib, but Devrin let fly the lasso, entangling Morgan's hind leg. The ferret pulled up short as the three mice grabbed on to the rope. It took all their strength to hold her in place.

"Exsolve!" Morgan hissed.

She was trying to do magic. She waved her paws in the air in a complicated pattern and attempted to pull free again, but the rope held fast. Her spells weren't working.

Galahad and the Grail must have stripped her of her magic, trapping her in the Manderlean's form.

With a snarl of frustration, Morgan lunged at the rope with her teeth, snapping it cleanly in two.

"Run, Calib!" Devrin shouted.

He had no more time to think, as Morgan darted toward him, impossibly fast. He turned and ran for the river. Not daring to look behind him, he scrambled up the trunk of a fallen tree that stretched out across the rushing waters. Its narrowest branches reached almost as far as the opposite bank. The tree was rotted through, its bark crumbling in places and slick with spray in others. A heavy rain would probably send it over the falls for good.

Calib ran as fast as he could on the treacherous surface, but he almost lost his footing twice. He was halfway across the river when he heard the scratching of Morgan's claws on the bark just behind him. It was time to stop running.

He turned to face Morgan. The ferret slowed her pursuit, eyeing Calib carefully as she closed the remaining distance.

"There is nowhere to go." Her voice dripped malice. "Call off your armies if you value your life."

Calib was trapped. He thought back to what Galahad would do in this situation. An idea came to him. Calib lowered his head carefully, as though considering Morgan's offer. His paws were shaking. He saw Morgan relax her defensive stance slightly.

"All right, I surrender," Calib whispered to himself. "For Camelot."

He looked up at Morgan and took a step. The ferret smiled a victorious smile, full of teeth. That was the moment Calib lunged.

He ran as fast as he could, plowing into Morgan's side. She gave a surprised yelp of pain as she twisted, trying to catch her balance, but she lost her footing on the wet bark. An instant later, she was falling, and Calib was falling with her.

The water was cold. It was all Calib could do to keep his head above the surface. Swimming against the current was impossible. Morgan's paws flailed wildly, but she was making no progress.

The river was carrying them both toward the waterfall. It was all Calib could do to keep his head above the surface. Morgan's paws flailed wildly. She was struggling as well. Calib knew he could not stay afloat for very long. Though the Grail might be able to heal injuries, he wasn't sure how much protection it would offer from a plunge over a cliff.

A few more seconds, and they would go over.

"Calib! Catch!"

Calib saw Devrin standing on the riverbank, almost at the top of the waterfall. She was spinning her rope once more. Calib kicked toward her with all the strength he had left, and as the rope arced out over the water, he leaped for it. He had the rope between both paws and between his teeth, and he held on for dear life as Devrin, Barnaby, Thomas, and Cecily pulled him to safety. Behind him, he heard one last angry shriek from

Morgan as she plummeted over the edge.

"Nothing that goes over ever comes back," Cecily said grimly.

Camelot's greatest enemy was defeated. For the first time in what felt like years, the burden of protecting Camelot lifted off Calib's shoulders. His castle was safe again, and he had fulfilled his promise.

"We did it," Calib whispered, overcome with emotion. "We've saved Camelot! We've stopped the prophecies!"

"Not yet," Cecily said, her eyes suddenly wide in horror.

The dragon, still impaled on the bell tower and abandoned by its controllers, began to list sideways sharply. Finally, it ripped away from the tower.

Calib watched as the dragon fell, like a slayed beast, onto the boats moored on the river.

The sound of splintering wood was followed quickly by a gigantic *BOOM!*

It shook the ground beneath him, and a blast of debris showered the battlefield. Humans and animals alike rolled away from the barricade.

Fiery bits of paper dragon fell all around Calib. The mouse watched in horror as the thatching on the roofs, and the hay in the stables, caught on fire. The fire jumped from roof to roof, the dry straw acting like kindling.

Camelot was burning.

CHAPTER
46

alahad slid to the ground like a rag doll, barely clinging to consciousness and only vaguely aware of the remaining Saxons turning from the flames and fleeing. The dark, terrible visions he and Guinevere saw in Merlin's Mirror were coming true.

The Saxon animals ran for cover, taking shelter in the Darkling Woods. Some of the Two-Leggers, who were too terrified, simply jumped into the river or laid flat in the tall grass, hoping for cover from falling debris. The flames danced like a rage-filled demon, consuming everything they touched.

Even with Morgan le Fay gone, the world was filled with many dangers. Galahad wished he were able to help the kingdom in this next fight for survival, but . . .

His body had gone completely numb. He could no longer feel the Grail or Excalibur in his hands. Everything went very cold and distant. His mind felt removed from his body. He thought how wonderful it might feel to shuck his body away, like a corn husk, and float freely into the lands beyond.

But where do you belong? a voice inside him asked. It sounded very much like his mother's. Galahad could almost sense her warm hand brushing out the knots from his hair.

The king's sudden grip on his arm brought Galahad's mind crashing back down into his body. The pain followed immediately. Galahad grit his teeth. The king was repeating some question.

"How did you do it?"

Arthur lay next to Galahad, his face deathly pale. Blood trickled down from his arrow wound. The king looked at Galahad with astonished eyes. "How did you do what Morgan could not?"

"A mouse told me that the Grail's power cannot be taken," Galahad said. The weariness had settled into his bones and made it hard to talk. "You must offer it something of great value."

"What did you give it?" Arthur's breathing was also becoming labored. He coughed up some blood. The arrow must have punctured his lung. He did not have long to live.

From afar, Galahad could see the first of Arthur's men trying to climb over the wall of debris Morgan had created.

The world around Galahad faded in and out of darkness. He was tired, so very tired. All he wanted to do was let the darkness take over. Let it take everything he had left, and let him rest.

"My life," he whispered.

Smoke filled his lungs, making him cough. He was dimly aware that somewhere behind the debris, the castle still burned. He could hear the shouts of men and animals trying in vain to put out the flames with water.

Galahad wanted to do more to help. Perhaps he could use Excalibur to raise the water from the river. He tried once more to draw power from the legendary sword, but it was useless.

Without words, King Arthur took the Grail from Galahad. He gripped it so tightly, Galahad could see the whites of his knuckles. It looked like a small child's cup in his hands.

"Please save my people," he whispered to the Grail. "Save Camelot."

With a gasp, Arthur shut his eyes with sudden pain. His hands went limp, and the Grail rolled away, falling with a small splash into the river. Neither Arthur nor Galahad made any attempt to retrieve it. They were too weak.

These were probably their last moments, Galahad realized. This was where it would end, with everything still in the balance.

Nothing happened for a few breathless seconds.

Perhaps it was too late, Galahad thought. Arthur had already been dying when he offered his life. Perhaps the Grail would only work once.

Suddenly, a crack of thunder and lightning rent the sky in two.

At long last, a steady rain began to fall.

CHAPTER
47

The rain dampened the flames and kept them from spreading into the town. But where the grand castle once stood was now a blackened husk of rubble and brick. The castle would become an old ruin like St. Gertrude, lost to time and memory.

Calib buried his head in his paws. It was too painful to watch. His beloved home.

Tears mixed with rain as Calib mourned.

"Calib, look." Cecily pointed over his shoulder. "Something is coming."

He turned to where Cecily was directing him. At first, Calib thought it was a moving cloud, but as he watched, a silver boat sliced through the mist and smoke, flying through the air like a dragon.

The boat approached Camelot, sailing high in the sky.

At the sight of the ghostly ship, the remaining soldiers who were standing on the cliffside fell into a stunned silence. Like a gentle leaf, the boat descended onto the river. It floated against the current, skimming the churning surface.

One by one, Saxons and Britons alike fell to their knees at the impossible sight of this ship. Some trembled with fear; others had their eyes wide-open with ecstatic wonder. Even Leftie and the rest of the animals fighting the flames had paused to stare.

"A miracle."

"Merciful heavens."

The awed whispers grew among the gathered crowd, reaching Calib's ears as the passengers of the boat came into focus. The ghostly outlines of an egret and a wolf stood side by side at the prow. He recognized Howell and the Lady of the Lake. The raw magic of their combined presence made Calib's whiskers burn and tingle. It felt like being struck by lightning all over again, but painless.

The boat stopped before Galahad and Arthur. The egret spread her wings and took off from the deck, alighting on the shore before the fallen heroes. As her feet touched the soil, she folded her wings over her face and body. The egret began to change shape, growing taller and sprouting human limbs where there once were wings. The feathers gathered to form an elegant long-sleeved white dress. The long beak shrank back into a pale human nose set in a stern visage. A silver diadem in the shape of an egret appeared on the ageless face of a woman with long gray hair.

"The time has come for Arthur Pendragon and Galahad du Lac to journey to Avalon," the woman began in a watery, faraway voice. The Lady of the Lake looked nearly translucent, a mere echo of herself on Avalon. "Their time among mortals is at an end."

Her words hit Calib's chest, cold and final. She couldn't mean what he thought she meant.

The Lady of the Lake took a step toward the Two-Leggers. She moved her hand in a complicated gesture, and Arthur's wound closed. The king still looked to be in great pain.

"Wait!" A panicked Calib ran forward to step between them, but someone else got there first.

Queen Guinevere drew and aimed an arrow right at the Lady of the Lake. "No," she said firmly.

"No?" The Lady of the Lake sounded taken aback. No one had dared defy her in a long time. A blush of anger rose to her cheeks.

"You are not taking them." Queen Guinevere pulled the arrow taut against her bowstring. "We still need them here. Back away!"

"I'm afraid that is not for you or any mortal to say," the Lady of the Lake replied. "They made a deal with the Grail. They belong to Avalon now."

Guinevere's hand trembled slightly. "I don't understand. What deal?"

"It's true. In exchange for saving Camelot . . . I . . . We gave up our places in Camelot. It was the only way to defeat Morgan. . . ." Galahad struggled to tilt his head up. He tried to prop himself on his elbows but fell with a squelch back into the mud. Calib ran to his side and placed a protective paw on his forehead.

"Shhhh," Calib said. "Stay down. We can take it from here." To his distress, Galahad's skin was ice cold to the touch.

Lancelot appeared beside Guinevere and raised his sword at the Lady of the Lake. "I don't care what you think you are owed. You have no claim here. Our kingdom needs a leader. And I need my son!"

"Peace, Guinevere! Peace, Lancelot!" The wolf stood up now. "Perhaps I can explain this better, Nimue."

Howell leaped gracefully from the boat and onto land. When his paws touched ground, they transformed into booted feet. The fur on his body grew long and knitted together into a white robe. Howell's long snout shrank back to form a Two-Legger face with a ragged beard and shaggy eyebrows. The Two-Legger's eyes were mismatched just like Howell's: one sea green and one icy blue.

Calib gasped as he beheld Howell in his human shape— Merlin, the greatest wizard who ever walked the Earth.

He looked around with his mismatched eyes. The burned castle, the ruined ships beached on the rocks, the many injured men and animals.

"It was too good a place to last forever," he said wistfully to Guinevere. "You saw it in the mirror many times. You knew this would come to pass."

A grief-stricken Guinevere lowered her bow and arrow.

"Why, Merlin?" she asked, her voice breaking with sorrow. "Why come back now, when it is too late? You could have done something."

"A new Britain is coming," Merlin said. "It was time to let this age pass."

Beneath his grief, Calib felt a flash of anger. It was not fair. Everything he and his family had sacrificed, it was all for nothing.

"Then what was the point of it, if Camelot was always going to be destroyed!" Calib burst out, surprised at how angry he sounded. "Why did you send me on these stupid quests to try to save it?"

Merlin turned his attention to Calib. "You misunderstand,

mousling. You have ensured Camelot's survival for eternity."

"My dear Calib." A familiar, warm voice stopped Calib's heart. "You have much to learn about what Camelot is and could be."

"Aye, not that we had enough time to tell him of course," responded another voice that spoke to him from a long-lost past. Calib turned to see who the voices belonged to.

A stout, barrel-chested mouse stood on the shore. His golden fur was tinged at the ends with silvery-gray hairs. He wore a simple brown robe, the kind he always chose when he did not want to be noticed. Beside him stood a noble mouse-knight, dressed in the Christopher colors. His coloring matched Calib's. He was the spitting image of a certain tapestry of which Calib had memorized every single detail.

Calib rubbed his eyes, barely able to speak.

"Father? Grandfather?"

CHAPTER
48

"But how is this possible?" Calib whispered. His mind couldn't comprehend what his eyes were seeing. He staggered forward toward Yvers's and Trenton's outstretched arms. And like a waking dream, everything and everyone else seemed to melt away. When Calib's paws grasped theirs, and the familiar scent of his grandfather and father reached his snout, tears overwhelmed him. His greatest wish, even more than becoming a knight, came unbidden to his lips.

"Will you stay this time?"

Sir Trenton and Commander Yvers looked at each other sadly.

"I'm afraid we are here only for a little while," Yvers said. He looked longingly at their surroundings. "Given my abrupt departure, I had wanted to see Camelot one last time."

At the thought of the ruined scene behind them, guilt flushed Calib's cheeks red. For generations, the Christopher mice had protected the Grail, and with it, their castle home. And now both were lost.

"I'm sorry I let you both down." Calib could no longer look into his grandfather's kind eyes. "I've failed to live up to the Christopher name. Failed spectacularly."

Calib unbuckled his chest armor with the Christopher crest and tried to hand it to Sir Trenton.

"No, Calib, you haven't," Yvers said, staying Calib's paw. "In fact, you've done just the opposite. You've saved us all."

"I don't understand," Calib said. "The visions in Merlin's Mirror came true. Camelot burned no matter what I tried to do to prevent it."

"Camelot was never about a castle or a piece of treasure, but its people," Trenton said, coming forward to place the armor back on his son. "In each of your adventures, haven't you noticed? You've united the Darklings, the Two-Leggers, and even many of the Saxons, all under one banner. You've truly made Camelot stronger in ways we never could have done by our keeping secrets and distrusting others."

"I knew that night you first stumbled into my cave that you were destined for greatness," Merlin said, having returned his attention to the mice. He sat himself down on the ground. "You have always been brave, strong, and wise, Calib Christopher . . ."

"And that is the mark of a true Camelot knight," King Arthur finished.

Everyone looked surprised that the Two-Legger king could suddenly understand what the mice were saying to one another without the aid of Excalibur.

"Under the circumstances of our gathering, all may speak and be understood freely here," Merlin clarified.

"I remember you," Guinevere said to Calib. "You upset an entire meeting of the Round Table before my cat, Lucy, ran off with you."

"He was the one who unlocked the Sword in the Stone." Galahad was awake now. "He's the whole reason any one of us has survived this long."

"And to think, Lucy nearly ate a knight." Queen Guinevere patted Calib on the head.

"Thank you, Your Majesty, but I am no knight," Calib said, bowing sheepishly to the king and queen. "I'm just a squire."

"Well, that won't do." Arthur crooked a finger to the mouse. "I can change that, you know."

"You mean . . . ?" Calib looked at Yvers and Trenton in disbelief. He didn't think he would ever be knighted after everything that had transpired, but somehow, Galahad's praise also rang true. All this time, he thought he was failing to live up to what he thought his grandfather and father would do. But perhaps he had found his own path.

"The Crown now calls Calib Christopher before this court and company," King Arthur said.

Calib stepped forward. With his father and grandfather watching on, he felt dizzy from joy.

Queen Guinevere helped prop Arthur up. Trenton handed Arthur a sword. Calib recognized it as Darkslayer, which he had sacrificed to call forth the Lady of the Lake. His father's sword.

King Arthur held it between his thumb and forefinger.

"With this sword, do you swear to be brave, strong, and wise, and to uphold yourself to the qualities befitting a knight of Camelot and Britain?"

"I do." Calib thought he had never said truer words in his life.

King Arthur smiled. "I dub you Sir Calib Christopher, guardian and defender of Camelot ever after. Rise, sir knight, and claim your title."

Calib's eyes were bright as he stood and accepted the sword from King Arthur. It felt good and right in his paw. He looked around at the gathered group. Color was returning to Galahad's face. Arthur and Guinevere were holding hands. Maybe, just maybe, everything would be all right. Life could go on without the castle.

A peaceful silence settled as the sun began to set.

"It's time to go now," the Lady of the Lake said. "Our magic will only last a short while. Arthur's wounds are deep and beyond the physical. Morgan buried all her hate into that arrow. He will need healing from the Sisters, and our magic is not what it used to be."

"And what about Galahad?" Calib asked.

"Galahad will heal faster because of his youth." A new voice entered the conversation as a Two-Legger woman emerged from the boat. She was dressed in an all-white habit, one that resembled the Lady of the Lake's feathers. "But it will still take time. And there is no better place to heal than home."

"Mother!" Galahad stumbled forward, and mother and son embraced.

"Avalon is my home now, and yours as well," Lady Elaine said. "We, the sisters of St. Anne, have taught you all you needed to know about the need for peace, while your time with your father in Camelot has taught you what it means to be truly brave. Those lessons will serve you well, but as beings of magic, we belong on Avalon."

"Will Galahad ever come back?" Calib asked.

"Perhaps one day, when the world is ready again for magic," the Lady of the Lake said. "Galahad and Arthur will both return, but perhaps not in the forms in which you see them now."

"Will we be able to visit?" Calib asked. "We made it to Avalon once."

Merlin and the Lady of the Lake looked at each other uncertainly. "I'm afraid," she finally said, "we will need to cut Avalon from this world in ways that cannot be undone. Two-Leggers do not know how to handle magic."

"That's not true. Look at Galahad," Calib said.

"But look at Morgan," the Lady of the Lake said. "It's too dangerous to keep magic in this world."

"Men will go on to do great things on their own," Merlin said. "They don't need magic anymore."

And though he did not wish it, Calib knew it to be true.

"So I guess this is good-bye for now," Galahad said to Calib. "Thank you for everything you've done. I won't forget you, ever."

Calib struggled to come to grips with saying good-bye to his best friend. He thought back to the first time they had met in the throne room so long ago. There, Galahad had invited him on to his palm on the night of their first encounter. Calib had been terrified then and ran away from him.

But now, as Galahad opened his palm again, Calib bounded up to his Two-Legger friend without hesitation. Calib took off his helmet and placed it on Galahad's thumb.

"Remember, you will always have a friend in the woodland realm."

Queen Guinevere looked at her husband. "All our long years together. I did not think there would come a day when you would not be by my side." The queen placed her hand gently on Arthur's cheek, letting her own tears fall on his face.

"I am sorry," Arthur said. "You deserved better."

"No," Guinevere said. "We deserved each other. And for as long as I live, I will find a way to honor the legacy that we built here."

The king and queen embraced for a long time. Finally, she let go and allowed Lancelot and Merlin to carry King Arthur to the boat. Galahad stood on his own and began to follow them toward the ship.

"Good-bye," Galahad said, stopping in front of Sir Lancelot. The knight wrapped Galahad in a strong hug. "I'm sorry I never followed in your footsteps."

"Son, you were meant for a much greater purpose than I could ever imagine," Lancelot said. "I could not be prouder of you than I am now."

The knight looked at Lady Elaine with tears in his eyes. "Thank you for looking after our son."

Merlin and the Lady of the Lake beckoned to the mice. Commander Yvers and Sir Trenton lingered by Calib's side.

"You take care of yourself, young Christopher," Yvers said, giving Calib's paw one last squeeze before they boarded.

Together, the animals on the shore watched the boat to Avalon sail downriver, carried by the rushing waters.

Many warriors had gone this path to the Fields Beyond. And the thought filled Calib with hope.

Just as the boat looked like it might tip over the waterfall, it took off soaring in the twilight air.

Camelot—beast and man—watched it until it became a small speck on the lavender-blue horizon and then disappeared.

"I will go help the others clear out the debris," Lancelot said softly. His eyes stayed on the horizon where the boat had gone. "But eventually, we will need to address the issue of succession."

"We will rebuild," the queen said. "But I have no interest in ruling over a new Camelot. There will never be another Camelot, nor would I dare try to recreate it. It lives on in our stories, and that is enough for me."

"There may be a fight for power," Lancelot began uncertainly.

"I will see that through," Guinevere said, and gave Calib a smile. "With the help of some very sage advisers."

Hours later, when the last of the embers had finally died out, the animals of Camelot went to see what they could salvage. Calib found himself walking through the tapestry hall once again, taking an old, familiar path. Most of the tapestry was irrecoverable. Only a blackened, charred splotch on the wall marked where Sir Trenton and Lady Clara's tapestry once hung.

He was soon joined by Cecily, Commander Kensington, Sir Alric, and the rest of the Camelot mice.

Together, they began to sweep up the dust and ashes in silence.

"Leftie has offered us a home in the Darkling Woods," Commander Kensington said. "There is room in the caves. Plenty of space. It can shelter us for a time."

Viviana von Mandrake placed her paws around Cecily's shoulders. "We will go. I've been thinking about starting my own inn again."

"The caves are near a river," Barnaby added. "It's a good place to launch ships."

"There are hot springs, too," Dandelion said as she and her reunited cousin, Fennel, filled a bag with ash.

"How luxurious!" Ginny exclaimed. "We could start a bath spa!"

"I've read about those," Thomas said. He helped lift the bigger pieces of debris while Rosy and Silas tumbled about, fetching water for the working mice.

One by one, all the creatures of Camelot agreed. They would join the Darklings.

"What do you think, Calib?" Cecily asked, putting her paw in his.

It was true what his grandfather and father had said. Camelot was not a place but an ideal. It would have to live on only in stories. Calib looked into a nearby mirror and thought he saw Galahad waving back. He blinked and realized it was just his own reflection.

He smiled and nodded.

He was Sir Calib Christopher, brave, strong, and wise. And through him, Camelot's glory would never fade, no matter where he lived.

EPILOGUE

"The Hurler only looks intimidating, but just keep your eyes on the berry." Calib repositioned little Gala's paws farther apart on the wooden sword. "Draw your strength from your shoulders, not the arms, just like your mother taught you."

Gala made a few practice swings. They were strong and sure. Calib was impressed but not surprised. She was her mother's daughter, after all, and Lady Cecily Christopher was the greatest swordsmouse of her generation. There was a bright eagerness in Gala's eyes that reminded Calib so much of himself at that age. An ache built in his throat.

He turned to face the direction where Camelot once stood. Some mornings he believed he could still see the castle, its proud turrets ever reaching toward the sky.

After so many years, and a smattering of gray whiskers around his cheeks to show for it, Calib had come to accept that a new world had dawned on their Britain.

"Okay, I can do this," Gala said, and ran to line up with the other first-years about to face the Hurler—the

Two-Legger slingshot that shot berries and acorns for target practice.

Calib surveyed the new recruits, taking pride in seeing all the different animals represented: mice, hares, weasels, owls, crows, otters, and more.

They had gathered to train in the knightly qualities first established by the mice of Camelot: bravery, strength, and wisdom. Though Camelot was no longer a physical place, Calib knew that its name would never be forgotten as long as these virtues held true for the woodland realm and beyond. Under Commander Calib's steady paw, they would become defenders of Camelot, all of them.

Owen—Ginny and Admiral Barnaby's son—was up before Gala. He missed his swing at the last moment and got splattered in the face with a hawthorn berry.

"Not bad!" Owen said, wiping off some of the pulp from his fur and sticking it into his mouth. "They're extra ripe this year."

Gala scrunched up her snout, just like Cecily did when she wasn't impressed. Even though she shared the Christopher coloring, right down to the white patch on her ear, she was a Von Mandrake through and through.

Ginny came up behind them, pushing a cart with a large trencher of savory turnip soup and a salad of carrot peels. Since taking over for Madame von Mandrake in her retirement, she went by Madame Ginger instead.

"Care for some lunch, Commander?" she asked.

"I'm fine, thank you." Calib shook his head. He kept his eye on Gala, who now approached the Hurler with a steely determination. "Any word from Lady Cecily yet?"

"She and Macie have just arrived. I've set them up with a late breakfast in Leftie's old cave."

"What news from Lady Guinevere and Lady Britta?"

"The visit went well, I think. The peace reigns steady. To hear Cecily speak of it, the Saxons have become as much a part of Britain as the Britons are. And Lord Mordred has been very helpful in achieving that peace, opening up the mountain passes for trade and convincing Theodora the hawk to ally with the owls."

Calib nodded. Indeed, that was the way the world always worked. When people opened their hearts to those they once feared, the fear tended to vanish.

"I'm ready!" Gala cried out.

Thomas Steepaw poked his head out from behind the Hurler.

"Is that Gala Christopher I hear? Are you sure you've gotten enough practice?" the weasel teased.

"Aye, Sir Thomas!"

The weasel had become one of their best weapons trainers. He'd taken to squire training soon after he'd joined them. Now, Sir Thomas went behind the Hurler and let loose a berry that barreled toward Gala faster than a blink.

Calib watched his daughter's arms tense and her eyes focus. She hacked the berry in half, cleanly, with barely a grunt.

Applause rang out from the other first-years.

"*Brava.*" Calib clapped alongside the others.

"Just like her parents, that one," Ginny mused.

Gala's smile lit up her whole face. She began to chant, "Together in paw and tail! Lest divided we fall and fail!"

The rest of the first-years joined in a resounding chorus. Calib's heart swelled to their steady rhythm.

The Darkling Woods have much to say, if one knows how to listen.

And if you listen carefully, the drumbeat of Camelot marches on in the heartbeats of all creatures.

ACKNOWLEDGMENTS

At the closing of this tale, I wish to express my deepest gratitude to the following Two-Leggers:

To my editors, Kamilla Benko and Andrew Eliopulos—my story wizards for three books running. Paw over my heart, I bow down.

To the wunderkinds of Glasstown Entertainment: Lexa Hillyer, Lauren Oliver, Alexa Wejko, Adam Silvera, Stephen Barbara, and Emily Berge. I await these book warriors in Wordhalla.

To the flawless team at HarperCollins Children's: Rosemary Brosnan and Bria Ragin in editorial; Alexandra Rakaczki in managing editorial; Megan Barlog in marketing; Olivia Russo in publicity; Andrea Pappenheimer and her team in sales; Erin Fitzsimmons and Cat San Juan in design; and Lindsey Carr, the illustrator of the series. To make books is to build worlds, and what they do is nothing short of pure magic.

To my agent, Wendi Gu, esteemed queen of encouragement and brilliant insights.

Thank you to the patient staffs at Swallow Cafe and

Vineapple Cafe in Brooklyn for hosting me during long stretches of writing this book. Your coffee-enhanced sanctuaries helped keep me sane and focused when the world seemed the exact opposite.

And finally, to my husband, Kyle, without whom I would have perished from a diet of microwavables by now.

READ THEM ALL!

There can be great power
even in the smallest warriors.

You may also like

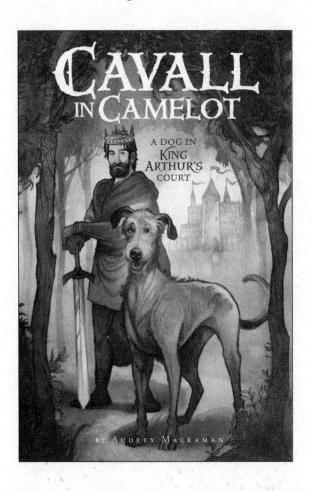